THE CHILDREN
HUDDLED TOGETHER
AS IF FOR WARMTH.

They sat on the edge of a cot, not daring to move, while the woman went about her business. . . . Her high heels went tickedy-tack, tickedy-tack on the wooden floor.

"Come, Georgene, come, Tammy. . . . I'm leaving for work now. Come kiss Mummy good-bye."

The children rose dutifully and came to the arms of the woman who forced them to call her "Mummy."

"Good-bye," the children chorused. Obedience, they had learned, was the best way. As long as they were good, they would not be punished. There would be no thrashings with the wooden spoon, nor being made to stand in the scary corner with the spider webs; nor would they be sent to bed so hungry that they cried all night instead of sleeping.

The high heels went tickedy-tack, tickedy-tack to the elevator. "Bye, my precious darlings." The woman waved, and the children waved back.

The elevator creaked and groaned and rumbled. They continued waving until they were sure they were alone.

HIDE-AND-SEEK

Lindsay Maracotta

PUBLISHED BY POCKET BOOKS NEW YORK

Another *Original* publication of POCKET BOOKS

POCKET BOOKS, a Simon & Schuster division of
GULF & WESTERN CORPORATION
1230 Avenue of the Americas, New York, N.Y. 10020

ISBN: 0-671-83622-6

First Pocket Books printing April, 1982

10 9 8 7 6 5 4 3 2 1

POCKET and colophon are trademarks of Simon & Schuster.

Printed in the U.S.A.

Once it was called Hell's Hundred Acres, a rotting industrial slum of a neighborhood that lay like an abscess between the great glass towers of Wall Street and midtown Manhattan. But that was before the artists moved in—before the galleries and cafes and spectacular shops proliferated, and coach buses full of goggling tourists began to cruise day and night through the suddenly famous streets. That was long before the neighborhood became known as Soho, the center of all that was unconventionally chic.

And now, on this sparkling afternoon in early April, West Broadway was jammed with strollers—so many that, from a distance, it looked as if a small, smartly clad army had recently broken ranks. Prompted by the first real day of spring, they had traveled from distances near and far to see for themselves what they had heard so much about. A trio of Westchester matrons marched Indian file through the pristine doors of O.K. Harris; across the street, a Japanese businessman aimed the long lens of his Nikon at an elaborate "Bishop's Crook" lamppost. Two Californians, tanned, slender,

1

and gorgeous, emerged jubilantly from a shop named "iFooo"—they had left behind a thousand dollars' worth of traveler's checks for two quilted leather jump suits and thought nothing of it. And a boy, fresh off the bus from Bayonne, New Jersey, laid down his duffle bag and simply breathed, feeling that at last he had come home.

No one among the milling parade on West Broadway noticed the green school van that pulled up to the corner of Spring Street. It was too mundane a sight in a neighborhood that abounded in the exotic to catch anyone's eye.

The driver of the van turned a weary face to her fourteen squirming charges. "Lisa Wyle," she called. "Your stop."

A thin, pretty child gave the boy sitting next to her a strategically aimed punch on the shoulder. As he howled, she snatched back her blue Danish book bag and darted up the aisle.

The driver peered out at the sidewalk with a dull frown. "No one here to meet you today, Lisa?"

The child shrugged. "Sometimes my mommy gets busy with work and forgets to look at the clock. My mommy's an artist," she added importantly.

"This is the second time this month no one's been here. Ain't no good for a first-grader to be walking by herself."

"It's okay, Mrs. Mosely. I'm allowed to go lots of places by myself."

The driver shook her head. "You just be careful, now."

"I *will!* Bye, Mrs. Mosely."

Lisa descended from the van and began to thread her way up West Broadway, swinging her schoolbag as she went. Several people smiled indulgently as she passed by—an unusually pretty child dressed in a grass-colored handknit sweater, a Casper the Ghost T-shirt, and Jordache jeans, her wavy light-red hair a ripple of sunfire. She was not unaware of their admiration—at six and a half, Lisa was already a full-fledged coquette. She knew precisely what privileges she could extract from her parents and their friends with her dimpled smile, and the cool, green-eyed glance she directed at the men was the calling card of a natural flirt. More than one adult had been prompted to exclaim: "She's going to be a heartbreaker when she grows up!" and Lisa accepted the prophecy with complacency. Though she had no use for the boys in her first-grade class—they were silly beyond belief!—she knew well that when they tried to tug her hair or purloined her erasers it was because they liked her the best.

But at the moment she was too busy nursing a grudge to be enjoying the effect of her charms. Mrs. Mosely treated her like a baby! This was a monstrous injustice —especially in light of the fact that everyone else told her how very grown up she was. She could read all of *Where the Wild Things Are* without having to ask any of the words. And when her parents had parties at the loft, she was allowed to stay up as long as she liked and watch their friend Jonas roll joints. And sex—she knew all about the penis and vagina and the seed that swims up to the egg. Her mother, while illustrating a child's book on human reproduction, had used the opportunity to explain everything quite matter-of-factly, and Lisa hadn't been upset at all. Not like Aaron Shapiro, who called her a liar and started to cry when she repeated the information. Now *there* was a baby! But Mrs. Mosely never picked on *him*.

Her thoughts were distracted by an object in the window of an art gallery—a shimmering crescent moon made of vermillion neon tubing. Lisa thought it was beautiful. The gallery was called "Let There Be Neon," and Lisa had been in it several times with her parents. It was like being inside her aquarium at home—sort of dark and spooky, with the bright bits of sculpture flashing by like incandescent fish. She was strictly forbidden to enter any shop by herself; but maybe no

one would find out if she slipped in now. Just for a
moment . . .

Eyes were watching her. Not the casual eyes of the
distracted stranger, but the eyes of someone who had
watched her many times before. Someone who knew
her name and the pitch of her voice, her height and her
weight. Someone who had studied the small body as a
scientist studies a rare specimen: passionately, yet with
the cold, clear will of the ardent researcher.

The eyes narrowed. Eager slits, a cat's eyes at noon.
The mind behind the eyes thought: *For it is written:
vengeance is mine, I shall repay. And for the children of
harlotry I shall have no pity.* So many weeks spent
waiting, watching, biding time until just the right
moment, when nothing could go wrong. *There is a time
for every matter under heaven.* And now the moment
had appeared. All those patient weeks of careful
preparation were about to see fruition. *A time to reap
and a time to sow.*

Closer now. Close enough to see the stitching of the
grass-green sweater. To smell the dark, sleepy odor of
fine hair. Close enough to stretch out a hand and touch,
oh, so gently, the sharp twin blades of perfect
shoulders . . .

"Lisa!"

The child looked up with a start. She had the terrible
impression that the stranger who had appeared beside
her and spoken her name had also read her thoughts—
knew that she was planning to sneak inside the gallery.
Her heart racing, she waited for chastisement.

"How are you today, Lisa?"

"Fine," the child said meekly.

"You look very pretty today. Is that a new sweater?"

Lisa relaxed. She nodded, then added, "We had a
substitute at school today. Miss Locker's got a cold."

"That's a shame. And where is your mommy this
afternoon?"

"She's at home. She's working on a big commission for Mr. Rizzetti." Lisa shot a discreet glance up at her companion to make sure the word *commission* had been duly appreciated. But the sun caught her eyes; she blinked and looked away.

The stranger leaned closer. Lisa drew back a little. She was used to unfamiliar grown-up faces—friends of her parents were forever coming and going from their loft. But this one wore a fuzzy close-fitting cap and funny sunglasses that reminded Lisa of a cat.

"Listen, Lisa. How would you like to come have an ice cream soda with me?"

"I've got to go home," she declared.

"We'll only be gone a short time. I promise."

"My mommy gets mad if I don't come home right away." Lisa backed off another step, but a large hand closed firmly around her wrist.

"Well, as a matter of fact, I just talked to your mommy. She said it was okay this time. She wants more time to work on her commission."

Lisa hesitated. Only yesterday her mother had screamed at her for barging into the studio while she was working.

The hand on her wrist gently tightened. "What's your favorite flavor ice cream, Lisa?"

"Pistachio."

"What do you know? That's mine, too! Let's go get some, okay?"

"I don't want to."

"You want to do what your mommy says, don't you? You don't want to make her mad?"

"No."

"Then come on. It'll be a lot of fun."

"Okay," the child said listlessly.

She was led quickly to the curb. There was a big, dirty-looking car idling there, and she realized that was where they were heading. It reminded her of the car they took her Grandma Macy in when she died last year. Maybe there was a dead person in this one, too.

Her friend Jennifer was always telling her what happens to dead people after the worms start to eat them. Their eyes and noses fall off, and their tongues turn black, and yucky old holes start growing all over them.

She pulled back. "I don't want to go in there!"

"Don't you talk back to me! *Thou shalt obey thy father and thy mother!* You'll do whatever I say!"

Lisa was suddenly thrust into the car, the door locked beside her. When the door on the driver's side slammed, they began to roll away.

And as West Broadway slipped by in all its vivid diversity of color and invention, one scared white face against a blackened window attracted no attention.

Part I

SOHO: A HISTORY
By Day McAllister

To begin with, there really is a spring at
Spring Street. It burbles steadily beneath
Manhattan's mile of concrete and asphalt,
where it is sewered out to meet the Hudson. But
every now and again it reasserts its presence
by flooding a basement or seeping up through
the cracks of a broken sidewalk. When it does,
it reminds the city that—incredible as it may
seem—this was once an island of virgin fields
and forests, hills and streams.

Back in the days when the spring flows
freely, the part of Manhattan that will one day
become Soho is a pleasant valley, cut off from
the first Dutch settlement by a vast
marshland. Its first inhabitants are
Canarsee Indians, who hunt the fields and fish
the spring-fed pond; it is to protect

[MORE]

9

themselves from this tribe that the Dutch
build the famous wall of Wall Street.

New Amsterdam prospers, the last of the
Canarsee disappear, and the valley becomes
farmland granted by the benevolent directors
of the Dutch West India Company to slaves freed
after twenty years of bondage. It is the first
free black settlement on the island, and there
will remain a black population here until well
into the 19th century.

But more powerful eyes soon come to rest on
the valley's rustic charms. Dutch merchants,
their money made in slaves and furs and indigo,
claim sumptuous country retreats in the area.
They, in turn, are succeeded by burghers of
English ancestry.

But the bustling township that is New York
pushes inexorably northward, and with it
brings its commerce and industry. Tanneries
and iron foundries spring up on the sites of
former farms. Fields give way to stables and
inns. The uncobbled country lane called
Broadway, which leads to the sleepy hamlet of
Greenwich Village, is quickly becoming dotted
with the townhouses of prominent men.

But prosperity has its price. The
once—pastoral marshland has become a
dangerous and festering quagmire. The Collect
Pond, on which children once skated and
sailed, is now clogged with garbage and its
banks strewn with the maggot—ridden carcasses
of animals. Cows and dogs wander into the bogs
and are lost; the summer breeds swarms of
mosquitos that spread the deadly yellow fever

[MORE]

3–3–3–3

plague. At the petition of the landowners, the pond is drained; the gentle hills surrounding it are leveled and the soil used to fill in the marshes.

Now there is nothing to separate the valley from the ever–expanding city. The stage is set for a new age.

[MORE]

The bright spring sun, filtered through grime-encrusted windows, created a false twilight inside the loft. Gil Cassidy moved carefully until his vision became accustomed to the low light. He was a tall, lean-limbed Oklahoman with a face that seemed carved from the West: his features were as spare and resolute as the high desert plain, and in his clear gray eyes were the reflections of vast distances. As such, he seemed distinctly out of place in such a stark industrial setting. His hand-tooled Lucchese boots tramped through the detritus of what had recently been a factory: heaps of dilapidated crates and rotting boxes and scattered shards of a soft pink plastic. The cuffs of his worn deerskin jacket collected dust from the edges of ancient machinery. The silver buckle of his belt made only a feeble shine in the gloom.

But despite all appearances, Gil was very much at home here. At thirty-three, he was a partner in an architectural firm that was rapidly becoming known for quality renovations. The firm had just been contracted to convert this former factory into a lavish residence.

The budget for the conversion was high enough to afford a rare and luxurious freedom in the work.

Already Gil had mentally stripped away the industrial trappings and was busy appraising what was left—the raw space, as it was called. The flooring was yellow pine, a beautiful hard wood, which, when sanded and polished, would glow with a high shine. To buy such boards today would cost a fortune—if you could get them at all. The ceiling beams were also yellow pine, pitchy and aged hard as steel, so that you couldn't ask for a more sturdy support. And the columns that ran the length of the loft in a double row were slender and fluted—an enviable architectural detail.

And then there were the windows: great, crescent-shaped windows with northern, eastern, and southern exposures. When fitted with new panes of glass, they would flood the loft with dazzling sunlight and afford great sweeping views of the Manhattan skyline, which, as far as Gil was concerned, rivaled any natural spectacle on earth.

The inventory left him excited. In many ways this was the best raw space he had seen in months. It suggested endless possibilities; in his mind's eye, he began to throw up skylights, partition off space for a darkroom, a sauna, lay out a sumptuous roof garden with a glassed-in conservatory. Then he stopped himself, remembering that it would be one of his four junior associates who would actually be doing the design. His partner, Albie Knowlton, had convinced him that their own time was far too valuable to squander on design work. They had other plans now—plans that, if successful, stood to make them very rich men indeed.

But still he couldn't help thinking, almost wistfully, that it would be fun to do the drawings on this project. There was that odd trapezoidal space behind the air-shaft, for instance. It just begged for imaginative treatment . . .

A rumbling sound behind him meant that the old freight elevator had been engaged. This would be his client, a woman named Tracy Sherrill. He knew nothing else about her except that she had paid the $220,000 purchase price for the loft in cash. He waited with curiosity for her to appear.

She was much younger than he had expected—not more than twenty-seven—and certainly more attractive: tall, blond, and with the polished, insouciant air of a rich kid come of age. At her heels was a superbly groomed Brittany spaniel, unleashed and collarless.

She stood hesitantly in the open cage of the elevator. "It's dark in here!" she said.

"That's because the windows are so filthy."

"So you *are* there." She squinted as he came toward her. "I can hardly see you."

"Your eyes will adjust. But watch your step—God knows what's all over these floors."

"Rats?" she gasped.

He laughed, untactfully. "No, ma'am. Just old boxes and bits of stuff. Nothing likely to bite."

"Well, how should I know?" She took several purposeful steps into the room. The spaniel followed his mistress's lead and trotted off to explore on his own. "My god!" she said. "This is awful. Am I really supposed to live here?"

Gil glanced at her. "You haven't seen it before?"

She shrugged. "Sally Libscher's supposed to be the best real estate agent in New York. When she said this was a great buy, I took her word for it."

"Sally earned her commission. You've got a beautiful loft."

"Are you joking? It looks like a factory."

"That's exactly what it was three weeks ago."

"Really? And what did they make, if I might ask?"

"Nipples. For baby bottles."

"How very touching," she said sourly.

For some reason he enjoyed seeing her nettled.

Something about her face—perhaps the arc of her perfectly tweezed brows or the petulant bow of her upper lip—insisted that self-indulgence had been granted to her as a birthright. It might be satisfying to prove her wrong.

But she was an important client; he couldn't let himself forget that. The businessman in him sought to mollify her.

"By the time we're finished there won't be a trace of the factory left," he continued crisply. "Try to visualize the way it'll be. Once we rip out the elevator and the walls are replastered . . ."

She began to laugh. He turned to see the spaniel squat, a yellow puddle spreading under its haunches. On those gorgeous Georgia pines! he thought.

"Shocked?" she asked.

"It's your property, Miss Sherrill," he said stiffly.

"Oh, call me Tracy. And you're right—it's my goddamned factory." She laughed again. Then she stood for a moment, lips pursed, studying him. Gil withstood her scrutiny confidently. Since his days as a track star in his west Texas high school, any number of women had studied him in just this same way. And generally they liked what they saw. There was the contrast between his easy, affable manner and the hint of something remote in his eyes that made him uniquely appealing.

"You don't look like an architect," Tracy pronounced. "You're not straightedged enough. And there's no M.I.T. stamped on your forehead."

"I went to Rice. Sorry."

She drew out a pack of Gitanes. He shook his head when she offered the pack.

"I quit," he said.

"Really? How long?"

"About five months now."

"You'll go back."

The smug assurance in her voice made him itch to smack her hard. But then he realized he had wanted to do that almost from the minute he'd seen her. Partly because of her supreme insolence. But partly, too, because he wanted to test the spring of her flesh—to feel the womanly give beneath the sleek, taut, young boy's smoothness of her skin. Watching her walk away from him, he had to admit that he found her extremely attractive. She wore a skimpy camisole beneath a pale, elegant Adolpho suit, seamed stockings, five-inch heels on peach kid pumps—teasing touches hinting at the availability of the body beneath. Tantalizing touches. A look that only the most self-confident woman would dare to adopt.

A look, Gil thought, that Cynthia would never choose for herself.

The thought of his wife was involuntary and brought a crease to his forehead. Cynthia, with her drab "good wools," her sensible shoes, and her sweaters chosen for warmth. Cynthia, who wore her hair clipped back in the same miserly knot whether going to the market or to the opera. No, Tracy's style would never suit her. Yet when he had married her seven years before, she had been a beauty, vivid and laughing, her rich brown hair threaded with skeins of mahogany, auburn, and nutmeg.

Even now, if you looked closely enough, you could see that her features were actually quite lovely. It was just that no one bothered to look past the mousy facade. And so her drabness became a screen—one that served to protect not only herself but also their daughter Alexis from the glare of the world's notice.

Yes, it was for Alexis's sake, Gil thought bitterly, that Cynthia had signed away her life. For a child who would never know enough to appreciate it, would never be able to thank her.

For a long time he had tried to coax his wife back to beauty. He brought her presents: filmy lingerie, stylish blouses, exotic jewelry. He ordered subscriptions to *Vogue* and *Harper's Bazaar,* leaving them opened to layouts of fashions he thought might tempt her. He made appointments for her at Suga and Helena Rubinstein for hairstyling, facials, makeup advice. But the appointments were canceled, the magazines ignored. The clothes she invariably returned and with the money bought countless "educational" toys for Alexis, always nourishing her futile dream that this time they might do the child some good.

And then, abruptly, Gil gave up. He found himself spending more and more time at his office, avoiding going home. As his career absorbed him, his ambition grew, until it became an intoxication, the driving force of his existence. Everything he had went into his work, and an evening spent at home became an extremely rare occasion.

As for his marriage . . . He stared across the loft at Tracy's slender silhouette, not wanting to admit what he felt—that his marriage existed in name only.

He felt something nuzzle his knee and bent to stroke the silky head of the spaniel. "Hey there, old gal," he said.

"Cholly usually hates strangers." Tracy's voice rang with an echo as she crossed the room. "Especially men. I've seen her snap the sleeves off men who've tried to touch her."

"They say an animal takes its behavior from its owner," Gil said.

"I'm also very discriminating—if that's what you mean."

"And what do you look for?" he pursued.

"It varies. There's no one type. Just a certain signal I respond to."

"That's not very helpful."

"It wasn't meant to be." She dropped her cigarette and ground it out with her toe. "Let's go. I've seen all I need of this place."

"Wait a minute," he called. "We haven't even started to talk about what you want done . . ."

She shrugged coolly. "Why don't we both assume you know your job—where to put all the bathrooms and things. Okay? Come on, Cholly."

Bitch! he thought. In one stroke, she had deflated his function to nothing more than plumbing installer. A concise way of letting him know he was just another servitor in her life. What a pleasure it would be, he thought as he followed her into the elevator, to put her in her place.

Outside, a maroon BMW crouched beside a fire hydrant in front of the building. Tracy snatched the parking ticket from the windshield and tossed it into the glove compartment. The spaniel jumped into the front seat beside her.

"What now?" she asked Gil.

"My people get to work. When the drawings are done, you'll be called in to approve them."

"When do you and I meet again?"

He smiled. "Since you have no ideas you want to contribute, it won't be necessary . . ."

She revved the engine and peeled out into traffic.

Gil laughed, feeling he had scored a point. His spirits revived, he decided to walk the seventeen blocks to his riverside office. Soho: it meant south of Houston Street—an ugly name for what was in many ways an ugly place. The streets were narrow and littered, the buildings were blackened with a century's coat of grime. Yet how did that explain the excitement, the energy—even the glamour—that lingered in its corridors? It was as if some invisible alchemist had turned these iron landmarks into pure gold, pouring riches into the pockets of those who knew how to mine it. As he walked along, Gil saw his future stretch giddily before him.

Then, abruptly, his spirits dampened. There was a new poster in the window of an espresso bar. The child, Lisa Wyle, was still missing; the reward for her return had been upped to $25,000. Gil stopped to study the picture on the bill. The girl's elfin face laughed out at the world, eyes precociously sultry, the snub nose dusted with freckles.

It had been three weeks since she had disappeared. In the first few days the whole neighborhood had mobilized for the search. Gil had been among the many volunteers who had trudged from door to door, questioning the occupants of apartments and lofts for clues—an exhausting, and ultimately futile, labor. As the days slipped into weeks and still no trace of the child turned up, more and more volunteers abandoned the search to the police. The ones that continued, began to hunt for a dead body rather than a living child—deserted junkyards and open shaftways were combed, parts of the Hudson and East River dredged. And by now only the most stubborn optimists believed she was still alive.

A shame it had to be such a pretty kid, he thought. And bright too, according to the news reports. It seemed so damned unfair. If it had to happen, why couldn't it have been to a kid like Alexis instead?

He had no sooner thought this than he was shaken with horror. Had he really wished his own child dead? Christ, what kind of a monster was he getting to be? To first deny his wife, then his child . . .

He fished a vial of Valium from his jacket pocket and swallowed one of the small yellow pills. But guilt continued to gnaw at him. *Monster. Unnatural father.* He walked several blocks at a swift pace, trying to shake it off, but it was no use. What the hell. He stopped at a phone box, made a few calls, then hailed a Checker.

As he got into the cab, a car idling its motor across the street suddenly took off. An unusual model: fifties vintage DeSoto with a new black paint job. Gil realized he had seen it before—just fifteen minutes before, in fact, as he and Tracy had been coming out of the loft. A chilling thought struck him. Could it be following him?

He immediately admonished himself. Just what he needed—a good case of paranoia on top of everything else.

He shut the cab door and gave the driver the address of the King Street brownstone in which he lived.

Thia Cassidy peered anxiously over the spiral staircase that led to the upper floor of the duplex apartment. "Oh, it's you," she said with relief.

"Who did you expect? Jack the Ripper?"

She refused to be teased into a smile. "I didn't expect you. It's not even seven yet, is it?"

"I know. I had a meeting and a dinner thing, and both canceled out on me. And I was just too bushed to put any more time in at the office."

He saw she didn't quite believe him. But she said only, "I'm giving Alex her bath."

"I'll be up in a minute. I want to unwind first."

He showered in the downstairs bathroom, finding a fresh flannel shirt and pressed jeans stacked on the dryer in the adjacent laundry room. He recalled that they had just hired a new housekeeper. She seemed to be efficient. But the child's constant noises and disturbing behavior taxed the nerves and patience of even the most stolid of these women. He wondered how long this one would stay.

He took a light beer from the refrigerator, then settled down to catch Walter Cronkite—for all the world, he thought, like any work-a-day husband relaxing on a normal evening at home. He stared at the glowing screen. Terrorists, campaign rhetoric. Flooding and tornados in the South, poor bastards. And that's the way it is. Bayer aspirin.

He stayed seated through ten minutes of a wildlife show, then reluctantly turned off the set and went upstairs. His daughter, in her room, was asleep in her trundle bed. He stared for a moment at the beautiful, pathetic face, touched her hot forehead. He tried not to think.

His own bedroom was a spacious square room granted charm by a large domed skylight centered above the brass bed. The furniture was period Art Deco—the height of fashion, he knew, but never really his style. He had always intended to sell it and construct clean, functional shelving in its place.

Thia sat on the bed. She had just bathed and was wrapped in a long white terrycloth robe. Her face was flushed pink; tendrils of damp hair clung like dark lace to her valentine-shaped face. If only the world could see her like this, he thought. If only they could know how desperately lovely she *could* be . . . He realized that for the first time in months he felt desire for his wife.

"I looked in on Alex," he said awkwardly.

"You didn't wake her?"

"No, I was careful. How was she today?"

"Much better," Thia said. "You really should have seen how well she ate her supper. It's the first time she ever picked up her milk all by herself. She's really starting to improve, Gil!"

He grunted. Why did she insist on interpreting these grotesque parodies of normal behavior as triumphs, signs of improvement? Why couldn't she accept what was real?

She touched her damp hair, testing for dryness. "Since I didn't think you'd be home for dinner, I only bought a tiny London broil for myself. But I could cut it up for shish kebab."

"We can run out for a bite later. First, let's talk."

She glanced at him warily, knowing well what talking had led to in the past.

"I've been thinking," he began. "What if you were to go back to work?"

"Do we need the money?"

"Of course not. I just thought that, since Alex is going to this day-care school and there's this new gal for the cleaning, you might want to. You were doing so well at that literary agency before you quit. But you don't have to go back there. You could do volunteer work. Or go back to school for a while . . ."

"My job's right here," she said flatly. She went over to the dresser, a lacquered half-moon, and picked up a wooden hairbrush. "Is this what you wanted to talk about?"

"Not really. I want to talk about us. The way we live."

"Do you want a divorce?"

The question took him by cold surprise. "Christ, no. Why did you ask that?"

She turned and faced him, her eyes the color of topaz in the lamplight. "I've been getting used to being alone."

He sighed. "I know we've been growing apart, and I'm willing to admit a lot of it's my fault. But there's a lot going on at the office right now. Albie's putting together a development deal that could swing us right into the big money. We could be rich, Thia!"

"That's never been what I've demanded."

"I know, but don't you see what it could mean? How much more we could do for Alex? Get her the best specialists . . ."

"It's *us* she needs, not more paid substitutes!"

It was going wrong. They were skidding inexorably back into the ruts they had already worn so deep. "I don't want to argue," Gil said. "All I'm asking is, should we give it another go or not?"

Thia paused a moment. "It's best for Alexis that we stay together."

"And is that the only reason you'd stay with me?" he demanded. "Honestly?"

Her eyes met his. "No," she admitted.

She turned back to the dresser. Gil had a sudden terror that she was about to bind back her hair and put on one of her frumpy housedresses, and that the luminous beauty he glimpsed now would suddenly be gone again. He went up to her and parted the collar of her terry robe, revealing her delicate collarbones. "I love you in white," he said softly.

"It's just a bathrobe," she protested.

"It's gorgeous. You're gorgeous." He kissed the collar playfully. Then he untied the sash, and the robe fell open. As always, the flushed nakedness of his wife's body overwhelmed him. He cupped the full undercurve of her breast, half expecting a rebuff, but she stood motionlessly, her eyes opaque. Eagerly, he let his hands explore. Such opulence! he thought, grateful that it should belong to him.

He undressed beneath the dark dome of the skylight, then, naked together, embraced his wife, pulled her down onto the bed. His rangy body eased over hers. He caressed her and, finding her wet and ready, filled her. So perfect. Sex with other women—those he'd indulged in affairs with—now seemed in memory dry and hostile. It amazed him that he should ever have been tempted.

Afterward, she whispered, "Let's always be like this."

"We will," he assured her.

But from behind the closed door a child began to cry.

Kermit the frog was riding his bicycle. He waved, and she waved back, so very glad to see him. But suddenly she realized it wasn't Kermit at all, and there was no bicycle, only a huge, horrible elephant with big teeth coming closer and closer to her. She tried to run, but she was too sleepy to move her legs. It was going to get her!

Lisa woke with a start.

"Mommy!" she cried out. No one answered her cry.

She sat up, wiping her eyes. Why was it so pitch black in her room? Where was her Gladys Goose lamp, and what happened to the streetlight that usually shone through the cracks of her curtains? *"Mommy,"* she cried again, louder. Her bed felt funny too: it was softer and narrower and had a funny kind of smell. I'm at camp! she thought suddenly, and a warm joy flooded through her.

But then she remembered and abruptly her joy vanished. She wasn't at camp at all. She was in the big room with the boarded-up windows and the spooky rustling sounds in the walls. She remembered the floor that gave her splinters, and the big crack in it that grinned up at her like a crazy smile. And she remembered how scared she was. Scared to be left alone with the spooky sounds and all the creepy shadows. But scared too whenever The Person came back.

She saw a flashlight beam floating toward her. It was The Person holding out a glass of water. Lisa didn't want to take it—but she was *so* thirsty, so very thirsty. She drank deep. And before she could wonder why the water tasted funny, she was once more sound asleep.

Susan Capasian was a dealer of art, and so it was not surprising that her appearance was a triumph of imagination. She wore antique jackets paired with jewel-colored silk harem pants, embroidered smocks over hand-stitched Victorian petticoats, boots of dyed canvas or leather. Her wrists displayed ancient ivory bangles carved in Nairobi, and from her neck hung lavish silver necklaces from Afghanistan.

But such costumes, no matter how adeptly coordinated, might have appeared merely bizarre if Susan hadn't also possessed the kind of looks necessary to carry them off. Her wide-spaced cat's eyes seemed stolen from a Modigliani portrait, and her mouth was the full crescent of a Raphael; and though she wasn't tall, her long legs gave her the appearance of being so. And her hair: it fell in a cascade of poured honey to her waist, the perfect bridge of innocence between the almond eyes and gorgeous, exotic clothes.

It was a look that was beyond fashion and therefore always, uniquely, in style. Heads turned when Susan walked into a room. People asked to meet her and, when they had, did not easily forget her face.

But at the moment she would have gladly exchanged her vivid outfit for a sober dark suit. She sat staring at her friend Carla Wyle, shocked by how much she had changed.

Carla was a calligrapher and book illustrator; her husband, Donal was a weatherman on a local news program. Susan had known them as a gay and attractive couple, famous for their loft parties at which people were encouraged to act outrageously—in the tradition of Scott and Zelda Fitzgerald—while Donal recorded their antics with a Betamax half-inch video camera. They had been like the slick, two-dimensional characters of a hit TV series—somehow unaffected by the drearier, more mundane problems of life.

But then their daughter Lisa had disappeared after disembarking from a school bus scarcely two blocks away. And in the four weeks since the Wyles had become almost unrecognizable. Carla seemed to have aged ten years—she had lost a good deal of weight, and there were deep grooves around her mouth that hadn't been there before. Donal's puckish face had collapsed, giving him the look of an unnatural, dissolute child.

Both of them were trying hard to be animated for Susan's sake, but their efforts had little success. Carla chain-smoked, while Donal helped himself liberally to a bottle of Jack Daniels; both their voices cracked with fatigue. Their grief was like a living thing in the loft, slavering over Susan with its heavy breath.

"The worst part of it," Carla was saying, "is having to drag out our entire lives for the police. Anything we remember might be a clue. We can't keep any of our memories of Lisa private."

"And the press keep hounding us for new photographs," Donal added. "And the police keep wanting better ones. So we have to keep *looking* at her."

"It must be hell," Susan murmured.

"You can't possibly imagine," Carla said. "There are times when, just for your own sanity, you wish you could forget. But then something pops into your mind

—some detail you hadn't thought of before—and you've got to concentrate on it."

"Everything's got to be checked out," Donal echoed. "But there were all those people at all those fucking parties—I mean, it's impossible."

Carla's stubby painter's fingers tapped out another Marlboro. "The first week our phone rang off the hook—people with leads to report. We had four officers from Missing Persons here to man it. And now we get maybe three calls a day."

"And all the leads were dead ends?" Susan asked.

"All of them. Most were from people who meant well but were just wrong about their information. Though, of course, we've had our share of cranks."

"And sickos," Donal said bitterly. "Some bastard telling me in explicit detail what he'd like to do with our kid when she was found. A six-year-old kid, for Chrissake."

"Donal, please!" Carla's voice was nearly a shriek.

"Sorry, Carly. It's just that when I think of that creep, I want to put a bullet down his goddamn throat."

Carla took a deep drag of her cigarette and blew the smoke out in a violent, focused stream. "Lord, it's so easy to get morbid sitting around this place. Let's talk about something else. *You* talk, Susan. How's Joey?"

"Oh, she's fine," Susan replied uncomfortably. It seemed cruel to dwell on her own daughter, safe and well at home, with Lisa missing. But Carla seemed eager for her to continue. "I'm enrolling her in the Synergy Center—that day-care place on Houston Street everyone's been raving about. They say it's a great preparation for grade school."

"I wish you'd brought her. People have been avoiding us lately—especially the ones with kids. They seem to think we're under some kind of a curse, and it could be contagious if they get too close."

"But so many people pitched in to help," Susan said.

"Sure, at first." Donal's voice grew taut with bitterness. "The whole damned neighborhood turned out.

Five hundred people—knocking on doors, passing out fliers, searching rooftops. Bringing us *fruit*cakes, for Chrissake! But you know what happens. People get bored. More important things come up. Like a good movie on TV or a chance to go roller skating."

"Oh, Donal, you're being too hard. You know there was really nothing left for them to do." Carla turned wearily to Susan. "If Donal seems especially negative today, it's because he's worried about his job. The station's been wonderful, though. They've told him to take as much time off as he needs."

"Hoping it'll be forever," he muttered. "If you think they want me back, you're crazy. People don't want to hear it's going to rain from some guy with tragedy hanging over his head. A weatherman's got to be up*beat*, for god's sake."

"I know how he's feeling," Carla sighed. "I haven't touched a brush since this whole thing started." She gave a dismal laugh. "Maybe it *is* a curse on us."

Her husband drained his glass. "Or maybe it's a judgment," he said.

She looked at him. "What's that supposed to mean?"

"You ought to know."

"Well, I don't," she said slowly. "So maybe you'd better tell me."

"I mean, if you had spent half the time thinking about your daughter that you do running around with your goddamned friends . . ."

"*My* friends! Oh, that's sweet coming from you. From old Donal Wyle and his one-track mind. Don't you think all of Soho knows how you spend *your* time?"

"Just what are you insinuating?"

"I'm not insinuating anything, darling. I'm *saying* that we all know how you were spending your extracurricular time. You're nothing but a damned *rabbit*!"

"And you, I suppose, are the virgin princess? Have you forgotten our last party, when you and Freddie Dugan were locked in the john for an hour?"

"You bastard!" she shrieked. "You son of a bitch . . ."

The green wall phone began to ring. Carla caught herself with a gasp and stared at it, her face a mingle of hope and terror. Then, with a sudden movement, she snatched up the receiver.

"Yes?" she breathed. She listened a moment, and her eyes began to glow with new life. "Yes, that's right, she does. Wait a minute, let me get a pencil." She began scribbling furiously, as if the pencil had a movement of its own and her fingers could barely keep hold of it. "I've got it," she said at last. "Thank you. Oh, god, thank you!" She hung up. "They've seen her!" she breathed. "Some people have seen her! In Hoboken— that's right across the river! They described her perfectly—even the little freckle above her eyebrow. And she's all right! She's in a hotel with some old couple. They must've found her wandering around somewhere and don't listen to the news."

Donal rose, unsteadily. "Darling, let's not get too excited. We've had promising leads before that turned out to be nothing."

Carla shook her head furiously. "This time it's true. I can feel it. I know it is. I've got to call the police and have them pick her up." She reached for the phone again.

"Should I go?" Susan asked softly.

Donal looked at her with surprise, as if he'd forgotten she was there. "No, stay. It could be a while before we hear anything more. I'll get you another drink."

Susan remained on her stool at the butcher block-topped kitchen bar. The Wyles' loft was like dozens of others she had been in—a long white rectangle done in "High Tech" style—the stark, streamlined industrial furnishings and fixtures that were currently the rage among the most fashionable architects and decorators. And the Wyles themselves were no different than so many Soho residents—career-oriented people conditioned to putting their own ambitions and pleasures before everything else.

She glanced at Carla on the phone, her knuckles white where they gripped the receiver, and at Donal trying hazily to open a bottle of wine. Did she blame them for Lisa's disappearance? She honestly didn't know. Certainly they loved their daughter—but they did seem to regard her with the same careless delight with which they enjoyed their other possessions—their Art Deco Wurlitzer jukebox, or their Betamax video recorder, or the vintage player piano they had had so lovingly restored.

Yes, careless—that was a good word for them. They acted upon whims and rarely gave a thought to the consequences. Until, of course, it was too late.

But blame them or not, Susan couldn't help a slight feeling of envy. They were together. However much they might wound each other, at bottom they were always each other's support. Susan thought of her own struggle—to raise Joey, to get the gallery off the ground—with no one to help her, no one but herself to lean upon. Years of juggling feedings, baby-sitters, and playgrounds with the constant demands of artists, collectors, museum curators, and doing it entirely on her own. Not that she was complaining—she had received ample reward for her struggle. It was just that every now and then she wondered what it would be like to have someone to help her.

She was an unwed mother. The phrase itself sounded so corny here in tolerant Soho, where people actually congratulated her for her independence. And most of the time she gave no thought to it. But other times she was plagued by uncertainties. She would recall snippets of articles in the moldering *Reader's Digest*s she used to find in the beach cottages her own family rented on the Carolina coast. The ones that quoted ominous statistics to support their moralizing conclusions.

How ironic! she thought. Susan Capasian, owner of

one of the most powerful galleries in Soho, dressed in fantasy clothes, surrounded by glamorous and eclectic friends—who would ever guess that what she dreaded most was becoming another statistic in the *Reader's Digest?*

Her thoughts were interrupted by Donal placing a glass in her hand. "Drink up!" he exhorted with faked gaiety.

She smiled up at him encouragingly. How selfish of her to be dwelling on her own vague problems in the face of her friends' very real tragedy.

Carla, having finished on the phone, joined them. The three sipped the wine and waited through what seemed an eternity. Susan, at one point, heard herself talking about the gallery—she was opening a show on Saturday that she had particularly high hopes for—but neither Donal nor Carla was listening. Their eyes lingered on the clock, willing the stubborn hands to move faster.

At the sudden rasp of the door buzzer, they all gave a start.

"They've brought her!" Carla cried.

She flung open the door. All three waited breathlessly as heavy footsteps clumped up the three steep sets of stairs. A tall man in a herringbone sports jacket appeared at the door.

"Sergeant Donner . . ." Carla began. She peered around him as if to find her daughter lagging on the stairs.

The detective shook his head. "It wasn't her, Mrs. Wyle."

Carla seemed not to understand. "You . . . you talked with her?"

"We sent an FBI man—the address you gave us was out of state. He found the girl. She was from Quebec, traveling with her grandparents. Apparently there was a resemblance, but she wasn't Lisa."

Carla's face turned a dead white. She broke into

convulsive sobs, and her husband rushed to cradle her shoulders.

"Come on, honey," he said tenderly. "I'll get you a pill, and then you'll lie down for a while." He led her off to the bedroom in the back of the loft.

Susan got up and went over to the detective. "I'm Susan Capasian, an old friend of Carla's," she said.

He put out his hand. "Kerry Donner, Missing Person's Bureau."

"I know this is a difficult question, but what are the chances . . ." She hesitated, unable to put her fears into words.

"Do you want me to be honest? We're up a creek. There's been no ransom note—hell, there's been no evidence that any crime's been committed at all. There's just a kid missing." He scrunched his hands in his jacket pockets as if angrily. "For all we know, she could've wandered off somewhere and gotten stuck in a shaftway or an abandoned old refrigerator. Or she could've fallen into the hands of a sexual psychopath— some guy who looks as normal as you or me on the outside. Either way, our hands are tied; there's no way we could trace her. Which means all we can do is wait for the body to show up in some trash heap or suburban woods."

His words startled Susan. Such insensitivity, she thought, was despicable. But then she noticed the acute pain that had surfaced in his eyes and realized she was wrong—if anything, Sergeant Donner had been too affected by this case.

She studied him more closely. She saw a rugged-looking man in his mid-thirties with a rather lopsided face—yes, one eye was definitely slightly larger than the other. And he had the appearance of someone who despised looking in mirrors—tie, shirt, and jacket were a clash of prints and patterns, and his shaggy brown hair was finger-combed at best.

But for all that, she decided, she wouldn't call him

ugly. He had a strength about him that superseded all his other features. It was a quality too often missing from the men who habituated her own circle. She found it attractive.

Donner walked to the window and peered out to the street. "It's this neighborhood," he murmured. "It's too damned unnatural. People living in factories. Shops selling truffles and marmalade where a month ago there was die cutter . . ."

"Are you saying," Susan cut in, "that it's the neighborhood's fault that Lisa is gone?"

"Not exactly. But it's no place to raise kids."

"And why not?"

"Kids need structure. Rooms with four walls. Furniture that looks like furniture and not"—he gestured—"the insides of a munitions plant. They should know that when they go out to go to school in the morning the printing press across the street will still be a printing press and not suddenly a sidewalk cafe."

"How many children do you have, Sergeant Donner?"

He looked up, slightly startled. "None. I'm not married."

"Well, I have a daughter. And I wouldn't bring her up anyplace else in the world."

"How can I argue?" he said. "There's a saying—I think it's from Goethe—'All theory is gray beside the golden tree of actual life.' "

It was the second time Susan had cause to stare at him. "Is *Faust*," she asked, "required reading at headquarters these days?"

"No, it's just bachelor living. I read a lot." He looked at her. "Now I know why your name's familiar. The gallery . . ."

"You know it?"

"I'm afraid that since working on this case I've gotten to know everything around here. Including the galleries."

"You don't sound very complimentary."

"Should I be? Some of that stuff they call art—I call it the hoax of the century."

The quick temper Susan inherited from an Alabama-born mother flared. "That's a ridiculous opinion," she snapped.

"Is it? There's one gallery room filled up completely with dirt—nothing but sterilized dirt. They told me it cost over fifty thousand dollars to set up. Maybe they can't think of anything better to do with fifty thousand bucks, but then maybe they haven't been to the South Bronx lately either."

"I think you should find out more about it before making such a sweeping generalization!"

He glanced at her and gave a sudden, brief smile. "Maybe you're right. Anyway, I'm always ready to learn."

She liked his smile. As a rule, Susan was cautious about men. There was never any lack of candidates for her attentions. She had been pursued by actors and industrialists, a rumored embezzler, a Pulitzer Prize winner, and any number of artists. Sometimes she responded, but only up to a point—she never let herself fall in love. When it looked as if there would be a danger of that, she ran. It was for Joey's sake, she told herself. She couldn't allow herself to become involved with anyone who wouldn't be totally devoted to her daughter. And, as a result, she often picked her escorts from the wide pool of gay men at her disposal—men who were handsome, witty, eminently presentable—and, above all, safe.

The thought now crossed her mind that perhaps with a man like Kerry Donner she wouldn't have to play it quite so safe.

But that was ridiculous! she immediately chided herself. They existed in different dimensions; they had as little in common as a Hottentot and a man from Mars. In another minute he'd walk out the door and she'd never see him again.

Why then did she hear herself saying, "I'm opening a

show Saturday evening that I think is first-rate. If you care to come by, I might be able to convince you that it's all not such a fraud."

"Sorry," he said, "I'll be on duty."

She didn't know whether she was sorry or relieved. But then Donal emerged from the bedroom. He seemed sober now, but his face was taut and gray.

"Carla's lying down," he said. "It's the best thing for her. She's been up till dawn every night this week."

"I guess there's nothing more I can do," said Donner.

"No, but thanks for coming by, Sergeant. She couldn't have taken hearing the news over the phone."

The detective nodded and left. Donal turned pleadingly to Susan. "You'll stay awhile, won't you, Susie? I can't stand the thought of staring at these goddamned walls."

"Of course I will," she replied.

"Georgene!"

Lisa rubbed her eyes. She was still so sleepy, even though it seemed like she had been in bed for days and days.

"Are you awake, Georgene?"

"I'm Lisa," she said. She sat up. "Where's my mommy?"

"I *am* your mommy, sweetheart."

She looked up, and it *was* the face of her mother, merry and comforting and warm. She reached out for a hug, but something was different—big, squashy breasts —it didn't feel like her mother at all. It felt like Constanza, who used to do the cleaning for them until her daddy fired her for stealing jewelry. But Constanza used to hug her just like that.

"It's time for your bath," her mother was saying.

Lisa climbed out of bed, still rubbing her eyes. She was glad she was having a bath because she felt so hot and sticky. But there was a big black pot on the floor, like the kind the turkey at Thanksgiving was cooked in. She wondered why she was being made to take a bath in the Thanksgiving pot.

Her nightgown was pulled over her head. "Climb in," her mother told her.

She stepped into the pot. "It's too cold," she complained.

Her mother's fingers fluttered in the water. "Don't be silly, it's just right. Sit down."

But it was too cold, freezing, and Lisa began to shiver. Her mother gave her something—a green rubber frog that was dirty and all chewed up and ugly. "This is yucky," Lisa said.

"But you love your Hammy. You never take a bath without him."

"He's not mine, and I don't want him," she insisted. The cold water was clearing the sleep from her eyes. She held up the ugly frog to show her mother she had made a mistake. But her mother had disappeared, and in her place was another person—one with big awful eyes, and teeth, and a huge red mouth like a crocodile.

She began to scream.

"I'll have a beer," Bob DeRitis said.

The butler seemed to flicker a moment, then withdrew on muffled cat's feet. He rematerialized minutes later bearing a crystal Steuben mug on a lacquered tray. The mug was filled to the brim with a dark, foaming liquid.

Unreal, DeRitis thought.

He took the mug, tasted—it was Watney's ale, served barely cooled in the proper British tradition. Delicious. Still, he'd have been more than satisfied with an icy can of Bud.

But, of course, a lowly domestic beer would never do in a joint like this. It wouldn't go with the English Regency furniture or the magnificent Aubusson rug—or, for that matter, with a butler who looked at Bob as if Bob were single-handedly lowering property values. The whole setup, Bob thought again, was too pissing unreal. Here was a baronial manor squat in the bowels of lower Manhattan; not only that, but it was a manor that had once upon a time been a flophouse. That's right, an honest-to-God Bowery-style flophouse. These very walls, now the backdrop for framed and

incandescent old masters, had once sheltered the dregs
of humanity as they coughed, spat, and guzzled their
final days away. Their stinking pallets had once lain
right where that Steinway grand now so magnificently
presided.

But what made it even crazier was that this whole
wonderland was now the property of Coy Seiglitz, his
classmate of twenty years before at the Rhode Island
School of Design. The kid with the goony grin and the
perpetual neck rash, who could never score on his own
but had to be set up with the easiest lays in Providence.
The kid who would have been voted least likely to
succeed if there had been such a category.

But that kid was dead, he reminded himself—
murdered in cold blood by the charming, calculating
stranger who sat across from him now. The celebrity
who called himself "Spetzi," well known to gossip
columnists, talk show hosts, and tabloid readers—the
fixture at Studio 54, the intimate of socialites and film
queens. The once skinny frame had been fed, exer-
cised, and oiled to robustness.

Of course, Bob had known about his friend's meteor-
ic rise to fame—with all the publicity the man courted,
it was impossible not to know about it. And Bob had
also heard all the rumors that had come down on the
ever-active art world grapevine about Spetzi's reputed
gangland connections and about his penchant for young
girls—there had been a hushed-up scandal two years
ago concerning the thirteen-year-old daughter of a
British viscount. But somehow Bob had never been
able to connect the smooth visage in the newspaper
with that of his former classmate.

Until now, that is.

"I've gotta hand it to you, Coy," Bob said. "You've
come a hell of a long way."

His host winced slightly. "Please, old boy—nobody
has addressed me by that barbaric name in half a
decade. It's Spetzi, if you please."

"If *you* please." Bob shrugged.

"By the way, Bobby, I haven't congratulated you on your recent success. I read the reviews of your show in Chicago. Very impressive."

"What was really impressive," he laughed, "was that after eight years of nothing I came up with anything at all. The critics had long ago given me up for dead."

"It sold well, I trust?"

"Well enough to get me back to New York. It's been a long time."

"So it has. Here's to your return." Spetzi lifted a fluted glass filled with a dark green liquid.

"What's that you're drinking?" Bob asked.

"A purée of carrot, spinach, celery, and wheat germ. My usual afternoon cocktail."

"Christ, don't tell me you've quit drinking?"

"Not entirely. I take two glasses of a good Latour or Margaux at dinner. The latest research shows that people who drink three ounces of alcohol a day stand the chance of living the longest."

"That so?" Bob said. "Well, my own research shows that none of us are gonna live forever. So here's to you." He drained his mug. The ale emboldened him; he blurted out, "What do you know about Susan these days?"

"I was wondering when you'd get around to that," his host said smoothly. "Susie Capasian—she's become quite a muscle in our little art world, as I'm sure you already know. A regular wheeler-dealer."

"And the kid?"

Spetzi glanced at him shrewdly. "I always figured it was yours. And I'll bet she's soaked you plenty for it over the years."

"She's never asked for a cent," Bob said gruffly. "Not that I had anything to give her anyhow."

"And you never will—not if you keep doing those absurdly detailed paintings. Who do you think you are, old boy, Jan van Eyck?"

"What's that supposed to mean?"

"I'm talking economics. Look, how many paintings can you turn out a year? About a dozen?"

"About that. I've been doing a couple of gouache studies for each."

"That's only one show a year. And after the gallery takes its forty percent, Bobby, old pal, you're not left with enough to shit on."

He laughed uneasily. "That's a damned mercenary way to look at it."

"The only way to look at it. Face it, kiddo, the value of a painting these days is only as great as its price tag. And a painter's only as successful as his bank account." He set his glass on a spindly tripod table and rose. "Come on, I'll show you my studio."

Bob followed him up a circular brass stairway into a vast skylit atelier. There was a time, he thought, when he'd have given his left nut for a space like this to work in. Funny how things like that seemed to matter less and less as he aged. There wasn't much chance he'd make it to the age of seventy; but if he did, he imagined his wants would be pared down to a few bodily necessities.

He walked through the studio, looking at the canvases. Those that were finished were stacked against the wall; the rest sat on easels. They were Spetzis, all right—the style was now as familiar to the average American as the Coca-Cola logo or McDonald's arches. They were sketchy, psuedoartistic renditions of subjects stolen from the Impressionists. The colors were the bright, ingratiating colors of advertising illustrations. It was a style that pandered shamelessly to the popular taste, while pretending to be something more. The man on the street—the guy who watched the national average of 6.4 hours of television a day—could look at a Spetzi and feel smugly that it was art he could understand.

There wasn't, Bob thought, an honest brushstroke in the entire studio.

"You don't have to tell me what you think," his host said. "The critics have a label for it. They call it 'trash.'"

"But Christ, Coy, you used to be a damned good draftsman. You could really draw."

"Sure I could. And that entitled me to starve. Face it, Bob," he said bitterly, "the art world is crap. If Michelangelo came along today, the critics would kill him. 'Too academic,' they'd say, 'No respect for the picture plane!'"

"You don't know for sure," Bob mumbled.

"Oh, but I forgot—you're the darling of the critics right now. They're giving you straight A's. But you better watch out, old boy. Tomorrow they might decide that you're out and somebody else is in. And *then* try to peddle your precious pictures!"

Abruptly, the bitterness vanished from Spetzi's face, replaced by the slick, professional smile. "Of course it's trash!" he said genially. "Utter, irredeemable trash. And you want to know something else? I don't even do it anymore. I've got an assistant—a very talented boy—turning it out for me. When Willie's feeling inspired, he can knock off three original Spetzis a day."

Bob burst into laughter. "You're an even bigger whore than I thought!"

"I'll accept that as a compliment." His soft, manicured hand fluttered to rest on Bob's shoulder, like an overfed bird alighting on a ledge. "Bobby, my old pal. You're the only one from the old days I wouldn't just as soon see frying in hell. I like you, laddy. And I'm going to let you in on something that could make your fortune."

"What's that?" Bob asked warily.

"A little real estate deal. If all goes well, it could return millions. Absolutely millions."

"Christ, Coy," Bob said, "you've got so damned much money already. Why the hell do you need any more?"

"Why? Because money is power. And when you've

grown up the runt of the litter, you know there's no such thing as too much power."

The butler's crisp voice broke in on an unseen intercom. "Excuse me, sir. The film crew is here."

"Send 'em up." Spetzi turned to Bob with a shrug of apology. "Sorry, old man. I'm having a documentary done on me—the artist and his work and all that—sort of an autobiography on film. So I'm afraid . . ."

"You want me to get lost. No problem."

In burst four young men hauling a profusion of lights, cameras, silver film canisters, and miscellaneous equipment. They fanned quickly through the studio as if it were familiar ground and began setting up.

Bob's earlier feeling of being in a dream began to return. He moved somnambulistically toward the stairwell. Suddenly he wanted to be out of this room. As far away as possible from this building and everything in it.

He was beginning to be sorry he had come back to New York.

From a block away Day McAllister could hear the shrill shouts of children at play rising above the horns and the grinding gears of Houston Street. She quickened her steps until she came to an ugly chain-link fence; then she peered through the links at the children congregated in the day-care center yard. Her heart gave a leap as she spotted the dark-haired man squatting in their midst.

It was strange, she thought, that even though she had been living with Eben Link for nearly eight months, she still felt a thrill whenever she looked at him. But then he was incredible. He had the sort of long, lanky, muscular body that made jeans and a workshirt the sexiest outfit a man could wear. And a generous, strong-boned face with a cap of tangled curls and lazy, lazy eyes. "Indecently attractive" was how a friend of hers had once described him, and Day felt that that about accurately summed it up.

She loved to walk down the street with him just to watch the reactions of other women. They would stare at Eben with damp, sulky eyes that nevertheless couldn't conceal the interest behind them; then the glance would slide to Day as if they wondered how on earth she had managed to snare such a prize. And, in truth, sometimes she wondered herself. Oh, she was pretty enough—especially her eyes, which were a deep, inconstant gray—and she knew as well as anyone that her figure did ample justice to a bikini. But she wasn't *gorgeous*. She didn't radiate the sort of physical beauty that fulfilled people's fantasies—as Eben indisputably did.

But that wasn't the way in which they were most mismatched. There was their backgrounds. Day was the only child of a Short Hills banker, and her childhood had been cradled in all the material comforts of upper-middle-class suburbia. She had been a Girl Scout, a cheerleader, and she had made her debut at the Junior Assemblies. For her sixteenth birthday she received an envelope containing the keys to a pineapple-yellow Mustang. And for graduating fifth in her class at Briarcliff her parents gave her a chaperoned tour of France and a check for $5,000 to "set herself up in the city."

And Eben. He was one of seven kids raised willy-nilly by a discouraged widow in a dying New Hampshire mill town. A high school dropout who had thumbed his way through all forty-eight states before he was seventeen and who had held every odd job under the sun—from caddy to grave digger—though none for longer than six months.

And he had spent nearly two years in jail.

It was so ironic, Day thought, that she—the coddled, overprotected debutante—was sharing the bed and board of an ex-con. A "jailbird," as her father would say. And yet such was the fact.

About two years ago Eben had been doing some dock work in New Haven, mixing with a fairly rough crowd. It was a late Saturday night. He had been letting off some steam at a downtown bar and caught a ride back with a man on his crew, a guy who was still pumped up, looking for some more action. He got into a drag down a side street with another buddy who had pulled up behind, took a bad turn, and skidded into a telephone pole. Eben woke up an hour later in a local hospital. He had a small concussion—nothing serious. But there were two cops standing over his bed, and they were more than a little interested in a plastic bag containing three grams of cocaine that they had found in his jacket pocket.

It had been a plant—either by the guy driving the car, who needed to get it off himself, or by one of the cops who was looking for a hot arrest. But it wasn't Eben's—of this Day was absolutely sure. Despite his unconventional lifestyle, she knew how essentially straight he was. He didn't smoke, hardly drank at all. And he never used drugs—not even the marijuana that inevitably circulated at loft parties.

But, whatever his past mistakes, to Day they were no longer important. What mattered now was that she have his long, hard body to hold in the night, his arms around her, his hungry mouth at her breast. And that mattered to her more than life itself.

Now, as she watched him, he finished buttoning the sweater of one child and rose to attend a pudgy Oriental boy who had been tugging importunately at his shirttail. Day started to call out to him, but stopped. There was something thrilling about watching him like this—as if she were watching him perform something intensely private, like making love or praying. He grabbed the Oriental boy, swung him twice around, then set him down and made a mock lunge at another child. Both children ran off, squealing with delight. It was obvious that they worshiped him—he was Spider-man, Han Solo, and the Incredible Hulk all wrapped into one. And he, in turn, seemed happy in his role as their guardian. Who'd have thought, when the parole board found him the job, that it would suit him so well?

Still, Day knew that it wouldn't hold him. It was only a matter of time before his restlessness would seize him again and he'd be off in search of whatever was to come next. She felt the chill of a familiar fear—if only she could be sure that what came next included herself.

He had noticed her and, waving vigorously, jogged over to the fence. "Hello, love of my life," he said.

They kissed through the fence. The metal link pressed cold against the warmth of his lips.

"Just like old times," he said. "Experiencing life from behind bars."

"Oh, Eben, don't . . ."

"Hey, just kidding." He grinned. "So what brings you to this neck of the urban jungle?"

She beamed back at him, never able to hold out against his smile. "I'm on a story, naturally."

"Another piece on the center? Wasn't it just last month you ran one?"

"Typical male ego—thinks the whole world revolves around himself. Couldn't possibly imagine there's another newsworthy establishment in the entire neighborhood."

"Guilty as charged! Okay then—let me guess what it is." His eyes swept the street mischievously. "Got it! The Chinese laundry—it's a front for a ring of international smugglers, and the *Soho Sun* is going to crack it wide open."

"Do you know you are completely crazy?"

"It *has* been brought to my attention."

"I'll bet," she laughed. "But you know something else? I wish it were true. I mean, if I could break a really big story, I'd have a good shot at the *Times*—or at least the *Daily News*—and not have to keep working my ass off for a community newspaper."

"Don't knock your paper. You said yourself it does a damned good job for something its size."

"It does. But it's still small time. And so am I as long as I'm working for it." She focused on the children playing behind them and drew a discouraged face. "The Lisa Wyle case is the biggest thing to happen in Soho in years. I keep thinking that if I were really any kind of a reporter—a Woodward or a Bernstein—I'd have turned up something on it. But I spent three solid weeks and came up with even less than the police. Maybe I'm fooling myself. Maybe I'm just not cut out to be an investigative reporter."

"Hey, now, listen." He reached through the fence and touched her shoulder. "You're good, baby. You're damned good. And whatever you want to do, you'll make it. I'm betting the rent on that."

He was like that always—supportive, ready to brace her confidence whenever its foundations seemed shaky.

"No kidding, now, what's this story you're doing?"

She brightened. "There's a synagogue on the next block that's been vandalized about a dozen times this year. It's only got a handful of a congregation, and the rabbi says he may be forced to just shut it down."

"Too bad."

"Eben, it's tragic! If he does that, they might knock the building down and put God knows what in its place. The kind of craftsmanship that went into that synagogue doesn't even exist anymore. It would just be another score for big money at the expense of everything old and beautiful!" She gave a little laugh, slightly embarrassed by the heat of her outburst. "It's the piece I'm doing for the *Sun* on the history of Soho—it's got me thinking about buildings and neighborhoods and things. You think I'm crazy to care about that stuff, don't you?"

Christ, no. I love you for it. But, baby, you know how I feel. When it comes to the system—*their* system —I just don't want to be involved."

A voice broke in from behind him.

"Excuse me, Eben."

They both turned. It was a tall, square-faced woman, her arms folded like a cincture at her waist. Day recognized her as one of the afternoon volunteer workers at the center.

"What is it, Caroline?" Eben asked.

"It's Alexis Cassidy. The Siegler twins are teasing her again. Poor little thing. It's criminal that they send her here instead of someplace where she could get proper care."

"What are the twins doing to her?"

"When they think I'm not looking, they snatch her pail and throw it back and forth to each other over her head."

"The little monsters. Look, stay with Alexis. I'll be there in a second to take care of the twins."

"Really, Eben. I can't stand guard over one child and look after all the others, too."

"One second, I promise."

Her flat eyes shot a quick, disapproving glance at Day. Then she nodded curtly and walked back through the yard. Day watched her bend over an angelic-looking little girl with ash blond hair.

"I don't like that woman," she declared. "There's something peculiar about her."

"Oh, Caroline's all right. She's just a duck out of water. A straight-laced Midwestern spinster who somehow wound up in the middle of Sin City. But she's great with the kids. You should see the way she looks at them sometimes—like a jeweler looking at a string of perfect pearls."

"Um," Day murmured. She glanced at Caroline again and noticed a thick strand of silver glistening in the woman's long reddish hair. Suddenly she realized what was bothering her. Caroline was dressed in the mode of the late fifties or early sixties—a long, full, swirly skirt with a short-sleeved taffeta blouse. Her makeup dated from those years, too—eyebrows tweezed and penciled to slim parabolas, mouth a clownish slash of red. And her hair was pulled up in a girlish ponytail. The look had recently become popular again with kids in their early twenties—the "punks" who wore it in the spirit of rebellion and mock nostalgia. But Caroline was hardly a kid—she was a good forty-five if she was a day.

"I still think . . ." Day began.

The angelic-looking child in Caroline's charge let out a piercing scream.

"I'd better go," Eben said. "Whose turn to cook tonight?"

"Mine. I'm planning to do my famous enchiladas rancheros. I picked up some fresh Monterey Jack at De Roma's."

"Can't wait. See you tonight, baby."

Day was keeping Rabbi Rosensweig waiting, but she couldn't resist lingering a moment longer. She gloried in the grace of her lover's movements, in the effortless way he attracted the love of those around him.

"Oh, Daysie," she told herself, "you're a very lucky girl."

But the strange eyes that followed her as she reluctantly drifted away wished her nothing but malice.

When Gil Cassidy had arrived in Manhattan to work as a draftsman with the prestigious firm of Gerald Arliss Associates, his country upbringing still clung to him like relentless prairie dust. He was an awkward sight on Madison Avenue in his two-piece double-knit suits that stopped short of his wrists and swamped his cheap, cardboardy wing-tip shoes. And his sandy hair, brushed flat with a healthy dose of Vitalis, gave him the look of a ten-year-old boy after an unhappy visit to the local barber. The splendid, ruthlessly chic creatures who glided past him on the avenues needed only a glance to place him as a hopeless unsophisticate—someone whose tastes ran to well-done beef and Worcestershire and French-fried potatoes.

It did not take Gil long to sense that he was out of step. He quickly began to absorb his new environment, letting it instruct him and polish him as he explored its myriad complexities. He learned to use chopsticks and snail forks—to eat sashimi, knedlík, caviar, and tofu. He learned to identify a *nouveau* Beaujolais and to appreciate glum Swedish movies with subtitles. Above all, he learned to recognize the symbols of rank and power upon which this most powerful of cities was founded: a fifty-year-old Patek Philippe upon a wrist, the telling finish of Savile Row tailoring, the scent of Joy, the white fire of a perfect diamond.

At the same time that Gil was falling in love with Manhattan, the city was cultivating its own ardent affair with the West. The boots and drawl and easy charm of his home state were suddenly in fashion. And so Gil discovered that his native style—the one that became him best—also gave him a ready status. His star was on the rise.

It was at moments like the present that he was most conscious of having transcended his hick-town roots. He was dining at The Four Seasons with a man so famous that his presence was the focus of the entire restaurant. People nudged each other, whispered, "That's Spetzi!" with the suppressed, almost embarrassed excitement with which New Yorkers recognize celebrities.

Gil gazed around his table with satisfaction. Across from him sat the artist, magnificent in Versace riding clothes, giving intricate instructions to an impassive waiter as to how exactly his salmi of duck should be prepared. Gil's partner, Albie Knowlton, sat on his left, nervously drumming his spoon on the table, his compact body tensed in preparation.

And then there was Thia. Here his sense of satisfaction faltered. It was true that the soft light coaxed the essential beauty of her features so that she looked lovelier than he had seen her in a long time. But she sat quietly, a dowdy white sweater pulled tight across her shoulders, as if she hoped to blend into the background. He wondered if it had been the right decision to bring her along.

The waiter collected the menus. Spetzi removed his gold-rimmed spectacles and with fussy precision settled them in their case. "Well, laddies," he said. "Shall we talk?"

"We're ready." Albie Knowlton leaned forward, his

fingers letting go of the spoon. "Let me fill you in on where we stand. We've purchased options on both the parking lot at 860 Broome and the neighboring Byer Thread Company building. Upon demolition of the building, we'll be in possession of a lot ninety-five feet by a hundred and fifteen. Using these dimensions, we're about to submit design-development drawings to the Bureau of Standards and Appeals."

He paused. Spetzi appeared momentarily absorbed in buttering a baguette.

Gil continued, "The plans call for a sixteen-story building that we're calling the Lower Manhattan Sports Center. Briefly, what it'll contain is six regimental tennis courts and eight squash courts, an Olympic-sized swimming pool, and four rinks for both ice skating and roller skating. There'll be four floors of gyms, massage rooms, saunas, and electronic game rooms. Also a quad cinema and a nursery—plus a full complement of pro shops, restaurants, and health food bars."

"And self-service indoor parking for two-hundred and eighty-five cars," Knowlton added. "The idea is to offer an entire day's recreation—from exercise in the morning to dining and dancing in the evening. And everything will be designed for optimum luxury. We're going for a top-class clientele. We're not competing with the Y."

Spetzi refilled his glass from a bottle of Lafite Roths-child 1959. He swirled the velvety wine, took a delicate sip. Finally he said, "This Dyer building . . ."

"Byer," Gil corrected. "The Byer Thread building at 864 Broome. It's been vacant for over a year."

"Uh-huh. But if I'm not wrong, it falls under the Soho landmark district designation. Tearing it down is going to present something of a problem."

"We've got a way around that," Knowlton said quickly. "We've got a licensed engineer willing to attest that the building is structurally unsound. In fact, ready to collapse any minute. You could say that our demol-ishing it would actually be a service to the city."

"Those old warehouses," Spetzi observed, "were built to last through the millennium."

"Maybe so. But I've also got a contact in the mayor's office who's willing to accept our proof. He'll help us override any objection the Landmarks Commission makes." Knowlton gave a short laugh. "Once we've got a go-ahead, we'll have the wrecking ball there and that building leveled inside of an afternoon. The Commission can raise all the fuss they want after that."

Gil stared into his glass, wishing Albie wouldn't be so blunt. His partner had long since convinced him that certain expediencies were necessary in this business. The dealing and bribes and kickbacks were the way things were done—it went on all the time, Albie insisted. Gil had developed a policy of letting his partner attend to such things, as if by not knowing about it himself he was not really involved.

He glanced quickly at Thia; but if she was listening, she gave little indication of it. She picked desultorily at the thin, nearly transparent strips of raw salmon on her plate, her expression immobile.

"You kids are pretty ambitious," Spetzi was saying. "You think big, and that's good. Let's hear what kind of figures you've come up with on this thing."

"We need," Knowlton said, "four-hundred and fifty-thousand dollars to buy out the option on the land, for which we've negotiated a ten-year balloon mortgage one point above the prime rate. Figure a quarter of a million for demolition. Then the construction will come in at around seventy dollars a square foot—or, say, thirteen million—for which the banks will fund forty-five percent."

"Uh-huh. And where do you boys figure on getting the rest of the financing?"

The two architects exchanged glances.

"It was our understanding," Gil said, "that you have access to investors with cash. And that your investors are specifically looking for a real estate venture."

The waiter set an oxtail terrine in front of Spetzi. He

sliced a forkful and brought it to his thin lips. "Perfect," he declared. "Just the right texture—not too coarse." He picked up his glass, but instead of drinking stared over its rim. "For the sake of discussion," he said, "let's say I did know some investors. Let's say they might be interested in some such venture as you've described. What kind of return could they expect to see on their money?"

Albie Knowlton placed his palms flat on the table. "For starters, we've got eighteen franchises for sale—food, equipment rentals, and pro shops. We've done some sniffing around, and already we've had positive responses from Jantzen, Adidas, and La Crêpe, just to mention a few. The sale of the franchises will give us immediate cash back, and the rent they pay will cover a good deal of the operating costs. Now, that's not even beginning to talk about membership dues, individual admissions, parking fees . . ."

"I see. And again, for the sake of discussion—what sort of deal are you offering?"

Knowlton smiled. "As our people have structured it, the investors would own sixty percent of a corporation . . ."

"No tax benefits in a corporation," Spetzi said sharply.

"Well, then . . ." Knowlton began.

"How's this for an idea? Let's say there's a limited partnership. Let's say that the investors would come in for—oh, eighty percent. You, of course, would get the rest, with your company acting as general partner."

Gil glanced up. "As general partner, we'd have full responsibility if anything went wrong."

"I can't think of a better way to insure that nothing *does* go wrong." Spetzi smiled.

"But that means . . ."

"Enough business!" the artist cried airily. "Surely we can come up with a more fascinating subject to go with this extraordinary meal. Art, of course. I think modern art has an obligation to readdress itself to the common man. Don't you agree, Mrs. Cassidy?"

Thia dropped her fork; it hit the edge of her plate and fell squarely into her lap. Her cheeks burning, she mumbled what she hoped was a coherent reply. Mercifully, Spetzi did not press her further, but launched into a long monologue punctuated with flamboyant gestures.

She shuddered with relief. But then she noticed that Gil was looking at her with an expression of disgust, as if he were ashamed to be with her.

She stabbed at the exquisitely prepared food on her plate with little appetite. Who was this anxious, ambitious stranger who called himself her husband? she wondered. What had he to do with the man she married?

She had a sudden, vivid memory of the first time she had seen Gil. She was twenty-three years old, an assistant literary agent for the William Morris agency, somewhat bored with her job, spending a restless lunchhour window-shopping and dreaming. In front of Radio City, a tall, country-edged young man asked her the direction to Fifth Avenue. It was such an obvious ploy to talk to her, but he was so fresh and unaffectedly eager, she couldn't help responding to him.

On their first date he took her to O'Lunney's, the only bar in Manhattan with live country music, afterwards steering her to the San Francisco Plum for French toast and ice cream. She had teased him about thinking he was still in Texas; and his embarrassment was so immediate and profound that she was sorry— she had only meant that she was having a good time.

But the next weekend he took her to see *Equus* on Broadway and then to a late supper at the Ginger Man. O'Lunney's was never mentioned again.

He spoke to her about his plans: buildings he wanted to do—significant buildings that would enhance the environment rather than plunder it; buildings that would change the way people live and think. Someday, he assured her, when his apprenticeship was complete, he would strike out on his own and forge his visions into brick and steel. She knew he dreamed of becoming another Frank Lloyd Wright, a Pei, a Venturi.

Somehow he had changed. It was partly the result of the seductive influences of Manhattan. The glittering image of success that the city held out to him drove his idealism into a far and vanishing future.

But the real change happened three years ago—when they first learned that their daughter, Alexis, was special. *Special*—that was the only word Thia could bring herself to use. There were other labels: "retarded," "autistic," but her mind firmly rejected them. Those words were for idiots, hopeless cases, morons. That had nothing to do with Alexis.

But that was the beginning of the nightmare. The rounds of pediatricians who shrugged their fat shoulders. "To tell you the truth, Mr. and Mrs. Cassidy, we still don't know too much about this syndrome." The EEG's and motor sensitivity tests and the endless rounds of psychologists' questions. The lack of answers. The shaking of heads.

She and Gil would straggle home after yet another day of fruitless efforts, and they would begin to fight. At first it was short spats over trivial things: a check she forgot to note in the ledger, his rudeness to a taxi driver. Then their quarrels grew longer, more heated, and more and more frequent, until finally it seemed they were fighting about everything. Their marriage was a battlefield on which there were no truces.

The pressures increased. It became awkward to entertain friends and have to explain why their three-year-old daughter wore diapers and screamed like an infant for a bottle; and so they stopped entertaining. Going out was another problem. It was difficult to get baby-sitters or housekeepers who would put up with Alexis's constant demands for any length of time—and,

anyway, Thia hated leaving her in the hands of strangers. She insisted to Gil that she preferred staying
home. And as time passed, he needed less and less
encouragement to go out by himself.

It was then that Albie Knowlton—another associate
at Gerald Arliss—had convinced Gil that they should
open up an office of their own. Albie instilled in Gil the
alluring idea that they could get rich by teaming up
together, and Gil threw himself into the project; as it
absorbed him, their fighting at home grew less and
finally stopped. And then one evening it erupted again,
viciously, out of nowhere; and in the heat of the
argument, Gil spat out that Alexis's condition was her
fault, that she was to blame.

Later he apologized, said he hadn't meant it. But she
had never forgiven him—because in her heart she—and
only she—knew it was true. Several months after the
baby was born, Thia had been feeding her in the living
room when the kitchen phone rang. She laid Alexis on
the couch—instinctively, without thinking, the way one
would lay down a book or some knitting. When she
returned scarcely a minute later, the baby was on the
floor whimpering. She had seemed unharmed by her
tumble, and Thia, after reprimanding herself, had
thought no more about it—until two years later, when
sitting in the office of a well-known child psychologist
and listening to him suggest, in his comical, lilting
Norwegian accent, that such a condition might be the
result of a fall on the head. At that moment she had felt
her world collapse.

Someone was hovering at her shoulder. She looked
up; it was the waiter.

"Dessert?" he asked. "I'd recommend the tea saba-
yon with fresh pears."

People were watching her. She forced herself to say,
"Yes, that sounds good."

The waiter moved away. Thia saw herself suddenly
through his eyes—a gray mouse of a customer to be
patronized for the sake of the more important people at

the table. She was sorry she had come. And yet there
had been a time when she loved going out—loved
dressing herself up in shimmering fabrics, courting the
passing admiration of strangers, flirting with her husband across a candlelit table. She hated how drab she
had become. But when she thought of making herself
pretty, she was seized by a paralyzing guilt. She didn't
deserve to be pretty—not after what she had done to
Alexis.

She raised her cup of coffee to her lips and found it
cold.

"You could've at least tried," Gil said sullenly. He
sat behind the wheel of the car, eyes fixed rigidly on the
road. The car was a '65 white Caddy convertible, which
he loved, but which had a gas mileage that horrified
Thia. She felt, when riding in it, that people stared
contemptuously after it and barely refrained themselves from throwing stones.

"What could I have done?" she said. "I don't know
much about your business."

"In these kinds of proceedings, it's not so much what
you say as the *way* you say it. It's a game—you go by
the rules. It was a distinct liability having you there not
saying anything." He took a turn in silence, then
added, "Spetzi went out of his way to draw you in. It
was damned nice of him. And you were hardly civil."

She considered saying, "Spetzi is a monstrous ego-
maniac who was merely looking for a fresh audience,"
but she remained silent.

Gil pulled up in front of the King Street brownstone
and waited.

"Aren't you coming in?" she asked.

"I'm going back to the office. There's a few things I
want to catch up on."

"But it's almost midnight."

"Yeah, but we're really under the gun with this deal.
Albie's probably there already."

An unsettling thought crossed her mind. Could he be

seeing another woman? A shock of jealousy ripped through her. She had guessed that he had slept with other women from time to time. But the idea that he could be actually involved with someone else was suddenly intolerable. She thought of the night before—she had responded to his lovemaking with a passion that had surprised her. It had rekindled feelings that had for too long been smothered. And afterward, sitting in bed eating sandwiches ordered up from a nearby deli, giggling at the television with the sound off—it had been almost like the first years of their marriage. If only they could be like that more often. If only he understood what she was feeling, and didn't leave her so alone.

She turned, meaning to ask him to stay. But a sudden surge of pride intervened, and instead she let herself silently out of the car.

It was quiet on the block. But as Gil pulled away she noticed a figure standing across the street, dressed in a raincoat and snug knit cap—odd on such a mild night. The person—she couldn't tell if it was a man or a woman—began to quickly walk away, and Thia imagined there was something familiar about the slouching, ungainly stride. Was it someone watching her?

It's just nerves, she told herself, and hurried into the house.

In every neighborhood there is one intersection that constitutes its heart—a corner from which all activity seems to radiate and where the gatherings are always the thickest. In Soho, it's where the fat, white ribbon of West Broadway crosses its skinnier sister, Spring Street. From here you are within stone-throwing distance of the most important shops and galleries, the best known of its cafes.

A couple stood on one curb of this corner as if transfixed. Though the day was warm, the woman had a lynx coat shrugged over her shoulders; the man held a folded Burberry trench coat as if it were a precious substance.

Bob DeRitis suddenly realized they were staring at *him*. What the hell? he thought. Then it came clear—it was because he looked like an artist. Baggy paint-spattered jeans, inside-out sweat shirt, torn Nikes. Flecks of pigment in his wiry, graying hair. He was exactly what they had come downtown to see: a tourist attraction!

Christ Almighty!

He cupped his hands to his mouth and shouted,

"Take a picture and stuff it!" Really witty, he told himself. A put-down worthy of Oscar Wilde.

It amazed him how much the neighborhood had changed in the six years of his absence. Changed for the worse, in his unabashed opinion. All the cutesy little shops, the atmospheric restaurants that soaked you fifteen bucks for a slab of pot roast with a phony French name, the tourists wrapped in the skins of endangered species, the shoppers swaddled in credit cards, the gallery hoppers stark naked under their pretensions. You could take all of it and send it back to Bloomingdale's, as far as he was concerned.

To be fair, he had gone through some changes himself. Two years ago, he had been a washed-up bum, exiled in Chicago, tending bar for a living and drinking up the tips. Not having exhibited in five years, he'd imagined that every now and then someone in New York would ask, "What ever happened to DeRitis? He was so promising."

And then, one March while the ice floes still glistened on the rippled lake, he managed to stay sober long enough to begin a painting—and finish it. It was one of the diaphanous nudes that he had once had a reputation for, but rendered now with a new and subtler perspective—something mature that he had acquired in the tough years of his exile.

Encouraged, he began another, then had a relapse and went on a drunk. It was a pattern that continued for over a year, the relapses becoming further apart, until finally he had done enough good canvases to comprise a small show.

He went, hat in hand, to a second-rate dealer and begged for a show. The dealer grudgingly granted it, though demanding 60 percent—"Sixty percent of zero is zero," he had quipped, while Bob barely restrained himself from a vigorous reply.

Astonishingly, miraculously, the show was a success. A small but glowing review in the *Tribune* touched off an avalanche of others. The critic from *The New York*

Times flew up to see what all the ruckus was about and went home with a pad full of superlatives. The paintings, originally priced at $1,200, began to sell for $5,000, then edged up to $10,000.

And three weeks later Bob was back in Manhattan. Success continued to breed itself. He received daily invitations to receptions at ritzy places for people he had never heard of, offers to teach at distinguished academies, commissions from the cream of society and the aristocracy of finance. And, of course, the top galleries had opened their doors to him.

But so what? he thought. It could all blow out tomorrow. Spetzi was right; the art world was a fickle place—one day you're adored, the next you're lower than rabies. He knew what it was like to fall from grace—better never to have been there at all.

He felt a sudden surge of nostalgia for the way things used to be: back at the start in the late fifties, when soaring rents forced him—along with hundreds of other artists—out of their studios in Greenwich Village, with nowhere else to go. They needed large space and plentiful light; but both are costly commodities in New York, and artists are perpetually short of cash. The crampy dark brownstone apartments they could afford in run-down neighborhoods just wouldn't do.

And so they discovered the lofts in the forgotten iron valley—vast open spaces with rows of oversized windows that flooded them with light, spaces that could be had for a song.

But there was a hitch. The area was zoned only for light manufacturing. The buildings were short on fire prevention and often had no plumbing at all; living in these lofts was strictly illegal. But artists are imaginative people. They quickly developed elaborate subterfuges to conceal their living arrangements from the prying eyes of fire wardens and health inspectors. Refrigerators and stoves could be hidden away in closets, mattresses covered by day with slabs of plywood. Clothes could be easily stored in boxes marked CANVAS or ELECTRICAL SUPPLIES.

Bob grinned, thinking of the first place he'd had down here. It had been an old spool factory on Wooster Street, and the ugly aluminum bins that still lined its walls were very convenient for sorting his laundry. The place was blazing hot in summer, freezing in winter—his only heat source was a tiny potbellied stove and three thin cats who slept on his feet at night. No plumbing—he pissed in an old kettle and used the toilet of a nearby gas station to take a crap. And once a week he commuted seventy blocks uptown to a friend's apartment to indulge in the luxury of a shower.

It had been tough; but at the same time there'd been something nice about it—a feeling that they were somehow all in the struggle together. They partied together, drank together, swapped supplies and stories and sometimes even spouses. And when anyone seriously needed help, everyone pitched in and gave a hand.

Who would do that now? Bob glanced down the swarming avenue. Expensive people looking for pleasure met his eye. Now a child disappears, he thought, and everyone's too busy spending money to care.

The light was failing; a block away, the first streetlamp blinked on. If he wanted to get to Pearl Paint before it closed, he'd better hurry.

But he had come to a large black door with the name Susan Capasian printed on it in Roman lettering. He stopped, realizing he hadn't come out to buy new stretchers after all. He hesitated, then resolutely pushed open the door.

The gallery was mobbed. It took him a moment to realize he had walked in on the middle of an opening. Just his luck, he thought, and started to back out. But then he reconsidered. Maybe it was for the best.

Faces swirled around him. Some he recognized from six years before, others—mostly younger—were unknown to him. He saw the flat moon face of a man he had once hated, though now he couldn't remember why. And the brittle face of a woman he had once pursued.

And then there was the face of a child with his own quick black eyes staring up from it.

He bent down to her, feeling suddenly light, as if the blood in his veins had turned to air. She had his eyes and tightly curling hair, but the rest of her features belonged to Susan.

"Hi," he said. "My name is Bob. What's yours?"

"Joey." The child solemnly extended her hand. He shook it with equal ceremony.

"Well . . ." he began. His mouth was suddenly full of marbles. All the speeches he had rehearsed for this occasion had suddenly vanished from memory.

"I'm getting a horse for my birthday," she stated.

"You are?" he asked, somewhat startled.

"Yes. I'm going to name him Pepper."

"But where are you going to keep him?"

"Oh, he'll have to stay outside. But if it gets cold, I'll give him one of my blankets. I don't care—I've got six."

Bob wasn't sure how he should respond. Kids, he thought—he didn't have much experience with them. But Joey, with a glance over her shoulder, announced, "I've got to go now." She gave a quick smile and trotted away.

He cursed himself. There were so many things he should have said. If only he knew how to talk to her. With a twinge of jealousy, he watched a young woman with a roan-colored ponytail bend over Joey and say something that made her giggle.

He began to feel suffocated by the crush. He pushed his way back to the door and burst like a drunk into the cool gathering dusk. Damn! He could have asked her what she liked to eat, what she dreamt about, what her favorite color was, whether or not she was happy. And instead he had just stood there stupidly.

Maybe he didn't deserve any more. He was the one who had abandoned her—hell, if it had been up to him she wouldn't even be alive.

But he had been in such a bad way back then. His work had soured, he was staring down the possibility of being forever washed up. The little money he had left he was rapidly converting to alcohol and pouring it down his throat. The thought of being tied down to the support of a family had spun him into a blind panic. He wasn't ready for it. He would have gone mad.

No excuse. Just honest admission of weakness. And a heartfelt resolution to start doing better.

Someone came out of the gallery. It was, he realized, the woman with the ponytail who had spoken to Joey. As she passed, he saw with a shock that she wasn't young at all—she was forty if she was a day.

What a remarkable subject she'd make, he thought vaguely. Without even realizing what he was doing, he began to follow her. He knew exactly how he'd pose her—on a single bed, naked except for a barrette in her hair, perhaps talking on the phone with her legs crossed. The lighting would be such that at first glance you'd think she was a teenager—but then you'd notice the middle-aged body. . . .

She whirled suddenly. "Why are you following me?" she demanded.

Bob glanced up as if snapping out of a dream. "I wasn't . . ."

"I crossed the street twice, and both times you did too." She put a police whistle to her lips.

"No, don't blow that," he said quickly. "Look, I was following you, but not for what you think."

She looked at him skeptically.

"I wanted you to pose for me," he went on. "I mean, I'm an artist. I've got a studio over on Prince Street. I thought you'd make a good model." Christ, it sounded lame. She'd probably have the entire First Precinct here in a minute.

But she dropped the whistle and stared at him, her eyes as flat and emotionless as a Byzantine icon.

"Look, it was a lousy idea," he stammered. "Forget it. I'm sorry if I scared you."

"You didn't," she said.

"Yeah. Well, sorry anyway." He edged away, then made off almost in a run, heading to the Spring Street Bar.

All things considered, he thought, *he could certainly use a drink.*

The show was going to be a success: Susan's finely tuned antennae had picked up enough signals to tell her so for sure. She had had overtures from both the rep of an important German collector and the art consultant for Pepsico; and she had seen the first-string critic of a major newspaper chain gaze at one of the most daring canvases in the show and nod. But most telling of all was a certain buzz in the room—an ineffable charge of excitement that always distinguishes the success from the failure.

Susan wedged her way through the crowded room, greeting old faces and new, accepting compliments, doing her share to promote the festive air. As she neared the door, she saw it open. Recognition of the man who entered made her smile.

Kerry Donner stood hesitantly by the entrance as if he weren't sure he was in the right place. His face relaxed as he saw her approach. "I was afraid I'd never find you in this mob," he said.

"Luckily, *you're* pretty hard to miss. Just how tall are you, anyway?"

"Six-four and a quarter. But I tend to slouch a lot."

"A little," she corrected. "Did you get off duty?"

"No, I'm working. But I had to stop in at the Wyles, and since I was in the neighborhood . . ."

"How are Donal and Carla?" she asked.

"Not great. Carla's lost more weight, and Donal's still drinking way too much. But they've decided to get some professional counseling, which might be some help to them. And," he added pointedly, "they could use a bit more company."

Susan dropped her head. "I know I haven't been back to see them. But I felt so helpless when I was there. If there were just something I could do for them . . ." She anticipated what he was about to say. "I promise I'll run over there tomorrow," she said. "Now come with me. I want to show you my favorite painting in the show."

She led him to a large canvas hung on the south wall. Huge bleeding blocks of yellow and red seemed to float beneath the surface of the canvas as if they were suspended in water. The colors caught and played off each other until it seemed as if the whole painting was in motion.

Donner gazed at it in silence for several long moments. "Remarkable," he said at last. "The longer I look at it, the more I see." He pointed to a red dot on the lower corner of the painting. "That means it's been sold, doesn't it?"

"That's right. To me—I bought it the moment I saw it." She laughed lightly. "Once upon a time, I'd put fake stickers on paintings that hadn't sold, just to make it look like the show was moving like hotcakes."

"What for?"

"The psychology of the collector. Hardly anyone buys a painting these days just because they like it. It has to be an investment as well. Something that will at least hold its price and hopefully become worth a lot more."

"So if it looks like a lot of people are buying it, then it also looks like a good investment."

"You've got it."

"You didn't care that it was somewhat—well—unscrupulous?"

"But I wasn't pushing schlock," she said strongly. "I was promoting work that I knew was good. Very good. And I was willing to do anything to get it to sell!"

He didn't reply for a moment. Then, glancing over her shoulder, he asked, "Is that your daughter?"

Susan turned. She saw Joey at the buffet table take a piece of sourdough bread and hold it out to the air in front of her. Her mouth moved, but there was no one there to listen to what she was saying.

"What's she doing?" Donner asked.

Susan sighed. "She's got an imaginary playmate she calls Tweenie. It's supposed to be a girl with green hair who comes from London. The rest of the details change from day to day. I don't know what to do about it."

"I've heard a lot of kids go through a stage where they invent imaginary friends."

"But it's not just Tweenie. Joey's started to make up all sorts of things. This morning she told me Peter Pan had been sitting in the window eating a Milky Way. She's got such an active imagination that I'm starting to have a hard time telling what's real and what's made up." She glanced hesitantly up at Kerry Donner. "I've had to raise her totally on my own," she told him.

"I noticed you wore no ring."

"You *are* a detective, aren't you?" she snapped. She was immediately surprised at her reaction. There had been no censure in his voice—nothing but a bland observation. To mask her confusion, she turned abruptly and said, "Let me show you my office."

They walked into a small, spare cubicle furnished with blue file cabinets, a metal desk, and a round, cherrywood antique table. "Here's where all the non-glamorous work gets done," she said.

He was staring at a painting that hung over her desk. It was an unfinished portrait in oil of herself, standing naked before a full-length oval mirror. The rendition of the double image of her body was overtly erotic. Light caressed the curve of her back like a lover's hand and lapped at the high breasts and converging thighs reflected in the mirror.

"Don't you like it?" she asked.

"It's a lovely painting. But . . . startling."

"Because it's a nude?"

A smile appeared briefly on his lips. "I know I'm a hopeless Victorian—totally out of step with the rest of the world."

"I'd think that as a policeman you'd see things a lot more shocking than this."

"See it, yes. But get used to it . . ."

She looked at him. He was a complete puzzle, this man. Each time she thought she had him neatly categorized, he said something or did something that shattered her conception. It annoyed her that she couldn't pin him down, just as it annoyed her that she liked watching for his rare, fleeting smiles.

He glanced at his watch. "Time for me to get back to work. And anyway, I'm taking you away from your guests."

"I *am* glad you made it tonight."

"So am I. I never like to back down from a challenge."

She had a strong impulse to ask if she would see him again. But then there were hands on her shoulder, a voice in her ear: "Susan, *cara,* you've been neglecting us all evening. And you know we're your most devoted admirers . . ." She was flanked by two young men fastidiously tailored in Giorgio Armani and De Noyer —they belonged to the network of elegant, affable gay men who composed a substantial tier of the art world.

"I was just leaving," Donner said awkwardly.

Susan was suddenly aware of how he stuck out in this crowd. His clothes were as hopelessly mismatched as before and his hair as disheveled. Her eyes fixed on his tie—a wide, paisley affair of the sort that went out with acid rock and student demonstrations. She felt a strange flush of shame for him. How could she have thought herself attracted to him?

"Good-bye, Sergeant," she said stiffly, and turned her face back to the glittering arena of her own world.

Lisa was all alone.

She knew it was day because all the lights were on. But she couldn't see the sun at all because the windows had big boards nailed over them. She wondered if this was a dungeon. If it was, then maybe she was a princess and a prince would come to rescue her.

But she didn't want a prince—she wanted her daddy. He was the best daddy in the world. He gave her rides on his back and told her stories about Pilgrims and people on other planets, like Saturn and Jupiter. And once he took her down to the studio and put her on television with him, so that all the other kids in her class could see her there.

She started to cry again, but she made herself stop. And she wasn't going to scream anymore, either. Because she knew that if she did The Person would come back and give her a drink of water, and then she would want to go to sleep again. Instead she was going to be very, very good and do everything she was told, and then maybe she would be allowed to go home.

Today she didn't complain at all when her hair was brushed and there were tangles or when this scratchy dress was put on her. She pretended that she thought the dress was beautiful, but it wasn't. It was old-fashioned, and it itched her legs when she sat down.

Maybe she could find her jeans. She decided to look. She knew they weren't in the dollhouse or under her bed or in the brown boxes next to the little stove and refrigerator. But there was an old suitcase next to where The Person slept. Maybe they were in there.

Lisa approached it cautiously, listening carefully for the sound of anyone coming. She knelt down beside it. It was so dusty and it smelled bad. She hoped her jeans wouldn't smell that way if they were in there.

She lifted the top of the case. But there were no clothes inside—just a bunch of old, beat-up toys, broken dolls, and games she had never heard of. And there was a photograph lying on top of them. It was old, too, and the bottom of it was all burned. She picked it up and looked at it.

It was a picture of a girl in the exact same dress that Lisa was wearing now. A little girl with hair like hers, and who looked exactly like herself.

Day McAllister awoke to the sound of bells from St. Anthony's in nearby Little Italy. Eben was still asleep, his hand shading his eyes from the sun, which poured, thick as buttermilk, through the tall windows.

She kissed his nose. "Morning, my love."

He murmured, then reached up and pulled her on top of him. Their mouths met, gently at first, then with urgency. She ran her fingers through his hot thick hair, softly pulling little curls; his hands stroked the down of her flesh. Their bodies moved sinuously, familiarly, against each other. Their rhythms were in sync—they fit so well together. With every thrust she felt herself fall deeper and deeper into a thick, sweet well; the waves lapped over her, shuddering, then subsiding.

She lay still in his arms. Sticky, sunny peace. "I love you," she murmured.

"Mmmm. Me too."

She couldn't help teasing. "You love you, too?"

"Oh, what a nasty girl! You know what I mean."

The second part of their Sunday ritual began. Eben smoothed the crocheted spread over the rumpled sheets and laid out the fat sections of the Sunday *Times*.

He flipped on the stereo, chose Pachelbel's *Canon in D Major.* Day arranged breakfast on a tray. This morning there were chocolate brioches, a thick slab of Crottin Poivre studded with peppercorns, delicate smoked chicken breasts with a homemade mayonnaise. She added a steaming Chemex of a fresh Nicaraguan roast and brought the tray complete with utensils to the bedside table.

They ate every last crumb, then settled back with the paper. An attempt to work the crossword puzzle was abandoned over an obscure South American parrot genus. The record clicked off. Both were too luxuriously lazy to change it.

"Trade you 'Arts and Leisure' for Section One?" Day said.

"It's yours. Nothing in here anyway but inflation and the usual politicians letting off wind."

Day skimmed the front page, fighting back a spurt of jealousy for the reporters whose by-lines appeared over plum assignments. You'll get there, she promised herself, turning the pages.

Her attention was snagged by a small item with the word *Soho* in the headline buried in the back of the section. She read it quickly. A sixteen-story public sports facility was to be constructed at 860-864 Broome Street. A public hearing was scheduled to determine if zoning variances should be granted to demolish the building currently on that site. There was a brief description of what the facility would contain and a quote from the architect, Albert Knowlton: "The Lower Manhattan Sports Center will be a valuable and important contribution to the growth of the Soho community."

Day tossed it to Eben. "Look at this."

He glanced at the item. "The wheels of progress," he said lightly.

"God, don't you realize what something like this could do to the neighborhood? Turn it into downtown Passaic!"

"Maybe. But Soho's getting pretty commercialized anyway."

"But this would destroy everything that's left." She turned to him with a frown. "Doesn't that bother you?"

He shrugged. "If it gets to be a drag here, we can pick up and go someplace else."

"Just like that?"

"Sure. Why not?"

"But we *live* here. This is our home!"

"If we move somewhere else, *that* will be our home."

His easy smile that usually thrilled her now stirred something disturbing inside her.

"Isn't there anything you'd fight for?" she asked.

He knelt beside her on the bed, suddenly serious. "You can't fight, Daysie. That's what I learned sitting up there in that shithole—Danbury. The system's too damned strong. If you try to fight it, it'll smash you. All you can do is try to stay free of it."

She was silent. He reached out and touched her cheek. "Hey. You're not mad, are you?"

She looked at him. Soft dark curls tangled with the thick fringe of his lashes. "No," she said slowly. "I just wish I understood you better."

"I wish I understood myself." He rose, stretched. "Listen. You know Rusty Klein, that guy who's into holograms?"

"What about him?"

"He told me that if I came by today he'd show me the process."

She glanced up. "I didn't know you were interested in holography."

"Sure, it's fascinating. You know I always thought I had it in me to be some kind of an artist." He laughed. "Employed or otherwise."

"Are you thinking of quitting your job?" she asked tensely.

"Not yet. I'm just browsing. But I think there'll be a lot happening with holograms in the near future, and it wouldn't be bad to be in on it." He picked up a towel. "Anyway, I told Rusty we'd be over around two."

"You go ahead. I've got that synagogue story to write up."

"Okay," he said cheerfully.

She watched him take a new bar of Pear's soap from a cabinet and disappear into the bathroom. Just once she wished he'd argue with her, try to make her change her mind. But she knew it was against his code—the one that said everyone should do exactly as he pleased without interference.

All right then, what did she want? Eben, of course. She wanted him desperately. But already she could sense him turning toward some indistinct future. She could no more cling to him than to a retreating wave. She could only hope to swim with him.

And if she couldn't? If she were to lose him? Well then, there was her career. Her dream of breaking a big story, of making it as a reporter.

She picked up the section of the *Times* that had slipped off the bed. She suddenly knew what she wanted to do.

She was going to stop the Lower Manhattan Sports Center.

It was Gil Cassidy's secret conviction that hiring Teddy Golfarb as an associate had been one of his most fortunate decisions. Not only was she a superior draftsman and a talented designer—she had been top of her class at Columbia Architecture—but she also handled clients with tact and efficiency. And, what's more, she appealed marvelously to his sense of aesthetics. She was built on long, crisp lines—not a beauty in the conventional sense, but sleek, perfect, breathtakingly clean. In this she matched the white-on-white offices that gave out onto the white snake of the Hudson. Both Teddy and the river view made him think of the word *purity*.

He wondered if it was strange that he had no desire to sleep with her. But though he sometimes squeezed her hand or playfully stroked the nape of her neck, the thought of any more intimate contact repelled him. What he felt for her was more closely associated to pride of possession. He liked just knowing she was around.

He was glad to find her in before him this morning, her lean figure, in a simple straight black skirt and

78

severe blouse, bent fluidly over a drafting table. As usual, they fell into the bantering routine they had developed over the year they had been working together.

"Tell me the truth," he teased. "Do you wear skirts like that just to drive us poor guys crazy?"

She straightened, grinned. "That's right, boss. I love to see strong men falter."

"Why, ma'am, I always knew you had a mean streak in you."

"Mean as they come," she said cheerfully.

"I suppose you were out all night bringing honest men to their knees."

"Don't knock it—I meet some of the best people on their knees." She laughed, shaking the thick, black bangs from her eyes. "Actually, I was here till almost one last night. The Sherrill project is turning out to be a bitch."

"I figured it would be. That's why I assigned it to *you*."

"You're too good to me."

"I know." He grinned.

He went over to a bank of wide, shallow drawers that contained the drawings of current projects. Seven of these were labeled SPORTS COMPLEX. He opened the top drawer and carefully removed the delicate sheets of drawings.

"Albie in yet?" he asked.

Teddy nodded. "I've got a feeling he was here all night. When I left, he was still working."

"That's funny. He told me he had a dinner date."

"Well, I can vouch for the fact that he was definitely burning the midnight oil."

"Then his date probably fell through." Gil took the plans into his office. They were due for final submission to the Board of Standards and Appeals, and there were several minor details of the lower floors he wanted to modify.

He studied the plan of the third floor, which was

designated for lockers, pro shops, and a long, curving health-food bar. He had an idea of how to make the same number of lockers more spacious—it meant a slight readjustment of the placement of the bar.

He worked through the morning, oblivious to the bustle and ringing phones of the office around him. At lunchtime he munched a dry ham and Swiss sandwich Teddy brought up for him. By two he had reworked the plan to his satisfaction; he stretched, then went out to get the drawings of the building's exterior.

He was particularly proud of his design for the facade. He had spent weeks wrestling with the problem of making a modern sixteen-story building conform to a neighborhood of low gingerbread structures. Finally he had hit upon an ingenious solution: a five-story false front, with the main bulk of the building set slightly back, out of the direct line of vision. Some simple, but graceful, detailing on the false front echoed the ornamentation of the older buildings around it.

He picked up the elevation. Then his fingers gripped the edges of it, as he could scarcely believe what he saw. This wasn't his work. These were plans for a grim, massive cinderblock rectangle—a monstrosity of a building, more suitable for a prison than for anything else.

He snatched up the sheet and burst into the adjoining office of his partner. "What the hell is this?" he demanded.

Albie Knowlton cocked his head. "I happen to know you're capable of reading an elevation, Gil."

"Don't be cute, Albie. Teddy told me you were here all night. Is this what you were doing? Changing these plans?"

"Don't you like my design? And here I always thought you respected my work."

"This is nothing but a hack job. The cheapest . . ."

"That's right. The cheapest." Albie picked up a Dunhill briar root pipe. He tapped the bowl lightly against the edge of the table and began filling it with

Capstan tobacco. "With this revision we can knock off close to a quarter million from our construction costs."

"For Christ's sake . . ."

"Sit down, Gil—you're getting excited." Albie gestured with the stem of the pipe. "Now listen. I've been in very close contact this past week with both Spetzi and his money people. They're not terribly sentimental. They're looking for the highest possible return on their money, and they're not interested in frills."

"Damn it, boy, I'm an architect. I don't consider good design a frill."

"Come on, Gil—all that noble theory was fine for architecture school. But now we're dealing with real clients—there's real money at stake. We've both been out in the world long enough to know we've got to compromise."

"It seems to me we've done a hell of enough compromising already."

"Oh, baby, we've only started. And I'm telling you now—I'm damned if I'm going to blow this deal over any half-assed issues like the shape of the facade."

"It won't be up to me anyhow. You'll never get this past the Buildings Commission."

Knowlton looked at him. "Maybe it's time you stopped playing the eternal naive, Gil, and started facing facts. I'll get it past the same way I got the Landmarks overruled on the Byer building demolition. My friend in the mayor's office is going to be well taken care of on this deal. He won't let me down." He laughed sharply. "Which is another goddamned reason to shave some of our other costs."

Gil had an urge to smash his partner square in the mouth—to send his pipe flying to oblivion. He stepped forward.

Teddy stuck her head in the door. "Gil?"

He wheeled, snarled, "What is it?"

She looked at him, startled. "Your wife. She's here."

Damn! "Be right out," he snapped. He turned back to his partner. "I'm gonna say this straight, Albie. Our partnership is in serious jeopardy. I'm not thrilled with the way you've been handling a lot of things lately."

"You poor damned dreamer," Knowlton replied.

Gil stared at him a moment, then strode out. He stopped by the water cooler and swallowed two Valiums. The vial was running low. He'd have to go back to that quack on West End Avenue and pick up another prescription.

Thia smiled eagerly when she saw him.

"What are you doing here?" he demanded.

Her smile faltered. "Don't you remember? You said you'd come with me today to pick up Alexis at the center."

"Well, I can't. I'm too busy."

"But we agreed it would be good for you to meet the people there . . ."

"I'll go tomorrow. Something important's come up."

"Is it more important than your own daughter?"

"Stop bugging me!" he screamed.

The room started to spin. He shut his eyes to stop the dizzying carousel; when he opened them, Thia was gone.

A child with the face of a Renaissance cherub haloed by pale gold hair stood motionlessly in a pool of sunlight. Her smile was of an unearthly radiance—the kind of smile sponsors dream about to sell a new gelatin dessert, before settling for more mortal substitutes.

Suddenly the smile twisted into a hideous grimace. The button nose scrunched up, the cheeks puffed out. The child made this distorted face twice, then began to rock rhythmically, from heel to toe. A sound formed on her lips: "Buh, buh, buh . . ." She sneezed and continued rocking. "Buh, buh, buh, buh, buh . . ."

Caroline Losey drew a linen square from the pocket of her dirndl skirt and held it to the child's nose. "Blow," she commanded.

The child complied.

"Good girl." Caroline tenderly dabbed the child's cheek. "Alexis is a good girl."

"Want ball!"

"No more ball. It's time to go home. Look, there's your mommy!"

The ethereal blue eyes of the girl focused on the familiar figure in the distance. "Tia!" she crowed.

83

"Say 'mommy,'" Caroline prompted.

"Tia," the girl insisted. She shook herself from Caroline's hands and ran to her mother.

Thia Cassidy bent to kiss her. "How's precious? Look, I brought you something!" She held out a plastic half-moon containing a cityscape. She shook it, sending flurries of snow above the tiny roofs. Alexis grabbed it and stared, mesmerized.

"She was very good today," Caroline said. "She ate her lunch all by herself, and she stayed seated almost all the way through music time."

"Yes," Thia said. "I expect she'll be showing a lot of improvement from now on."

"Let's hope so." Caroline let her large hand brush the child's aureole of pale hair. "Such a beautiful little girl," she sighed. "It doesn't seem quite fair, does it?"

Thia's eyes hardened. "What doesn't?"

"Why, Alexis—her affliction." Caroline stopped, confused. She was offering sympathy; why wasn't it being accepted? "I mean that it's tragic that such a pretty little thing will never"—she took a breath—"can't ever be normal."

"Mrs. Losey," Thia said slowly. "Alexis does have a learning disorder, but I am absolutely confident she can overcome it. But it's people like you, with your negative attitudes, who are making it much more difficult for those of us who are trying to help her."

"But I didn't . . ." Caroline began.

"In the future I'd like you to stay away from her and let the other staff members take care of her. I don't want her kept down by someone with your attitude."

Caroline was stunned. She could only watch stupidly while Thia whisked away her daughter.

She didn't have to say that, she thought. It wasn't true. Everyone knew that Alexis was retarded—that she'd never be normal, never! It wasn't just her attitude at all. In fact, she was patient with Alexis when everyone else had given up. She watched over the child. She was her protector.

Her arms cradled her thin chest. It was these New York women—they looked down on her, she noticed that. But they had no right—she had once been as fine and fancy as any one of them. There was once a time when she could hold her head up high and see nothing around her but respect.

Her name then had been Caroline Brigham. She wore her bright auburn hair in a ponytail, and she was as popular as any other girl in the tree-barren town of Prescott, Indiana. She had her share of suitors: good-looking boys in their fathers' Buicks eager to drive her to the Dairy Queen on Friday night, where, in the fluorescent glare of the parking lot, the cool kids—the ones who really counted—gathered to wrest some excitement from the bland prairie night.

And, after a time, one of those boys became more important than the rest. Steven Losey had a sandy crew cut, a chipped front tooth, and for two years straight had clinched the county high-diving medal for Prescott Senior High. They went steady. Caroline wore his ring on a chain around her neck; he wore hers on his pinky. And a week before the senior prom, in the rumpus room of a house where she was baby-sitting, he rolled her panty girdle down over her knees, fumbled on a rubber, and took her in four short, painful, bleeding strokes.

They graduated. Steven signed up for the Air Force, and Caroline went to work, 8:30 to 5, behind the pet counter at Sculley's department store. When his three years were up, Caroline quit her job, and they married in the peeling white Lutheran church behind the new Sears mall. The year was 1957. Buddy Holly sang, "That'll Be the Day"; The Bridge on the River Kwai won the Academy Award; and Caroline and Steven drove to a honeymoon in Minnesota in a spanking new black DeSoto, a joint wedding present from their parents.

They returned to Prescott—Steven to work at his father's drugstore by day and study accounting at night, Caroline to keep house. The years rolled by. Steve

*earned his degree and began to make money, Caroline
hired a woman to clean and busied herself with local
charities. And though, on the days marked with a red X
on their calendar, they faithfully performed what Caroline had come to regard as an arduous chore, they
remained childless. While America was fertile, producing its last bumper crops of babies after the long postwar
harvest, the Loseys were barren.*

*And then, after four years, a miracle: Caroline be-
came pregnant. She could hardly believe it was true,
even as day by day her belly swelled larger, until at last,
one midnight in July, she was rushed to the lying-in
hospital and delivered of a girl—a perfect baby, with hair
the color of a match flame and wide, elfin eyes. They
named her Georgene after Caroline's maternal grand-
mother, whom she resembled.*

The child! Caroline closed her eyes. She had almost
forgotten—the child was returned, and no one could
fault her now. No one!

"Are you Mrs. Losey?" asked a soft voice.

Caroline turned, and her throat constricted. There
was a young woman standing there with thick sheets of
honey-colored hair, dressed in a robe of gauzy ruby
fabric that seemed to float over her body. A luminous
creature whose appearance seemed to reproach Caroline's very existence. She felt suddenly weak, and her
mind began to race—words, phrases . . . *and I saw a
woman arrayed in purple and scarlet bedecked with gold
and jewels and pearls and in her hand a cup full of
abominations* . . .

"Who are you?" she gasped.

"I'm Susan Capasian. My daughter Joey started here
last week."

"Yes." Caroline paused, finding her voice. "I'll fetch
her for you, Mrs. Capasian."

"It's 'Miss,'" Susan corrected softly.

A thrill shivered through Caroline's breast. "You are
divorced?"

"I was never married."

For their mother has played the harlot; she that conceived them has acted shamefully! A thin smile of triumph rose to Caroline's lips. "And the father doesn't see fit to give the child his name?"

Susan stared at her in shock. "I don't see that that's any of your business! Now either tell me where I can find my daughter . . ."

"I will get her."

Susan watched her walk away. What a peculiar woman, she thought. So forward and nosy. She hoped she hadn't made a mistake in sending Joey here for the summer.

Each year countless thousands of college graduates pour into Manhattan armed with nothing more than B.A.'s and the vague intention of doing "something creative." Susan Capasian had been one of them. She had arrived from Kenyon with a degree in sociology and no firmer plans than to break into one of the glamour industries: publishing, art, theater, music. She had a misty conception of herself sitting in a Breuer chair, talking into a white touch-tone phone, negotiating something breathlessly exciting, dizzyingly cultural. Beyond that, the vision was bare.

She had one contact—a friend of a former professor who was a member of the New York City Council of the Arts. Through his influence she landed a job in the art-lending office of the Museum of Modern Art. At first she was elated; the job had cachet, it was creative. But there was a catch—it paid a salary of $95 a week. Not that she dared complain. Hadn't she been chosen over forty-three other qualified candidates? Weren't there hundreds more clamoring outside the door, desperate to step into her place? You're lucky to have it, her superiors constantly reminded her.

Half her salary went to maintaining a bleak fourth-floor walk-up on the Upper West Side. The other half barely covered the necessities of living. She found herself walking miles to save subway fare, lunching on an Almond Joy, buying underwear at Woolworth's and wearing it till it virtually disintegrated. And since most of the men she met were as young and poor as herself, she could rarely count on being entertained luxuriously. The typical date was a Godard or Buñuel film at one of the cheap revival theaters, then home to a bottle of jug wine and a mattress on the floor.

But her job had one important perk—invitations to gallery openings. At these she could mingle with exquisitely dressed people, catch glimpses of the mighty of the art world as well as scatterings of celebrities from other fields, and forget that the suede boots she was wearing were relics of college and had linings of newspaper to protect the worn soles. But best of all, she could drink her fill of white wine and gorge on the French bread and Brie and Black Forest ham that were generally provided at them. Sometimes she wondered whether if not for these events she would look like one of the children of Cambodia, who were dominating the media with their ballooning stomachs and matchstick limbs. How long could she survive on just Almond Joys?

Several months after she had begun working, she was invited to an opening in a 57th Street gallery. It was for a painter named Bob DeRitis whose work was being watched closely by the more powerful critics and collectors. He painted ordinary women posed in ordinary situations: scrubbing a wall, lugging overloaded grocery bags, wool-gathering over a mid-morning cup of coffee—ordinary except that they were nude. Their bodies were middle-aged, imperfect, yet rendered with a sympathy that made them startlingly beautiful. The flesh tones were especially accomplished; in them the artist had captured all the flush, pearly, delicate gradations of a Renoir.

But Susan hardly glanced at the paintings. She had eaten nothing for lunch but tea and a cellophane-wrapped package of Melba toast. She made straight for the buffet and began to feast as fast as she could, oblivious to the swirling activity around her. She crammed a hunk of bread into her mouth, reached for some more.

"I think you need this more than I do," someone said.

She glanced up and flushed a deep red. A man with broad shoulders and a mass of tightly curling, pepper-colored hair stood before her. He was laughing and holding out a huge wedge of cheese.

Such was the beginning of her life with Bob DeRitis. From that first moment he overwhelmed her. He was like no one she had ever known before—he laughed more, drank more, made love more. They made love on floors and tables, standing up, with and without their clothes on, and once in a coat closet with a party in full swing outside the door. He taught her to enjoy her own body. He insisted that she tell him exactly what she wanted, sparing no words, so that talking about the act, saying the words, became a part of the pleasure. Sex with Bob made all those nights on mattresses on the floor seem silly and rather dull by comparison.

He taught her too about art. He would stop her in front of the window of an exclusive Madison Avenue gallery and point to the painting displayed haughtily in a gilt frame.

"What do you think of that?" he'd ask.

"Well, I like it," she would reply hesitantly.

"Why?"

"The colors. . . . It kind of glows."

"It's pretty, right? You'd like to hang it in the living room?"

She would nod, pleased that she'd gotten it right.

"It stinks!" he'd roar. "It's wallpaper!" Then he would take it apart, element by element, breaking down the composition, criticizing the draftsmanship, until she could see what he did.

Gradually, she made a discovery: she had an "eye." At new shows she could predict with startling accuracy which canvases would be snatched up by serious collectors and museum curators, which would appeal to institutions looking to smarten up a bland reception lobby, and which, at the end of the show, would still be in the "collection of the artist." But after recognizing her ability she thought nothing more about it. There were too many other exciting things going on in her life.

Bob had a loft on Prince Street in the newly named district of Soho. To Susan, the neighborhood, with its narrow looming streets, so dark and deserted at night and clogged with trucks by day, seemed like the scariest place in the world. Then, suddenly, it was the most exciting. The people who lived here drew pictures on the asphalt and built musical sculptures on the sidewalks. Parties turned into happenings, mimeographed poems drifted down from windows, and, in the summer, the rich refrains of jazz and rock melted into the air.

For the first time in my life, she thought, I feel completely alive.

The job at the museum now seemed like just a dull routine. She quit and got three nights a week waiting on tables at the Bottom Line, a rock club that had just opened in the Village. The coordinated sweaters and skirts that had been the staple of her working wardrobe lay untouched in her closet as she let her taste run free. She discovered antique clothes from the thirties and forties—rich rayons with prints of rocking horses, daisies, apples, and oranges. She put them together with the accessories her quick eye picked out of thrift shop bins and flea market tables.

One night at the Bottom Line she was called to the table of one of the regulars, Gloria Ross, head of publicity for Elektra Records. Gloria was a tiny, cuddly brunette with blinking eyes and a voice that could carry distinctly across an eight-lane highway. She squeezed Susan's hand and turned to the balding man seated next to her. "I hate this kid," she announced in her megaphone voice. "Not only is she gorgeous, but her clothes are to *die* from! She's gotta have some terrific sugar daddy."

Susan laughed. "No one supports me, Gloria."

"Get her! I know we're big tippers around here, but I didn't think *that* big."

"But my clothes hardly cost me a thing." She briefly explained about her shopping methods and how she liked to experiment with old and unusual clothes.

Gloria rolled her eyes. "Are you listening to this? I drop five thou a year and end up looking like a zhlub, while this kid makes like a princess on nothing."

The right words came to Susan. "I've got a sort of sideline," she said. "Wardrobe consulting. I could put together an original look for you, probably from things you already own."

"Oh, yeah? What do you charge?"

Susan hesitated. "Twenty-five dollars an hour?"

"How about coming by on Saturday?"

In a matter of months Susan found herself with a thriving free-lance business. She had hit upon a very desirable service. Fashion, after the iconoclastic sixties, was in a strange state of flux. Women once again wanted to dress well, but they could no longer look to Paris to dictate a "uniform." Instead there was a bewildering freedom of style: long hemlines and short, big, oversized dresses and leotards, fluffy feminine clothes and severe man-tailored outfits. Only the most confident of women could feel comfortable with so much choice. There were many who turned gratefully to Susan for help.

She would have been happy except for one thing— the more success she had, it seemed the worse things became with Bob. He had hit a dry period in his work. He would begin a canvas with enthusiasm, working all

night in a high fever, but by dawn he'd be disgusted
with the results and slash the canvas to ribbons with a
hunting knife. He was drinking hard—a quart of Early
Times a day—beginning before breakfast and continu-
ing far into the night. And he would disappear for three
or four days at a time. Susan knew that during these
absences he'd be with a girl—one of the countless
artists' groupies who hung out at St. Adrian's or the
Cedar Tavern. When she could stand it no more, she
confronted him; they began to fight with the same
passion with which they had once made love.

Then, during one screaming session, he slapped her
across the cheekbone. She staggered back. Then she
ran to the tub and threw up in great, seemingly endless,
spasms.

When the implacable gynecologist in the Planned
Parenthood clinic confirmed her pregnancy, Susan felt
a tremendous relief. The responsibility would make
Bob shape up, give him an incentive for getting back to
work. She sailed out onto the frostbitten sidewalks of
Second Avenue eager to tell him the news.

"Get rid of it," was all he said.

Numbly she made another appointment at the clinic,
showed up at the scheduled hour. A dozen other girls
waited in the cheerful, unemotional reception room.
Girls in sweaters and jeans, their long hair loose, their
faces clean of makeup. Nice girls who had gone to
college, held good jobs, read books, attended the
theater. It must be all right, Susan assured herself—
these girls wouldn't be here if it wasn't.

A nurse gathered them together to explain the
coming procedure. There would be a slight prick when
the novocaine was injected into the cervix, two or three
minutes of discomfort during the sweeping of the
uterus, and slight cramping afterward. "It is far from
terrible, ladies," the nurse soothed. "Juice and cookies
will be served afterward." Susan stared at the freshly
painted blue wall. The words seemed thin and echoing,
as if coming from a great distance away.

Her name was called. She was ushered into a white room, laid on a table, feet eased into cold stirrups. The doctor was old. He looked as if he smoked too much, suffered from backaches. There was a machine; it looked like an industrial vacuum cleaner, the kind used by janitors in large office buildings. It was a vacuum, and the helpless thing inside her would be sucked away like lint from a couch, dust from a rug.

"No," she said, sitting up. She extracted her feet from the stirrups. "I won't do it."

But that was long ago. Not so much in years, which were only six, but in terms of everything that had happened since. Susan, working on her files in her office, wondered what had prompted this sudden flood of memories. Maybe it was watching Joey on the floor stack transparent Lucite bricks with a solemn concentration that reminded Susan of Bob. He had the same capacity to become totally—almost mystically—absorbed in his work.

But Bob had fled when she told him she was going to have the child. Fled to Chicago, leaving her $6,000—all the money he had left—and the only canvas he hadn't destroyed in the year since his last show—a magnificent, half-finished portrait of Susan standing nude before an oval full-length mirror.

Memories continued to crowd into her mind. Having Joey by natural childbirth, the pain greater than she had thought it would be, but somehow abstract, as if happening to someone else. Holding the ugly, beautiful, angry baby in her arms and becoming seized with overwhelming ambition. Suddenly wanting the world—for the baby and for herself.

Her wardrobe consultation business, though still thriving, was no longer enough. She searched her mind for something with unlimited horizons that she could do. That's when she remembered her "eye"—her uncanny talent for appraising art. Of course! It seemed so obvious. She would open a gallery.

She set herself to work. In the months that followed she pounded the dirty streets of Soho, carrying Joey in a sling papoose, looking at buildings. There was one she kept coming back to: a six-story warehouse on West Broadway, the widest and most traveled street of the neighborhood. She tracked down the owner, a former shoelace manufacturer who was about to retire to an adult community in Phoenix.

"I want to buy your building," she told him.

He stared at this rosy, colorfully dressed young mother, perplexed. What on earth could she do with a ratty, empty warehouse in the middle of nowhere? "Sixty thousand dollars," he said, shrugging.

"It's a deal," she replied.

As she had guessed, she had no trouble rounding up five people with $2,400 each to cover the down payment—artists overjoyed to find good space. In return for putting together the co-op, she received the lobby floor free.

But that left the problem of renovation. She had the money Bob left her; but $6,000 was barely sufficient to do the job. But she was not to be daunted. Though she had never before picked up a hammer, she now learned to wield one, along with all manner of saws, wrenches, drills, and chisels. She haggled like a French fishwife with electricians and carpenters and placed Joey in the arms of burly plumbers to soften their hearts. She combed the town for bargains in paint and lighting. And at three in the morning she found herself perched on a rickety ladder methodically rolling white paint onto the vast walls.

Little by little it took shape. It became a long, clean white oblong with scrubbed maple floors, smooth bare walls, recessed lighting. There was a semi-open office space in which she hung the double portrait of herself. And in the back, a large, closed-off room with a tiny Pullman kitchen and a Mediterranean-tiled bathroom where she and Joey lived in cramped comfort.

Yes, she said at last, it was a gallery.

Now there was more sidewalk pounding to be done—this time to the studios of artists. Susan panted her way up endless flights of stairs, subwayed to Brooklyn and Morningside Heights. She stepped over junkies sprawled comatose in the doorways of East Village tenements to get to the garrets of young men and women above. She examined the work of Pratt students and Yale dropouts; of a seventy-nine-year-old man who had taken up painting the year before and the fifteen-year-old winner of a statewide Draw Your Pet contest. She looked at paintings until the colors swam together like a madras shirt in the rain and the lines blurred like bad television reception.

Finally she made her selection: six men and four women, all in their late twenties or early thirties. There was no common denominator to their work except that each possessed something strong and original—something Susan knew instinctively would continue to develop.

She borrowed two thousand dollars to throw a spectacular vernissage—the christening of the Susan Capasian gallery. Five hundred people drank the Taylor champagne, consumed the crudités and Swiss peasant bread, the Bel Paese and Gouda. Person after person grabbed Susan's arm, oozing praises. "A stunning show!" they told her. She flushed with success.

The show ran for a month; not one painting or sculpture was sold.

When Susan had recovered sufficiently from the blow to be able to think again, she took a long night's stock of her situation over a bottle of Campari. She saw now that it had been foolish of her to expect instant results—so much work remained to be done. She made plans.

Beginning the next morning, she threw herself wholeheartedly into the frenetic task of promotion. She turned the gallery into a forum for live events: poetry readings, jam sessions, mime skits—anything that could lure the public and maybe attract a mention in the *Village Voice*. She deluged the mails with press releases written in a chatty, almost gossipy, style. And she attended every party, every opening, every obscure reception that came her way, just to meet people, collect new names for her mailing list, talk endlessly about the gallery until she thought she would explode.

The art world began to take notice. Commercialization! some cried. Cheapening the art with such tawdry show business gimmicks. Art should be above such things.

But whatever they thought of her hustling, no one could deny that the pictures, sculpture, and drawings Susan was showing were good. Some of them, in fact, remarkable.

It didn't happen all at once—not in the first year, nor yet in the second. But it happened. The Susan Capasian gallery became a success, surpassing even her earliest ambitions for it.

And yes, it was worth it, Susan thought now. Worth the fighting and the struggle and the despair. Worth every step of the way.

"Guess what I saw?" Joey asked.

Still lost in her train of thought, Susan glanced abstractly at her daughter. "What, sweetie?"

"It was a gigantic bird, and he was sitting on the roof of a house getting ready to pick up people in his beak . . ."

Susan frowned. "Joey, no bird is big enough to do that."

"Yes, they are." Joey began stacking the Lucite blocks she had scattered all over the floor into a precarious tower. "In paintings they are," she insisted.

"But paintings aren't real life, baby. You know that." Susan took the strip of slides she had pulled out of a filing cabinet and took them to the small round table. She pulled out a chair.

"Don't sit there!" Joey cried. "Tweenie's putting on her nail polish."

With a heavy sigh, Susan took another chair. She attempted to steer her daughter from the imaginary to the real. "Tell me about the Synergy Center. Do you like going there?"

Joey nodded. "Except when we have to lie down on blankets at rest time. The floor's too hard." She added, "When I'm fourteen, I'm going to get married to Mr. Link. He told me so."

"Fourteen is too young for people to get married, baby."

"I don't care, I love him. He lets me ride on his shoulders."

"What about Mrs. Losey?" Susan asked. "Do you like her, too?"

"Yeah, she's nice. But you know what?" Joey looked up, her eyes suddenly brimming with the importance of her news. "We've got a girl in our group who's a retard! She can't even go to the bathroom by herself. Somebody's got to take her."

"Joey!" Susan said sternly. "You are not ever to call anyone a name like 'retard'!"

"But that's what the other kids say."

"I don't care. It's wrong of them, too."

"But she's silly, mommy! She makes all these dumb noises all the time."

Susan got up and went over to crouch beside her daughter. "I'll explain it, baby. This little girl does these things because she can't help it. There's something wrong with her brain. Remember when you twisted your ankle that time and had to walk with a limp? Wouldn't you have felt terrible if somebody had called you names because you were walking funny?"

"I guess so," Joey said tentatively.

"Of course you would have. So you see, when someone has something wrong with them, you have to be extra nice to them. And remember to be glad that you're so smart and healthy."

Joey looked so suddenly crestfallen that Susan kissed the top of her head. "I know you didn't mean it, sweetie."

Joey smiled with the impish light in her eyes that, for

the second time that afternoon, reminded Susan so clearly of Bob. She had heard he was back in Manhattan and that he was showing again successfully. Remarkable that he had made no inquiries about his daughter nor attempted to see her. But no, she thought, that was just like Bob—the perennial Peter Pan, forever ducking out on responsibility.

Joey added a final brick to her spindly tower, and the structure came crashing down. Disconsolately, she piled the bricks back into their container. "Can I go out and roller-skate?"

"Okay. But only on this block. You are not to cross the street alone. Promise?"

"I won't. Can Tweenie go out, too?"

"Yes!" Susan cried with exasperation. She resolved that if Joey didn't snap out of this stage soon she was definitely going to take her to see someone about it.

She returned to her task of updating her files of artists' slides, working happily in peace. But she wasn't to enjoy her peace for long. The gallery was invaded by a women's culture group from Westport, Connecticut —thirty-two formidable ladies. Even Susan's assistant, Danielle, a normally unflappable Vassar graduate, showed signs of agitation under this assault. When at last the women departed, Susan and Danielle breathed a sigh of relief.

"We survived," Susan offered.

"Barely," Danielle replied. "I'm still checking to see if I've got all my faculties intact."

Susan laughed. She was quite fond of her assistant. Danielle was a collagist whose work had been developing brilliantly over the past year. Susan was saving as a surprise that she would soon start showing her work to collectors.

Later a young highly praised actor came into the gallery. Like many celebrities, he had taken up art collecting as a way to give his newly acquired fortune some of the status of old money. He was not yet rich enough to acquire old masters—that would take a stint or two in Hollywood. Instead he intended to dazzle the world with the finest collection of contemporary art his money could buy.

Susan led him into the back room, where she stored the best of her artists' work that wasn't currently on exhibit. The actor had a reputation as an incorrigible seducer of beautiful women. Business concluded, he set about living up to his reputation.

"You will come hang it for me, Susan, won't you?" he pleaded.

She smiled. "I'm afraid that once I ship it my job is done."

"Oh, but couldn't you make an exception? For me?" He was giving it his all. Plaintive blue eyes. Hurt little-boy smile.

Susan felt herself beginning to melt. "Well, maybe. It depends, of course . . ."

"On what?"

"Oh . . . on what kind of champagne you'll have to toast the occasion."

"How about Dom Perignon sixty-six?"

She made a mock moue. "I suppose I *could* rough it, just this once."

"Done, then! I'll call you Tuesday."

The effects of his charm lingered like a heady scent several moments after he had gone. Susan collected her thoughts, tapping her lower lip with an index finger. What now? A dozen phone calls to return. Finish those damned slides. Could it really be five o'clock already? First, call in Joey. . . .

She went out to the street. There was no sign of her daughter. That blasted kid! she thought. She walked from one end of the block to the other, becoming more and more angry. Joey had flagrantly disobeyed her order not to leave the block. She was becoming extremely willful—probably Susan's own fault. She had a tendency to be much too lenient with her daughter. Overcompensating for the lack of a father. But this time Joey would not escape punishment. Susan was firm about that.

She circled the block, then made a wider circle, calling Joey's name. There was no response. Her anger was giving way to a deep anxiety. Now don't panic! she warned herself. You know how damned independent she's become.

She darted into shops—Paracelso, Harriet Love, The Wine Bar. No one had seen Joey that afternoon. She saw two children with roller skates and ran to them. No, they said solemnly, Joey hadn't been with them.

Forty-five minutes had elapsed. How stupid of me! she thought suddenly. While I'm driving myself crazy out here, Joey's probably long been back at the gallery.

She flew back.

Danielle looked at her with shock. "Susan, you're white as a sheet! What happened?"

"Has Joey come in?" she panted.

"No. I thought she was with you." Danielle's hazel eyes became grave. "Could she have gone upstairs to your loft?"

"I know I locked up. She couldn't get in."

"Let me run up and take a look anyway."

"All right. But I'm going to call the police." Susan dialed the First Precinct. She took deep breaths, trying to stay back her fear as she explained her problem to the desk sergeant. As she hung up, Danielle returned, shaking her head silently. Don't panic, Susan exhorted herself again.

Danielle went back outside to search the block again while Susan waited for the police. In less than ten minutes there was a knock at the gallery door.

Susan answered. At the sight of Kerry Donner, she shrank back. "No!" she gasped.

"Susan, I came as soon as I heard the call . . ."

"I didn't call for you," she rasped. "This isn't like Lisa. Joey's just lost, she hasn't disappeared."

"I'm sure you're right," he said.

"Then what are you doing here?" Her voice was beginning to sound unnatural. Something delicate inside of her threatened to snap.

"It's a precaution. Since it is the same neighborhood, I wanted to be here . . ."

"Until her body shows up in some trash heap or suburban parking lot?" she shrieked. "Is that what you're waiting for?"

"Susan, stop it!" he said sternly.

Her hands flew to her temples. She stood trembling a moment. "I'm sorry," she whispered. "It's just that when I saw you . . ."

"I know. I should be shot for what I said to you that day at the Wyles'. Believe me, Susan, that's not going to happen." He grasped her upper arms. "Here, sit down." He helped her into the large front desk chair. "What happens now?" she asked.

"I've got three squad cars cruising the neighborhood and vicinity with her description."

"And if they don't find her?"

"Then I think our best bet will be to get the dogs here. It should be an easy trail for them to pick up."

Susan found it hard to voice what she dreaded. "What if she really has disappeared . . . ?"

"Then we start all over again."

"With everything you did for Lisa?"

"Everything and more. One thing we'd do is have a computer match up your lifestyle with the Wyles' and see where the intersections are. Acquaintances you have in common, similarities in your routine . . ."

"Would there have to be reporters?"

"Definitely. We'd want the public to be as familiar as possible with your daughter's face." He saw her go pale and said quickly, "Most likely it won't come to that. But if it should—I think it's better you know now what to expect."

She nodded. His strength supported her. He made her feel capable of withstanding anything. She thought of the actor she'd been flirting with—was it only an hour ago? He seemed like such a shallow charm boy in comparison.

"Is there anything we can do now but wait?" she asked.

"Yes—I want to investigate a very good possibility. Joey's father." Donner's eyes flickered to Susan's office. "He's the one who painted that portrait of you, isn't he?"

She glanced at him. "How did you know?"

"I don't know, I just did. Is he in New York?"

"He just returned. But . . ." She shook her head. "It couldn't be Bob. He's never even seen her. He ran away before she was born, not wanting to have anything to do with her."

"That doesn't matter. There's an established pattern of parents who abandon their kids and then years later become desperate to see them."

"But why would he just take her? Why wouldn't he let me know?"

"Guilt. Shame. The fear that you'd try to prevent him from seeing her. There are a thousand complex and crazy reasons." He made a gesture. "I suggest you try to get him on the phone."

Susan snatched up the receiver. The old number had never been changed when he sublet the apartment; now, as she dialed, the sequence seemed as familiar as the lyrics of a once-loved song. She let it ring thirty, forty times, not wanting to let go, not even as the first pair of uniformed cops arrived empty-handed at the door.

Johanna Elizabeth Capasian was having fun.

She loved riding in the big old-fashioned elevator—the kind with no ceiling, so that you could see the top of the building coming straight down at you. It was scary—the way the Ferris wheel at Great Adventure was scary—but fun, too, because you knew you really couldn't get hurt.

And then there was the room. At first it looked like the Synergy Center because of all the colored furniture and the beautiful pictures hung up on the walls. But it was much, much bigger, and there were big boards nailed to all the windows. Even though it was daytime, all the lights were on. Joey knew that was wrong. Mr. Link had taught them not to waste electricity.

But the sight of the toys made her forget everything else. There were millions and millions of them—all brand-new, like Christmas and her birthday all rolled into one. She ran into the midst of the shiny objects, touching things here and there, not knowing which to play with first. There was everything she had ever seen on television and wanted: Simon, and Miss Piggy Colorforms, and Baby Feels So Real. And, oh! a

104

dollhouse that looked big enough to walk into, with shutters that really opened and closed.

From out of the dollhouse came her friend, Lisa Wyle.

"Hi, Lisa," Joey said.

Lisa looked at her and didn't say anything. She was wearing an old-fashioned blue dress that looked like a boy's sailor suit and funny-looking shiny black shoes. What a dummy! Joey thought. She doesn't even know that everybody's been looking all over for her.

But then Joey saw something she had coveted for a long time. Charlie's Angels paper dolls. She had asked for them for Christmas and been disappointed when they weren't under the tree—but now here they were! She reached for one raptly. Maybe she'd be allowed to take them back to Tweenie.

Lisa came over and snatched the paper doll out of her hand. "Those are mine!" she declared.

The woman said, "Give then back, Georgene. You must learn to share your toys."

Lisa shook her head. "That's not my name! My name's Lisa, and I want to go home!"

"Are you going to start this nonsense again? I'm getting mighty tired of it, Georgene. You promised that if I brought your friend to play . . ."

"I don't want her, I want my mommy!"

"I'm warning you, Georgene. I refuse to tolerate such behavior. You're a very lucky young lady, and I expect you to show some gratitude for all your lovely blessings."

"I hate them, they're ugly!" Lisa shredded the paper doll in her hands and dashed the pieces to the floor. "There! I hate them and I hate you!"

"All right, Georgene. I have tried to be patient, but I can see that doesn't work with a spoiled child like you. Bring me the spoon."

"No!" Lisa shrieked.

She tried to run off, but the woman grabbed her and pulled her, hollering and squirming, to the back of the room. Joey could see the woman take a thick wooden spoon from a shelf nailed to the wall and raise it high. "Let me go!" Lisa screamed, but the spoon came down with a hard smacking sound against her thighs. The woman cried out, *Do not withhold discipline from a child and you will save his life from Sheol!* Again and again the spoon came down and Lisa's screams echoed from the four walls of the room. The woman cried, *If you beat him with a rod he will not die!*

And Joey stood very still, not daring to move, not daring to make a sound, until it was over, and Lisa lay sobbing on a tiny cot made up with Peanuts sheets. Only then did she tentatively pick up the crumpled bits of the paper doll that lay on the floor. She was very, very frightened.

"I think I'd like to go home now," she said.

Part II

SOHO: A HISTORY (continued)
By Day McAllister

In the early years of the 19th century, an immigrant fur trader with a coarse Heidelberg accent quietly snaps up huge tracts of land in the neighborhood that will come to be known as Soho. His name is John Jacob Astor, and, as in most of his other endeavors, he will prove to have the Midas touch. The area begins to develop at a bewildering pace; soon it is the most populous ward in the city, an enclave of the newly wealthy bourgeoisie.

But even greater things are in store for this hundred acres. In 1859 the great retailing concern of Lord & Taylor establishes itself on the corner of Broadway and Grand; its building is such an extravagance that the *New York Times* is moved to gasp: "It looks more like an Italian palace than the place for the sale of

[MORE]

5-5-5-5

broadcloth." Others follow: Brooks Brothers,
Arnold Constable, Tiffany & Co.; they are
joined by theaters and music halls and lavish tea gardens. Almost overnight Broadway
becomes transformed from a street of small
shops and foundries to a grand boulevard.
It is crowned by the vast and magnificent
St. Nicholas hotel, whose appointments—
down to the hand-embroidered mosquito net-
ting—are acknowledged to be worthy of
royalty.

But such days of splendor are short-lived.
Even as the St. Nicholas entertains kings and
queens, the tiny cobbled lanes behind Broadway
are becoming notorious for quite a different
sort of amusement. Here are the
brothels—dozens upon dozens of them—only
nominally disguised as "ladies'
boardinghouses." They are elegantly furnished
and cater to an epicurean variety of tastes, be
it for the "fair Quakeresses" of Mrs. C.
Hathaway, the "agreeable and accomplished
lady boarders" of Miss Thompson, or "Miss
Clara Gordon's Southern belles." Guidebooks
reviewing the quality of service at these
establishments are published for the benefit
of the browsing clientele.

With the coming of the brothels, the decay
sets in quickly. The crime rate soars; a
visiting dignitary, relieved of his money at
gunpoint, creates a ruckus. People of
respectability begin to shun the
neighborhood. The theaters close their doors,

[MORE]

6–6–6–6

the great retailers move uptown, and the
middle–class families flee to other,
less–threatening neighborhoods.

For 20 years the district suffers a decline.
Then a fresh turn of the wheel: the age of the
industrialist arrives. Men who made fortunes
in dry goods and textiles choose the area for
their factories and new warehouses. There is a
new building material called cast iron––its
strength as a skeleton allows them to build
vast interior lofts lit by enormous sweeps of
windows. Moreover, the facades can be cheaply
prefabricated to imitate any of the glorious
architectural styles of the past. The
Victorian merchants adorn their factories
with the graceful columns, pediments, and
arches of Italian palazzos, acclaiming them as
"cathedrals of industry," "temples of
manufacturing!"

The area hums with commerce. But behind the
opulent warehouse facades (painted creamy
white to simulate Italian marble), a scandal
festers. These are the sweatshops. Each day
thousands of men, women, and children plod
from squalid tenements on the Lower East Side
to be locked into 16–hour shifts for slave
wages. They are Jewish and Italian and Irish
immigrants, grinding out a futureless
existence, lives sacrificed to the greater god
of industry.

As if in retribution, the neighborhood
becomes destined to fail again. By the end of
the 19th century, all speculative interest

[MORE]

7-7-7-7

comes to an end. As the heart of the city shifts
relentlessly uptown, the prominent businesses
follow, and the cathedrals and temples of
commerce fall to the smaller, more sordid,
industries: the rag dealers, the box makers,
and the sullen purveyors of cheap underwear.

[MORE]

Everyone who worked in the office of Cassidy and Knowlton knew that a coolness had developed between the two partners. Until recently, it had been Albie's custom to burst into Gil's office several times an afternoon, brimming with ideas, questions, sudden inspirations. And Gil, as often, could be seen slouched against the partition of Albie's office, weaving his partner's slapdash ideas into breathtakingly workable form. Albie was the instigator, Gil the perfectionist; together their partnership transcended their individual talents. Many were the late nights they had spent working with heads together, engrossed in the sheer creativity of their collaboration.

But now all that had changed. Each one remained stubbornly sealed in his own office, communicating only through one of the associates. When they met by chance in the central drafting room or the tiny efficiency kitchen, only a curt nod passed between them. Though the employees tactfully refrained from asking questions, they guessed that the rift was somehow related to the design of the Sports Center. What a bitch! they agreed among themselves. This used to be such a fun place to work.

And so they took it as a heartening sign when Albie, returning from an outside appointment, bounced jauntily once again into Gil's office. The associates exchanged grins. Maybe, at long last, things were on the mend.

Gil glanced warily at his partner over the rim of a ceramic coffee cup.

"Break out the bottle, old boy!" Knowlton cried. "Put on your dancing slippers! We're home free!"

"What do you mean?" Gil asked.

"Come on, kiddo, let's not be so dense. We've got the money. Spetzi's people have committed!"

Gil rose from his chair, lightened with relief. "That's great," he said weakly.

"Yeah." Albie's grin was jubilantly self-satisfied. "You know what clinched the deal? They saw the way our plans greased right through the Standards and Appeals hearings, despite the heavy opposition from the local community board. That convinced them that my contacts had enough juice to get us where we want."

Gil let him gloat a moment. "What's the deal look like?" he asked.

"We're coming in as general partner for eighteen percent."

"Shit!"

Albie's eyes narrowed. "Look, I had to close the deal—we can't afford to carry those options too much longer. And this way we still stand to make plenty."

"But if anything goes wrong . . ."

"Nothing's *going* to go wrong. Stop being such an old woman."

Gil felt some of his anxiety begin to return. "When do we get started?" he asked edgily.

"All the principals are going to meet Saturday out at Spetzi's estate in East Hampton. There's a couple of minor details that still need ironing out. Then it's home free all." Albie scratched the side of his flat, boxer's nose. "Just one thing—until the construction of the Sports Center is finished, you and I have got to keep a strictly low profile. We don't want anyone getting too close."

"Why not? Now that the plans have passed, the construction's on the level."

"Not exactly." A smirk floated across Albie's face. "There's been a change in the deal. We're going for three extra stories on the building."

"Are you crazy!" Gil exclaimed. "Do you realize what it'll take to refile all the plans . . . ?"

"Man, you are being dense today. We're not refiling shit, buddy. Once we start building, we'll just keep on going up."

"But that's illegal!"

"So what? Once the thing's built, there's not much they can do about it, short of making us tear it down again. And they're sure as hell not going to do that. So we get fined—big deal. We'll be able to afford it."

Gil sat down again, his eyes fixed on his grinning partner. "This is downright insane," he said.

"On the contrary, it's the most rational thing I can imagine." Knowlton chuckled. "Think of it this way— the bigger the pie, the bigger our slice will be. So I wouldn't be so depressed, if I were you."

A blunt pain bore its way into Gil's left temple. He sat motionless after Albie left, eyes closed. His thoughts were confused. He hated what Albie had dragged him into. And yet another voice within him insisted that he couldn't entirely blame his partner—he had wanted to get rich every iota as much as Albie. And maybe Albie was right—maybe he *did* live with his head in the clouds. Maybe he was just an impractical dreamer, out of touch with the world. But was the only alternative to sell out as completely and as quickly as you could?

"I don't know," he said aloud.

His hand reached for the new vial of pale yellow pills

that lay on his drafting table. He hesitated, then shook out two, washing them down with the last dregs of his coffee. He vowed that from now on he'd start rationing them—they had been disappearing too quickly.

He sat staring for a moment. His office, the very focus and pride of his life over the last years, suddenly looked no larger than an architect's model of the real thing. There's not a spare molecule of air in here, he thought in panic. He bolted into the main drafting room.

Teddy Golfarb sat hunched over a drawing, her face hidden by the severe geometry of her hair.

"I've gotta go," he told her. "When you finish those revised drawings, run me a couple of copies for tomorrow morning, okay?"

"Don't you want to see them first?"

"Personally, I'd prefer never to see them again."

She shot him a worried look. "Gil . . ."

"Hey, pay no attention to anything I say today. I'm just in one hell of a mood."

He walked briskly for several blocks, then ducked into a bar, ordered, and tossed back a shot of tequila. He ordered another and settled in a corner, taking care to avoid the pencil-thin beams of track lighting that cut through the air like lasers.

It was the time of day when the energy dissipated by a long afternoon began to be rekindled—a wave of emotion rode into the bar like rumor on an election night, like the high gusts of wind before a thunderstorm. But Gil sat apart, disaffected. He stared from face to face, confident that he knew what each one was after: status, atmosphere, a quick pickup. They're all on the make, he told himself, every last one of them. I don't owe them a goddamned thing. Let them have Albie's mausoleum of a Sports Center. From now on, I'm strictly out for myself.

He thought briefly of Thia and his daughter. What did he owe them? Images floated into his mind: Thia dressed in a pale peach sundress, reclining on a porch glider, listening with radiant encouragement to his blustering dreams about the future. Thia staying up till dawn while he untangled some knotty problem of design or worried aloud about an intractable client. His pride the day his daughter was born, and the inviolate innocence of her face . . .

Certainly the memories, at least, should be worth fighting for.

Suddenly he noticed another face in the bar, one he couldn't readily categorize. It was a woman in outlandish harlequin sunglasses, hair hidden beneath a wrapped scarf, mouth a thin crimson gash like a sword wound. She stared at him, not bothering to turn away discreetly when his eyes fell on hers. She gave him the creeps.

Just another Soho weirdo, he thought.

Time was passing: people came and went, faces shifting like a kaleidoscope. But the face in the harlequin glasses remained fixed on him, steadily taking his measure. What did she want? He felt suddenly spooked. Hands trembling, he threw an uncounted wad of bills on the bar and bolted out.

The eyes behind the glasses closed briefly. Too many sensations, distractions. It was too hard to think. But she had watched him for many weeks now, and the evidence was almost complete. She had delivered her judgment: the child must be saved.

But it was difficult—he distracted her, this man. He brought on thoughts and desires that made it hard to concentrate on her purpose. The child—she must think of the child. And yet it was with the child that the torment of her desires had begun. The birth that had blessed her, also brought her bondage.

It had been an easy delivery, and Caroline made a quick recovery. The stitches of the episiotomy were removed, the incision healed cleanly, and she looked forward eagerly to the end of the ordered three months

*of sexual abstinence. For a strange thing had happened:
directly after the birth, she had begun to desire her
husband.*

*The magic night arrived; the scarlet X on the calendar
was bigger and brighter than it had ever been before.
Caroline turned to her husband in the solemn comfort of
their bed. He took her in his arms. But something was
wrong—he couldn't stay aroused. Trembling, she offered to do things she had never done before. But he
shook his head angrily, then broke from her and sat on
the edge of the bed.*

*"It's no use," he cried. "You've had this baby, now. I
can't do it."*

*"But the doctor said it's okay," she told him. "We
waited long enough."*

*"That's not it. I mean, you're a mother now,
and . . . oh, good lord, Carrie, I can't. Not with someone who's a mother. I mean, it's just not right!"*

*She was stunned and didn't know what to say. After a
moment, he got up, dressed quickly, and went out of the
house. She lay shivering beneath the sheets, listening to
the car's muffled roar from the garage, wondering what
she had done wrong and what was going to happen now.*

*No! This was all distraction, the work of the evil ones
keeping her from her purpose. She must concentrate
now and bide her time. She had only to wait and the
proper time would come. This child too would be hers.*

Susan Capasian dragged herself home from the station house. She had spent the morning flipping through mug books—a staggering and futile task that had left her drained. Could it really be only eleven o'clock—only a day and a half since she had first circled the block looking for Joey? She could hardly believe it.

But then she remembered reading somewhere that our most elaborate dreams—even the ones that seem to blow us over five continents and go on for hours—actually take place in a matter of minutes. If that were true, then of course a waking nightmare like this would seem to stretch into eternity.

But she was so tired. And she had still not gotten used to the strangers who had invaded her home. Someone jabbed a mike in her face, but she pushed past it; for the first time, she would have gladly traded her loft for a regular apartment—one with rooms and doors that could be shut and locked. She dropped into a chair and buried her head in her arms.

You've got to keep on going! she warned herself.

There was still so much to do. And only by endlessly

119

pushing herself could she keep her mind from snagging on the forbidden thoughts. The ones in which she saw Joey's body crushed and mangled beneath the wheels of a truck or torn to shreds by vicious dogs. Or saw her violated by a sexual psychopath, sold into a Chinatown sweat factory. Thoughts of open barrels of toxic chemicals, abandoned refrigerators, gaping shafts—thoughts that, if left unchecked, would surely drive her mad.

If only she weren't so desperately tired . . .

Someone said her name. Wearily, she lifted her head. Then the blood rushed to her face, and she gave a gasp. Bob DeRitis was standing in front of her.

"Hi there, kid. Remember me?"

"Bob!" She stared at him for a moment, unable to find words. He had hardly changed at all. Oh, there was a hint of a paunch, a bit more salt and pepper in his hair. But there was the same raggedy smile, the same sharp black eyes that seemed to X-ray the world. Six years suddenly melted away. She was looking at the man she loved, the one who meant life itself to her. A tumultuous rush of emotions swept her. She gave a smile.

"You look sensational, babe," he said. "You were a pretty kid, but Jesus what a woman you've grown up to be."

"Oh, no, I look a mess," she murmured.

"Not to me, babe. I like your place, too. It's got your feel for things—a lot of light and color. It's a hell of a good place to bring up a kid."

Her face turned bitter. "A lot you'd know about that," she said.

"Yeah, that's true. But—"

"Damn you, Bob, you've got a lot of nerve. You took off before she was born, and now that she's gone you come slinking back."

"I figured you'd think something like that."

"Did you? And do you have a speech all prepared? Something that will make me forgive everything and welcome you back with open arms? You were always pretty good at that."

"No. No defense, babe. I'm guilty as original sin."

"Goddamn you, Bob!" she said again.

"Yeah. But listen—for what it's worth, I did come to see her."

She glanced at him suspiciously. "When?"

"At that opening you had in the gallery last Saturday. I was there, and I talked to her. She's an incredible girl, Suzy. You've done a damned fine job."

"I don't know whether to believe you or not."

"Christ, do you think I'd lie to you?"

"It's been known to happen in the past," she said bitterly.

"Yeah. But this is straight. You can ask the cops— they got a couple of calls from people who saw me with her. They came by my place last night and tore it apart, then gave me the third degree till almost dawn."

Susan got up, her eyes pleading with him. "Did you take her?"

"Christ, Susan, I wish I had."

"So do I."

Bob scrunched his hands into the pockets of his workpants. It was a gesture so familiar to Susan that she shivered. "I swear to God, Suzy, I'll make it up to you. What I've done—"

"Oh, please, Bob," she said wearily.

"I know I've got no credibility. But I'll earn it. And till then I'll stay out of your hair." He leaned over and kissed her gently. "Hello and good-bye."

His kiss, at once familiar and strange, left her once again confused. But before she could respond, her attention was distracted by Kerry Donner coming into the loft.

Bob followed her glance. "Friend of yours?"

"No, that's Sergeant Donner. One of the detectives working on the case."

"And nothing more to you?"

She looked at him, puzzled. "What do you mean?"

"Nothing. Listen, take care of yourself, babe. And if you need me for anything, just give a call."

When he had gone, Susan hurried over to Donner. "Anything?" she asked breathlessly.

He shook his head. "But there's still a lot of calls coming through."

Disappointment made her snap at him. "Sure, every crazy in the city has made this his personal phone line."

"One of those 'crazies' just might have the answer, Susan."

"Oh, sure. Like the one who said the kids have been absorbed into the fifth dimension. Or the little old lady who thought she saw them under her couch."

"Don't let yourself get cynical. If you do, we're through before we've even started."

"But I can't help it! I *hate* what's happening! I want to scream and kick and bite and throw things! I want to hit someone hard—really goddamned hard!"

"Go ahead," he said.

She gave a wan smile. "I didn't mean it to be you. God, I'm exhausted. I think I'd better sit down."

He looked at her sharply. "Have you had any sleep since all this started?"

"Not much. Well, none at all, actually."

"You need some. Take a nap."

"I can't. The Wyles are coming soon for another brainstorming session."

"Then at least let me give you a back rub."

He began kneading her shoulders. She arched under his proficient touch.

"That does feel good," she sighed. "You know, it's horrible seeing them—Donal and Carla, I mean. It's like I'd been pitying someone with leprosy only to wake up and find the same symptoms in myself. But I've got to see them—and that reporter from the *Post* is waiting for another interview. And there's so much more . . ." Her voice trailed off, her eyelids slipped closed. She was asleep.

Donner stood watching her. The expression on his mismatched features was unreadable, but, for one moment, it appeared as if he would stay watching her forever. Then one of the uniformed cops manning the phones called to him. He glanced up abruptly and, after answering the uniform's question, made his way out.

The city, as Donner emerged onto the street, seemed despairingly complex—a maze more intricate than even Daedalus could have devised. An army could never search all its corridors or its honeycomb of rooms and cellars. It was a labor of Hercules—and all he had at his disposal were ordinary men.

He cursed himself for being a defeatist. The solution to this case did not depend upon a blind search. He had reason, logic, years of training and experience behind him. And there was the very real possibility that someone, somewhere, would come up with a real lead.

If the children were still alive.

Damn it, he thought, it was so easy to despair. But what was it Shaw had said—"He who has never hoped can never despair." Presumably it also worked the other way around—if you never despair, you can't hope.

For the third or fourth time that day he put himself through an exercise he had devised—he tried to think like a child. What if he were a bright, generally well-behaved six-year-old? What would possibly induce him to disobey his parents and wander off?

He ticked off several possibilities. A familiar face, someone he already knew. Another kid his own age. What else? Some irresistible temptation—the promise of candy or a toy he'd seen on TV? How about a puppy or a little kitten? Or an offer to go to the circus?

Being childless put him at a distinct disadvantage. And though the two precinct detectives—Snyder and Weitz, who were also assigned to the task force—were both family men with teenage kids, neither of them had much recent experience with children this young.

His thoughts broke off as he reached a tenement storefront with the name Synergy Center written in flaking red finger paint across the window. There was a door painted Chinese red. From the other side of it came an ungodly noise.

Donner let himself in cautiously. Some thirty children sat in a circle banging on pots and pans, basins, tom-toms, rhythm sticks, and—lacking an instrument —sections of the floor in front of them. In the center sat a young man, cross-legged, strumming on a guitar. He seemed oblivious to the racket around him.

Donner covered his ears and glanced around the room. He was uncertain about what he really expected to find here. The staff—three full-time workers and four volunteers—had been thoroughly questioned by two officers the day before. They had all given satisfactory accounts of where they had been at the time of Joey's disappearance. Maybe it was just the proximity to children that he hoped would be useful.

His eyes traveled back to the young man in the center of the circle. He was the type that women call a "stud"—lean, magnetically handsome—a definite sexual presence. Hardly the type you'd expect to find cooped up in a day-care center with little kids.

But a middle-aged woman in a short green pleated jumper was advancing toward him. Something of an odd duck, he thought. Too much makeup and outlandish clothes had an unfortunate effect on a woman her age.

"Can I help you?" she shouted.

Donner flashed his badge. "What's going on here?"

"It's our rhythm session. The children are learning about following a beat."

"I don't think it's working. They're not at all in time."

"No, no, we encourage them to improvise." The cacophony came to an abrupt end, and the woman lowered her voice. "There, that's better. You see, inspector, our goal here is to bring out the individual in each child. We encourage them to find original rhythms of their own—not to blindly follow the same one as everyone else."

Donner nodded dubiously. "You're one of the teachers?"

"We call ourselves guides," she corrected crisply. "I'm Mrs. Losey—one of the morning volunteer guides. I suppose this is about Joey again?"

"That's right."

"We've had so many policemen round to talk to us. Of course, we're all just shocked as can be." Her voice, Donner noted, was as bland as her appearance was bizarre.

The banging struck up again with alacrity.

Donner shouted, "The man who's with the children now . . ."

"Eben Link."

"Yes, Mr. Link. Has he worked here long?"

"He started just after I did—about six months ago."

"Does he get on well with the kids?"

"Beautifully! It's a pleasure to see a man relate to children the way Eben does."

"Do you think I could possibly talk to him?"

"Oh, I'm sure. We all do so want to help out, inspector."

She waded into the circle and spoke in Eben's ear. He looked up, scowled, then nodded. Moments later, the children were trailing Mrs. Losey out into the yard.

Eben approached Donner. "You want to see me?"

"If you don't mind. This is an interesting place. You like working here?"

"Yeah, sure. It's great."

"You like kids?"

"It'd be a bitch of a job if I didn't."

Donner grinned. "I'll bet. Plan to make a career of it? Child care?"

Eben gave a forced laugh. "I don't think so. The pay's not too good."

"Got any other plans in mind?"

"There's a couple of things I'm investigating."

"Care to be more specific?"

A sullen look crossed Eben's face. "Am I a suspect, Sergeant?"

"Why do you ask that? Do you mind answering questions?"

"I don't like my personal life picked over without a damned good reason."

Donner regarded him intently. "There's a couple of children missing. Don't you find that enough of a reason?"

"Not when I had nothing to do with it. I told the two cops yesterday everything they had to know. Why am I being subjected to this cross-examination?"

"The lives of those little girls could be in great danger. Unless we have everyone's total cooperation . . ."

"Look, Sergeant, I'm sorry the kid's gone. I really am. She's a great kid, and I hope to God she's okay. But I didn't take her. And it's not my fucking job to find out where she is."

Donner's lips tightened. "Yeah," he said, "but it is mine. And I damned well intend to carry it out. Thanks for your time, Mr. Link."

He turned and headed for the door. There was a tiny Oriental boy trying to reach a plastic bat on a shelf. Donner took it down for him, and the boy thanked him shyly.

"You're welcome. What's your name?"

"Gary Ying."

"Did you know Joey Capasian, Gary?"

The boy nodded solemnly.

"Did you know she was lost?"

"Yup. And I know where she is."

"You do?" Donner leaned closer. "Where is she, Gary?"

"She went up to heaven."

A chill went through the detective's spine. He placed a hand on the boy's head and went quickly out.

There was an Italian mom-and-pop on the next block that he liked to frequent. He stopped there now, put a call in on the pay phone, then ordered a provolone and tomato sandwich from old Mr. Lostrito behind the deli counter.

Groceries like Lostrito's were an endangered species. You could get anything you wanted, from the boxes of laundry powder and bleach on the jumbled back shelves to the spicy meats and aromatic cheeses behind glass in the front. But both Mr. Lostrito and his wife were over seventy. Having lived their full lives in Little Italy, they had seen no reason to learn any more English than the basic words needed to serve their customers. Their sons and daughters had long become assimilated in up-to-date suburbs of great American cities; they would never return to the old neighborhood, nor would their children.

Once the Lostritos died, their shop would be replaced by a spanking new Superette complete with automatic digital checkout for speedier service. But you would no longer be able to get the kind of provolone that spoke in blessings to your tongue.

Progress, Donner thought.

He was finishing up an extra-large slice of moist ricotta cheese cake when the pay phone rang back.

"Donner? Jim Rose here. We've got some information on your boy."

"Shoot."

"No record in the state, but the Feds had something. Eben Christopher Link released eight months ago from Danbury Federal Penitentiary. Served just under two years on a charge of criminal solicitation of cocaine."

"Thanks, Jimmy. I appreciate it."

Donner hung up the phone. Well, then, he thought. Where do we go from here?

He passed the day-care yard on the way back to his car. Preoccupied with his thoughts, he didn't notice that the woman in the green jumper was staring at him—nor did he see the way the hatred distorted her odd, ebony-rimmed eyes.

Joey Capasian was shaking her finger at an empty chair.

"Now you stop being a cry baby," she scolded. "Look at all the nice toys you have to play with. You should count your blessings, young lady." She picked up a doll, a beautiful doll with hair the golden color of a fairy princess's, and sat it carefully against the chair. She changed her voice from angry to soft. "You can have my favorite doll, okay? You can keep her from now on, and I won't even care."

But Tweenie wouldn't stop crying. Tweenie was sorry she had come. Her mommy in London had gotten another little girl and forgotten all about her.

"I hate you!" Joey said suddenly. She screwed up her nose and made a horrible face at the empty chair. "It's all your fault. You made me come here."

Tweenie was the one who had wanted to go with the lady, and that's why they had come to this place. This place was dirty and ugly—not like home, which was shiny and clean and filled with all sorts of wonderful things.

She wanted to go home. She missed her big green octopus and her own bed with the Turkey Claw patchwork quilt and Eleanor, her doll from Haiti. Most of all, she missed her mommy. Her mommy was beautiful and looked exactly like an angel. Not like this mommy, who was witchy and mean. This mommy said "Joey" was a sinful name for a girl and that from now on she had to be named Tammy. But Joey didn't want a new name. She wanted to go home.

"I hate you," she said again.

"What are you playing, Tammy?"

Joey gave a start. She hadn't heard the clickety-click of the high heels come across the floor. But now the big head bent so close to her that she could see big scabby flakes of powder on the face.

"Nothing," she said.

"But I heard you. Is it a new game? Can I play, too?"

Joey shrugged. The woman's eyes looked like finger paint, smudgy and weird, and Joey couldn't stand looking at them.

"Why don't you teach me how to play?" The big ponytail went bob, and the woman began to lower herself into the little chair.

"Don't sit there!" Joey cried.

She almost laughed to see the woman jump up so fast. "Why not?" the woman asked.

Joey put her fist to her mouth and stared down at the floor.

"Tammy. I asked you a question."

"Because that's Tweenie's chair," she whispered.

The smile suddenly flew away from the big face, and the eyes became squinty and mean. "Who is Tweenie?"

"She's a girl. I wasn't supposed to tell you she was here."

"There is no girl here."

"Nobody can see her except me."

The big face came really close again, all twisted and mad now. Joey began to tremble. *"The liar shall be brought to perdition, and his lies shall plague him till the end of the earth! Do you understand?"*

"Yes," Joey whispered. She didn't understand at all. She just wanted the face to go away.

"If I ever hear you make up stories again, I shall punish you. Do you hear me? You will be punished!" The voice came at her like the hiss the radiator made when it was cold.

Joey kept her eyes on the dusty brown floor. She heard the clickety-click of the heels going back across the room. The woman went all the way back to where the little stove was and began to take things out of the box that held the pots and pans. After a minute she began to sing, a happy song about a doggy in a window. Joey relaxed. She knew that for a while now it would be okay.

She got up and started walking. When she looked over her shoulder, she saw that Tweenie was coming too. "Stay back there," she whispered, but Tweenie wouldn't listen. Joey walked all around the big, smiling crack in the floor making sure she didn't touch it with her foot, and Tweenie did too. Then she came to the hole. It was a big sharp hole in the floor and very deep. When she looked down, all she could see was black.

"Don't get too close," she warned.

But Tweenie still wouldn't listen, and when she leaned down she fell right in and fell and fell until she smashed down dead on the bottom.

Joey's eyes began to water. Because now Tweenie was dead, and now her mommy would never see her again. Not ever.

Day McAllister had spent an exasperating morning on the telephone. She had placed fifteen calls to city agencies. At each one she had been transferred, put on hold, retransferred, cut off, and finally told by some petulant voice that they were very sorry, but they really couldn't help her.

It was so frustrating! All Day wanted was some information on 864 Broome Street, the building that was to be torn down and replaced by the Lower Manhattan Sports Center. It seemed a simple enough request. She had never imagined it would prove so difficult.

She had another reason to be in a foul mood: a letter from her parents this morning. They were coming to New York next month for a week's vacation, to do the sights, see the shows—and check up on their daughter. "I know how frugal you usually are, dear, so if there are any tempting restaurants in your neighborhood you've been dying to try, Dad and I would enjoy treating you . . ." Damnation! Their visit meant an entire week that she'd have to spend in that stuffy little decoy apartment uptown. An entire week without

Eben. She couldn't cajole him into even meeting her parents.

"It wouldn't work, Daysie," he insisted.

"Why not? They're nice people."

"I'm sure they are. But your old man would want to know where I went to school, and who I work for, and what my prospects are like. And he wouldn't be too ecstatic at my answers."

"They're not like that," she protested. But that wasn't exactly true. Her parents were kind enough in their own way—they certainly meant well enough. But they only knew one way of living, one set of values. Those were just the type of questions they *would* ask.

But someday she'd make Eben realize that it didn't matter what her parents thought about him, or her friends, or the rest of the world. She was proud of him, and she believed in him.

Listen to me! she thought. Sounding like some sappy housewifey country-and-Western song. "Stand by your man" and all that. And in the meantime, her own work was going begging.

Resolutely, she picked up the phone again. There was one more number on her list—the Landmarks Commission. The voice of the young woman who answered sounded different from those Day had been dealing with all morning. It was bright and alert rather than lethargic. She seemed actually anxious to be of service.

Her name was Celia Markson. "I know the building you mean. The old Byer Thread building. I'm glad somebody's finally asking about it."

"What do you mean?" Day asked her.

"Well—" There was a heartbeat's pause before she continued. "It struck me as peculiar. The developers submitted an engineer's report on structural defects in the building, proving it was unsound and in danger of collapse. On that basis, they were granted approval for demolition—even though the building is in a designated landmarks zone. We were going to contest that decision. But then something happened. Word came down from somewhere on high—probably the mayor's office. Our appeal never got off the ground."

Day's pulse began to race. "Are you suggesting that someone in the mayor's office might have been paid off to intercede?"

"Oh, no, I can't say that. I have no evidence of anything . . ."

"But you do seem to think the developers' claims might be false. What makes you think the building isn't structurally unsound?"

Again there was the barest hesitation. "How much do you know about those cast-iron loft buildings?"

"Not much," Day admitted. "Even though I live in one."

"Let me tell you about them. Most of them were built about a hundred years ago by the finest architects of the day. They were designed to hold four-hundred-gallon drums of olive oil and industrial machinery weighing many, many tons—and even for that they were overbuilt. Take them apart, and you'll find twenty-inch solid oak beams supporting four-inch-thick floorboards. They have vertical columns made of iron or oak aged hard as iron. They were literally built to last forever."

"I see what you mean," Day said excitedly. "It's not very likely then that this building is about to fall down."

"Not likely, no. Though, to be fair, there could always be a fluke. The beams could have rotted somehow, or the original architects could have made some mistake . . ." Celia Markson paused. "I really shouldn't be saying all this . . ."

"I always protect my sources."

"But it's all just speculation. I've got no proof of anything."

"But maybe I can come up with some. Any ideas on where I could start?"

"Well . . . you might try the original plans on file in the Buildings Department. See if anything looks fishy.

You could also do a title search. Maybe you could trace a connection to someone important in one of the previous owners."

"Great!"

"And listen—if you do follow up on any of this, would you keep me posted?"

"Will do. Thanks so much, Celia. You've been a great help."

Day stuffed a notebook into her purse, then dashed into her editor's office to inform him she'd be out for the rest of the afternoon. A stifling subway took her downtown. She finally found the Department of Buildings within the maze of public edifices. The clerk, a woman with lacquered hair and a mouth pinched to an O, brought her a roll of microfilm and showed her how to use the viewing machine. But the plans had been poorly photographed—so out of focus Day could hardly read them. She returned to the clerk.

"I'm sorry, honey," the woman snapped. "That's the best I can give you."

"Why can't I see the originals?"

"Because," the woman said with a look of long suffering, "they've been misfiled. And I can't be expected to go searching through hundreds of thousands of plans just to find one for you, now can I?"

It was hopeless, Day thought. I'm nothing but a pest to her. If she had a can of Raid, she'd probably squirt me with it.

She thanked the woman and left.

Her next stop was the County Clerk's office for a title search. An hour's worth of work yielded little. The building had been purchased by the architectural firm of Cassidy and Knowlton from the estate of an Indiana man deceased ten years. He in turn had acquired it from a bankrupt real estate firm, which had owned and managed it since 1931; that was as far as the records went.

She decided to take the bull by the horns and talk directly to messieurs Knowlton and Cassidy. But a call

to their office informed her that both architects were
out of town until Monday.

Oh, well, Day sighed. Might as well knock off. After
all, it was five o'clock on Friday night. Even slaves
deserve their rest.

She and Eben had dinner that evening with another
couple at Oh Ho So. Through it, Eben was silent and
distracted, not taking his usual lively part in the chatter
and responding only vaguely when one of the others
tried to tease him out of his mood.

He remained distracted until they had returned home
to their loft. He undressed silently, pulling off one item
of clothing after another in a methodical way, as if
according to a regulation. Then he lay back naked on
the bed, hands folded behind his head.

"I've been thinking," he said, as Day settled in
beside him. "This place is really starting to get claustro-
phobic."

She laughed lightly. "We've got enough space in this
loft for a roller rink."

"I don't mean the loft, I mean the neighborhood.
The whole scene. There's too much development going
on. I feel like we're getting squeezed out."

"That's exactly why I'm on this Sports Center thing,"
she said.

"But it's too late. You could stop a million sports
centers and they'd still keep coming. Take a walk
around—every old building you see's got a dumpster
parked in front of it. They're all being converted to
swanky residences for rich fucking lawyers and ac-
countants." He shook his head. "It won't be long
before they get their hands on this one, too, and we'll
be out on our asses."

Day felt a shiver of dread. "Do you have any
alternatives in mind?"

"I've been thinking about Alaska."

She looked at him. "Alaska?"

"Yeah. One thing they've got up there is space. And

from what I hear, you can get rich working the pipeline."

"But what about your work here?"

"I think the center could survive without me," he said wryly.

"That's not what I mean. You've been talking about getting into holography—what a great future there is in it . . ."

"Sure—in ten or fifteen or a hundred years. In the meantime, those guys are barely scraping by. I've got to live my life *now*."

Day held her breath. "What about me?"

"I'd want you to come with me, of course. But I wouldn't force you to. It's a decision you'd have to make for yourself."

Damn that philosophy! Day struggled to keep her voice light. "You think I could make it working the pipeline?"

"Oh, you'd find something," he said earnestly.

Something! She didn't want to settle for something. Especially not now, when things were looking so exciting. A hot wave of resentment swept through her. Couldn't she get it through his thick skull how much her career meant to her?

But then she looked at him—the handsome delineation of his profile, his long, athlete's body. She thought of his grace and how funny he could sometimes be.

Don't do this to me, she pleaded silently. Don't make me choose.

Suddenly she was afraid. She snuggled close to him, seeking to draw some reassurance from the physical presence of his body. He curved to accommodate her and she reached out for him; the flat of her palms planed the muscles of his shoulders and chest. He lay very still, as if waiting to see what she would do next. Her touch traveled downwards; her fingers sought him, but despite her caresses he remained unaroused. She slid down and covered him with light, softly blowing kisses, sensing it starting to work.

But then she felt his hands on her shoulders, drawing her up. "Do you think I could have a rain check on that, baby?"

"Don't you like it?" she asked.

"Of course, it feels good. It's just that I'm completely beat. It's been a long bitch of a day."

Her heart pounded. He had never rejected her advances before. "Is there anything wrong, Eben?" she whispered.

"No, nothing's wrong. Really, baby, I'm just tired. Those little monsters can wear you down after a while."

"Well, then, thank God it's Friday." Her voice feigned an airiness she was far from feeling. "Sleep well, baby."

She waited until she was sure he was sound asleep. Then she pulled on a sweat shirt and a pair of jeans and went out, needing to walk off the knot of tension that had gathered in her chest.

Despite the lateness of the hour, there were still many people on the street. Day left the crowded cafes behind as she turned onto Broome Street. After several blocks, she found the building she was looking for. Number 864. The words Byer Thread Co. were struck in copper lettering across the facade.

In the dark it looked very much like its neighbors— one more Italian palazzo building encrusted with grime. The top story windows were boarded up; that was the only thing to indicate that it was marked to be destroyed, that in a matter of weeks it would be smashed to rubble by the wvecker's ball.

But no, there was something else about the building —some quality of hopelessness that came from inside. The sense of this grew stronger the longer Day gazed at it. The boarded-up top story began to seem very spooky indeed. She thought of tales of haunted houses from her childhood, abandoned buildings occupied by horrible forces . . .

A white face appeared in one of the lower windows.

She stifled a scream. There was nothing there—just the reflection of a passing headlight. She was only frightening herself.

Yet she couldn't get rid of the image of something trapped inside, the white bloodless face struggling to get out. She shivered and went quickly home to bed.

The children huddled together as if for warmth. They sat on the edge of a cot, not daring to move, while the woman went about her business.

The woman put the big bag of groceries on the table and unpacked it briskly. Milk in the refrigerator, orange juice in the freezer. Oatmeal and Cream of Wheat on the high shelf. Oreos in the little white cabinet that was always kept locked. Paper bag neatly folded and stored behind the shelf.

And when the bag was done, she began to unpack herself. Off with the funny hat and out with the long reddish hair. Off with the sunglasses and eyes on, black and bright. Out with the big red mouth that turned up at the corners like the crack in the floor.

She walked back and forth across the room, collecting things for her big, shiny purse. Her high heels went tickedy-tack, tickedy-tack on the wooden floor.

"Come, Georgene, come, Tammy," she said, opening her arms. The big red mouth smiled wide. "I'm leaving for work now. Come kiss Mummy good-bye."

The children rose dutifully and came to her arms. The crimson mouth kissed their foreheads. "Good-bye, children," the woman said. "Good-bye, my darlings. Be good."

"Good-bye," the children chorused. Obedience, they had learned, was the best way. As long as they were good, they would not be punished. There would be no thrashings with the wooden spoon, nor being made to stand in the scary corner with the spiderwebs; nor would they be sent to bed so hungry that they cried all night instead of sleeping.

The high heels went tickedy-tack, tickedy-tack to the elevator. "Bye, my precious darlings." The woman waved and the children waved back.

The elevator creaked and groaned and rumbled. They continued waving until they were sure they were alone.

The pool at Spetzi's East Hampton estate was shaped like a palette, complete with a circular concrete island where the finger hole would be.

Gil Cassidy found it preposterous. He wondered if any of the other guests who sat around its turquoise waters found it so as well. They were an impressive enough crowd, drawn from the cream of the art and literary establishments; most of them could boast estates of their own nestled within the secluded back lanes of the Hamptons. But even so, they seemed, for the most part, extravagantly pleased to be here—to be lounging on Spetzi's striped canvas pool chairs, to be sipping his mint-garnished iced drinks, to be basking under his bright June sun.

Gil's fingers trailed into the water, creating softly coruscating rivulets in their path. Spetzi, in a flowered Hawaiian shirt, was weaving among his guests, playing a good imitation of the perfect host. He made sure every drink was freshened, distributed towels, dispensed the barbed charm that was his specialty. But there was just a shade too much solicitousness in his atttentions to be genuine.

143

Like the way he now hovered over Thia and Alexis, insisting on personally escorting them to the bath-house. Gil's eyes narrowed. It had to be a mockery.

A shadow fell over him. He shaded his eyes to peer up at Albie Knowlton.

"Why the hell did you bring your kid with you?" Albie demanded.

He gave a lazy smile. "I had to, Albie. Blood is thicker than business, you know."

"Funny, funny. Especially coming from you, the way you've been catting around town the last few years."

"Why, Albie, I didn't think you noticed things like sex. I thought you couldn't be bothered with anything except making money."

"Fuck off, Cassidy." Knowlton lit a cigarette, then glanced at his watch, a steel-cased diver's Seiko. "The lawyers should be getting here soon. I'm going to wait for them in the study. You coming?"

Gil tilted his head back to the sun. "To tell you the truth, Albie, I think I could use a little more color on my face."

His partner threw him a disgusted look and moved away. Gil laughed.

At the other end of the patio, he saw Thia emerge with Alexis from the bathhouse. Her hair glistened in the sun. The simple coiffure that seemed so drab in the city was becoming to her here, and the black maillot she wore set off her stunning figure. Gil felt a sudden jolt of pride—for both his wife and his daughter, a picture in her tiny gingham sunsuit.

There were murmurs from the other guests over the exquisite little girl. A thin, elegant brunette jumped up from a lounge chair and ran over to her. She was a woman Gil knew from the cocktail circuit around town, a former catalogue model named Lorraine Bellamy. For the past five years, she had been the mistress of Dick Tedesco, a world-syndicated political columnist. It was well known that Lorraine, pushing thirty-six, had no desire to become a publicist, photographer's stylist, or any of the other off-camera positions available to former mannequins. Her sole ambition was to get Dick Tedesco to marry her. To this end she had devised a strategy: she had become a paragon of domesticity. She cooked Cordon Bleu, studied interior design, was a smashing hostess—and she professed to be inordinately fond of children.

Gil watched her warily. She had hustled Alexis away from Thia and back to her own chair, where she sat her on her knee. Alexis squirmed to get down. But Lorraine was determined not to let such a gorgeous opportunity slip by; she pinned the child firmly to her lap.

"Isn't she precious?" she crooned loudly. "Did you ever see such a fairy-tale princess in your life? I could just eat her up alive!"

All of a sudden her expression changed. Her eyes widened to pools, her mouth twisted downwards. "You goddamned little brat!" she screeched. She yanked Alexis off her lap and leapt up. "Zandra Rhodes pajamas, six hundred and fifty dollars at Bergdorf Goodman's, and look what you've done!"

Alexis began to cry. Thia rushed over in alarm. "What happened?" she cried.

"Your damned brat wet on me, that's what happened. Look—look at that stain."

"It's not her fault. She didn't mean it."

"The hell she didn't." Lorraine glared at the child. "You're a spoiled rotten little kid, and you ought to be whipped."

"Don't yell at her," Thia insisted.

"I ought to do more than that!"

Gil came up to them. "Knock it off, Lorraine," he said. "I can't believe this is the first time you've had a golden shower."

Her eyes turned a venomous green. "How dare you!" she sputtered. "How dare you say that!"

He felt Thia touch his hand. It was the first time they had stood for something together in years. It felt surprisingly good.

The commotion had drawn the attention of the rest of the party. Spetzi emerged from the house with a maid. He assured Lorraine that her garment would be taken care of, and the maid led Thia and Alexis back to the house. Peace was restored.

But Gil's nerves were on edge. He had taken two Valium that morning, but he had to stay alert for the meeting; he couldn't trust himself to take another or have any more to drink. Someone had left a pack of Marlboros on a table. It had been nearly six months since he quit, but he reached for it.

The first puff was harsh on his throat. But as the tobacco filled his lungs, he figured that for now it would do the trick.

Spetzi had noticed the child the moment she arrived. A remarkable creature. Sultry in the way only girl children could be. The provocatively arched back and pouting tummy, and such a seraphic little face.

His interest was definitely piqued. Under the pretext of showing the mother to the bathhouse, he was able to examine her more closely. The child made crowing noises and flapped her arms up and down like an excited chicken. An idiot! Well, so much the better, he thought. A foolish flower.

And now that imperishable tart Lorraine had given him the opportunity to be close to her again—a pleasure worth the reimbursement of a dozen ruined dresses. The child was indeed enchanting. His eyes sought his present mistress sunning by the pool—a frail Japanese girl of seventeen who, in the proper clothing, could pass for twelve. How coarse and overgrown she now appeared.

But the child was being led away, and his illustrious guests required his attention. With a jaunty step, he returned to the party.

Coy Seiglitz, Jr., now known to the world only as "Spetzi," gloried in his possessions. They were the symbols of his success. Each costly artifact testified eloquently to the fact that the clownish, unpopular fat boy had finally triumphed. His celebrity was as tangible as the things around him—and for this reason he only acquired the best.

The East Hampton "cottage" was one of five properties owned for tax purposes by an elaborate corporation of which Spetzi was the sole shareholder. The main house was a fourteen-room structure of the shingle style built by Stanford White for one of the lesser Vanderbilts. It was nestled within six acres of prime oceanfront property; its five outbuildings—pool house, tennis house, sauna, gardener's shed, and gate house—were each large enough to house a family. The estate contained a museum-quality collection of Early American antiques and folk art. Each highboy, braided rug, posnet pot, and cow creamer had a pedigree as long and as distinguished as that of a Boston Lowell.

The feelings the artist had for the things he acquired extended to his guests. By accepting his hospitality, they belonged to him. No matter how rich or famous or notorious, he could make them dance to his tune.

He was especially pleased with the people he had gathered to pay him homage today—a carefully picked crop chosen to offset the tedium of having to do business. There was a game he liked to play. It involved seeing how close he could come to actual insult before any of his guests took offense. He strolled about the pool delivering scarcely veiled innuendos—to a Broadway lyricist about his secret alcoholism, to a young editor about her affair with her seventy-year-old publisher. It interested him to see that none of them dared rise to the bait.

But there were two of his guests who were not included in his game. When he spoke to them, there was nothing but unqualified respect in his voice. These were middle-aged men dressed in lightweight navy business suits, crisp white shirts, and sober ties. Their faces were bland to the point of anonymity. They did not mingle with the rest of the party, but sat at a small table in the shade abstemiously sipping imported Italian *limonata*.

"Is everything all right?" the artist asked them earnestly. "Is there anything else you'd like?"

"Nothing, thank you," they replied.

The obsequious smile lingered on his face until he was safely out of sight. In point of fact, he knew very little about these two men, but over the years he had been able to formulate a few assumptions. He guessed that each was worth at least as much as any other person here today; that together they represented more real power than all his other guests put together. He guessed, too, that their only social life was confined to family and those like themselves in Riverdale and Bay Ridge. This guarded cordiality was their only concession to the prebusiness amenities.

They had made him what he was. His fame, his possessions, his sycophantic followers—all of it he owed to them. And never for a second did he doubt that, should they so desire, they could take it all away.

The thought disturbed him. For comfort he returned to the house to check on preparations for dinner.

His Haitian cook, Samuel, greeted him with a grin.

"We are in luck today, Mr. Spetzi. Jimmy Jones at the game farm, he gave me the pick of the kill. Feel these birds for yourself, sir."

Spetzi poked at a plump breast. "Your judgment is, as always, impeccable, Samuel. Have you decided on a first?"

"I'm thinking a chilled cucumber soup with dill, followed by *salade mimosa*. And to finish, my *gâteau crème glacé*."

"Marvelous. And the wines—what do you say to the last of the seventy-one Montrachet for the quail?"

"Excuse me, sir, but I am thinking instead of the Haut-Brion blanc."

"You are perfectly right. Much more original."

Samuel beamed with pride.

Through the open half of the kitchen's Dutch door, the artist noticed someone leave the house. It was Thia Cassidy returning to the pool. The child must be still in the bedroom. He was struck by an urge to see her again.

He crossed the house to the east wing, trying several doors before finding the right one. She lay asleep on a canopy bed, undressed and covered with a white Porthault sheet. Her thumb was securely fastened in her mouth. Wisps of silvery hair clung to her moist forehead.

Hardly breathing, he touched her. She stirred but didn't awake. Gently, he pulled the sheet down, gloating at the flushed form, smooth and hairless as a boy's. But the plumpness was female, as were the twin rolls of fat between the small legs. So perfect, he thought. Such a delicate feast.

He was excited as he'd never been before. He glanced down the hall, then shut and locked the door. The child's an idiot, he said to himself. If she awakens she won't understand—she'll never be able to tell . . . He touched her, confidently this time, enjoying his prize. A milky odor arose from her. Inhaling, he could no longer restrain himself.

Suddenly the door opened. He whirled—damn these old locks. His blood ran cold as he met Thia's eye. The extraordinary instinct of the mother, he thought. She had seen nothing, yet had she a weapon in her hand he would be a dead man.

"Get out!" she hissed.

His lips froze in a smile. "I was merely making sure . . ."

"Get out before I kill you!"

He hurried past her, out the door, and took refuge in an unused servant's room. There he collapsed in a high sweat against a dresser.

All his thoughts were of the two somber men in the

dark suits. Good family men, protective of their children—this was the kind of thing they would never tolerate.

Once before he had come dangerously close to courting their displeasure. It had cost him seventy thousand pounds sterling to hush up his adventure with the viscount's little daughter, but even so, rumors had leaked out. And he had received warnings—subtle, but clear. That one had been thirteen. Whatever would they do if they found out about this?

He was sweating profusely. He could never go back to being just Coy Seiglitz, the nobody he was before. He'd do anything to prevent that from happening. Anything at all.

Some moments later, when he walked into his wainscoted study, there was nothing to suggest that he was in anything less than perfect control. His step was jaunty and his forehead was dry.

He gazed around at the assembled faces. "Well, boys," he said heartily, "do we have a deal?"

"Don't see why not," Albie Knowlton put in. "Give us seven days, and we'll have that building slapped down flatter than a pancake."

There was laughter all around, but it was Spetzi who laughed the longest and the loudest.

All the energy and ingenuity that had made her gallery a success Susan Capasian now brought into the search for her daughter. She pushed herself night and day, lighting fires under people when she sensed their interest flagging, talking into the telephone until it seemed like a permanent extension of her hand. She gave interviews to anyone with a pencil and pad and licked mountains of envelopes until her tongue adhered to the roof of her mouth.

And at the end of two weeks, she had nothing at all to show for her efforts.

Every morning Kerry Donner stopped in on his daily reconnaissance walk through the neighborhood. Susan found herself looking forward to his visits more and more with each passing day. He had become the mainstay of her support, bucking up her courage in a hundred different ways and sometimes even making her laugh.

This morning he ordered her to take a break. "Go to the zoo, take the Staten Island Ferry—do anything," he said. "If you don't, you're going to crack. You're not invincible, you know."

She started to protest. "Out of here," he commanded. "If you don't, I'll have to get tough."

She knew he was right. She decided to put some time in at the gallery.

Dani greeted her with an exuberant hug. "God, I've missed you down here," she cried. "It gets so lonely when it's just me and the Westchester luncheon ladies." She faltered as she noticed the utilitarian workshirt and jeans Susan was wearing.

Susan grinned. "I'll bet you didn't even know I owned such practical clothes, did you?"

"Uh-uh. But, damn it, you could wear a bedspread and still carry it off!"

Susan walked around the gallery, exploring. The vivid rectangular canvases floating on white walls gave her a momentary lift. "You've done a great job, Dani," she said.

"Oh, God! There's been about a dozen crises a day, but somehow I've managed to muddle through."

"You've been terrific." Susan entered her office. Something there struck her as wrong. Of course—the double portrait of herself was missing. "Where's my painting?" she asked.

Dani looked puzzled. "Why Bob DeRitis came and took it. I thought you knew. I mean, I'd never let him take it if I didn't think you knew."

Why would Bob take back his painting? Susan wondered with irritation. But it was just like him to pull something like this. He was obviously just as erratic and irresponsible as he had always been. Just as well he was out of her life.

But she couldn't worry about that now. "If we intend to hang a new show on Thursday," she said, "we'd better get to work."

For the rest of the afternoon she poured herself into the operations of the gallery and tried to keep her mind off Joey and the fruitless search. At six-thirty she dragged herself, bone weary, back upstairs. The officer manning the phones told her it had been a slow day. Only one caller, and that was an obvious crackpot who'd had a dream about children in a hayloft.

Susan thanked him, and he left. She turned on her television to catch an update on the case prepared by one of the local news programs. When it was over, she continued watching out of inertia. Sports, a theater review, and then the weather. Donal Wyle's face filled the screen.

Susan gasped. He looked as if he hadn't a care in the world. His eyes twinkled, his voice was as glad as a summer's breeze. "And for all you sun worshipers out there, it looks like another fine day for tomorrow," he chirped. "Though we might get a sprinkle toward late afternoon—just enough to give a drink to all those thirsty gardens. For the big picture, let's take a look at Mr. W's weather map . . ."

Susan snapped off the set, her body trembling. It was ghastly! How could he act so completely insouciant with Lisa still missing? Had he so little feeling for his daughter?

She imagined an answer. Life goes on. There are still bills to be paid, obligations to be met. You can't mourn forever.

But why not? she screamed silently. What's the use of all this senseless carrying on? Why can't we just give up and die if we want to?

"I must be going mad!" she said aloud.

The silence gathered. It was Saturday night. All over the city people were preparing to go out—to dance and dine and take pleasure. Where were all her friends? All the beautiful and exciting people who had cultivated her after her success? Why was her phone so silent?

Perhaps they thought it tactful to wait until she contacted them. Yes, that must be it! They were waiting for a call from her.

She picked up the phone. She would call Henry Lupino, an antiques dealer who lived in Soho and who professed to adore her in the way gay men often did. During the past year she had been in the habit of seeing Henry at least once a week.

But as her finger found the dial, she thought of Henry's nasal, insinuating voice and his cleverly devastating put-downs of people behind their backs. No, she couldn't bear that now.

She dropped the receiver back in its cradle.

Another name suggested itself: Kerry Donner. She thought of his strength and quiet humor. She had never met anyone who was so completely at ease with who he was—he never even tried to be anything else.

Could she be falling in love with him? She quickly dismissed the thought. If she was, it was only in the way women were always falling in love with their doctors and psychiatrists. It didn't really mean a thing.

Not a thing.

She went determinedly to the liquor cabinet and poured herself a stiff Scotch and water. The drink had become an evening ritual. But tonight, she decided, she wouldn't stop at just one.

It is a birthday party.

The children are scrubbed until their faces shine, and they are all dressed up in dresses of pastel organdy. On their heads are shiny paper cones held in place by elastic that snaps under their chins. They sit neatly around the table; at the places in front of them are paper plates decorated with clowns and balloons and little party baskets filled with plastic grass and jelly beans and silver-wrapped candy kisses.

They are singing "Happy birthday to you," but their voices are tentative and soft—hardly more than a whisper. The woman's voice drowns them out, booms out the words, "Happy birthday, dear Georgene. Happy birthday to you!"

"Hooray!" the woman crows and claps her large red-tipped hands. The children clap, too, but they do not cheer. "Blow out the candles, Georgene," she says. "Make a secret wish, and blow out the candles."

Lisa Wyle sits at the head of the table. She closes her eyes tight and wishes fiercely that her daddy will come to take her home. She puffs with all her might. But

155

when she opens her eyes, one candle is still brightly glowing.

"Oh, too bad!" the woman cries, "Georgene didn't get her wish. But don't worry, sweetheart, mommy will give you a nice big piece of cake instead. Pass your plates, children." She plunges a knife deep into the chocolaty heart of the cake and slices it into wedges.

The paper plates go round the table.

There is a gasp and a small cry. Joey Capasian has overturned her cake in her lap. She puts it back together on the plate, but there is chocolate frosting all over her dress; the more she scrapes at it, the more it smears into the pale pink organdy fabric. Her heart beats quickly; she knows she is in trouble even before she feels herself jerked to her feet.

"Look what you've done to your beautiful dress!" the woman is yelling. "You've dirtied it up just like a little baby. Like a two-year-old! Well, we don't want babies at our party, do we, Georgene?"

"No, ma'am," she dutifully echoes.

Joey is pulled rapidly by the hand toward a small chair in a corner. The frilly party dress is yanked up over her head. "Children who can't keep their clothes clean don't deserve to wear them," the woman declares. "Now you can sit here until you learn to appreciate the nice things you have."

Wearing only white cotton underpants, Joey sits down in the chair. It is damp in the corner; a draft blows from somewhere. She shivers, but she knows what will happen if she dares to complain.

The woman has returned to her seat. "Let's sing, Georgene," she is saying brightly. "Who knows a nice song? Oh, I know one! Let's sing 'How much is that doggie in the window?'" But the child doesn't know the words, and it is only her own high-pitched, eager voice that resounds through the loft, singing about the dog with the waggly tail.

The coffee was as vile as usual, but Kerry Donner had perfected the knack of swallowing without tasting. He grinned as Casiopo of the First Precinct slammed down his cup with a grimace.

"What's in this stuff?" he spat. "Carburetor fluid?"

Casiopo was new to the task force. He'd become inured to it soon enough.

Donner's grin faded as he glanced down at the clipboard on his knee. It contained the distillation of everything they had to date—and it could all be summed up in one word: zero.

The fact was reflected in the faces of the men who sat around his desk. They were plain, hard-working men, unaccustomed to the public spotlight the case had thrown upon them. The sacrifice of their peace and privacy only compounded their immense frustration. The case followed them everywhere. Reporters badgered them constantly, friends quizzed them about it, their wives demanded to hear every little detail. The strain was beginning to tell.

Twice a week the task force met to consolidate what

information they had acquired. Each time the meeting was shorter and more discouraging.

"We got nothing," Snyder declared bluntly. He spoke up against the constant background chatter of the Missing Persons Bureau—typewriters, teletype machines, the jingle of an AM radio station. "We got calls coming in from Greensboro, North Carolina, Salt Lake City—you name it—and not one solid piece of information in the whole friggin' mess."

Weitz nodded. "It's nuts. Some guy swears he's seen the kids driven by a little old lady in a Fairmont. Only then he's not sure if it's an old lady or an old man, or even if it's a Fairmont or maybe an LTD. So what do we do? Detain all senior citizens driving late-model Fords? I tell you, it's nuts!"

"I got paperwork up the ass," Snyder grumbled. "I can't handle no more dead-end leads."

Donner let them complain, knowing that when they got it out of their system they would go back diligently to their jobs. The talk turned to what had been done. The tedious process of checking out all delivery men to the area was just about completed but had yielded nothing. The papers had received no new calls, and nothing had come in that morning over the wires. Nothing. The word had become oppressive; it fell on their ears like a blow.

"Well, maybe today we'll get lucky," Donner ventured.

The men shrugged. Years of experience had taught them just how much you could trust to luck.

The meeting dispersed. Donner drove the now-familiar route uptown from Police Plaza to Soho. He parked the car outside a building with a cherry-red neon sign that flashed SOHO SUN.

As he went inside, he nearly collided with a young woman who appeared to be in a great hurry. She yelled "Sorry!" over her shoulder as she swept on by.

"Wait!" he called. "Could you tell me where I could find Day McAllister?"

She turned. "That's me."

"I'm Sergeant Donner of the Missing Persons Bureau. Could I have a word with you?"

"If it's about the missing kids, I'm not assigned to that story anymore. And I've got to go now, so if you've got some information, you can give it to . . ."

"I want to talk to you about Eben Link."

She glanced up in alarm. "Eben? Is he in some kind of trouble?"

"Probably not."

"Then why are you asking about him?"

"When he was questioned about the case, he seemed very reluctant to cooperate. I thought I might have better luck with you."

She bit her lip. "All right. Come into my office."

Her office was a makeshift cubicle with no windows. But she had conquered the cheerlessness of the space by turning the walls into a riotous collage of clippings, posters, snapshots, and Woolworth's counter plastic toys.

She perched on the edge of the desk, looking up at him. "What do you want to know?"

Her eyes were astonishingly lovely—almost too much so for the rest of her face. And unnervingly direct.

"How long have you been living with Eben?" he asked.

"About six months."

"The entire time you've lived in this neighborhood?"

"That's right."

"In this time, have you observed anything unusual in Eben's behavior?"

"Unusual like how?"

"For instance, sudden outbursts of temper or prolonged periods of depression or insomnia? Does he disappear at times without explanation?"

"No, to all of the above," she said firmly.

"When he's been out on his own, is he ever reluctant to tell you where he's been?"

"I'm not in the habit of drilling him on where he goes."

"Does he have a key to the apartment you keep uptown?"

"How did you know about that?" she began, then laughed. "Of course, you're an investigator. No, Sergeant, he does not have a key."

"But he has access to yours? He might easily have had one made for himself without your knowledge?"

"Eben wants nothing to do with that place uptown."

"You haven't answered my question."

She made an exasperated sound. "Well, of course, he has access to my keys, but . . ."

"How about his sexual behavior? Does he ever make any unusual requests?"

Her eyes hardened. "What do you mean?"

"I mean, is he kinky? Does he get off on bondage or more than two in a bed? Does he ever put on your clothes? You're of an enlightened generation, Miss McAllister. I'm sure you know what I mean."

"I don't see that I have to answer that kind of question!"

"You don't," Donner said. "I can bring your friend down to the precinct house and get some answers out of him there. And with his felony record . . ."

"Eben made one mistake! Is he going to have to be persecuted for it the rest of his life?"

"No. Not unless he's made a second. Will you answer the question?"

She hesitated. "He's quite normal in bed, if that's what you mean. Unless you happen to consider being gentle and patient on the list of kinky behavior in your 'enlightened' society."

He ignored her sarcasm. "Does Eben like his job?"

"I think so."

"Is he affectionate with the kids? Does he hug them, pick them up, that kind of thing?"

"Children need to be touched, Sergeant. They *need*

hugging and cuddling. Eben naturally responds to that."

"Sometimes a little too enthusiastically?"

"No!"

"Seems to cuddle with the little girls a bit more than the boys?"

"Stop it!" she cried shrilly. "You're trying to make Eben out to be some kind of pervert, and he's not! You barge in here accusing him . . ."

"I haven't accused him of anything, Miss McAllister."

"Bullshit! I know a leading question when I hear one." Her eyes flashed fury. "It's obvious what you're doing. You've gotten nowhere on this case, so now you need a scapegoat—someone you can drag through hell just to show the taxpayers you're earning your money."

Donner held her gaze. "Have you ever seen the body of a sexually abused child, Miss McAllister? Or, more likely, what's left of it? Because that's the real hell. And if you had, you'd know that no matter how many innocent people have to be dragged through purgatory to prevent that, it's worth it." He hesitated, as if to add something further, but changed his mind. "Thank you for your time," he said, and left.

But he felt far from calm as he returned to his car. Something in what Day had said had struck a nerve. He had gone after her almost viciously, even though his gut instinct told him that Eben was probably clear. It was as if this case was becoming his own personal proving ground—the means of finally proving to himself that the decision he had made ten years ago had not been wrong. For that he could not afford to fail. He had to have answers, and he had to have them at any cost.

His next stop was his daily morning check-in at Donal and Carla Wyle's loft.

Carla opened the door, her face flushed with excitement. "Madeleine Coffee is here!" she told him. "She's offered to help us find the children."

Donner frowned. Madeleine Coffee was a psychic enjoying a current fame. Her predictions concerning national disasters and the imminent breakups of various television stars' marriages were regularly splashed across the front pages of cheap weekly tabloids. Donner had worked on several other cases in which she had been called in to assist. In his opinion her "powers" ran heavily toward attracting publicity to herself and little more. Apparently, this hadn't changed. She sat surrounded by reporters and photographers, an obese, frizzle-haired woman wrapped like a bonbon in a voluminous candy-striped caftan. Her face was thrown back in an attitude of beatific concentration.

"This is absurd," Donner scoffed. "That woman is a complete phony."

Carla smiled. "She told us you'd say that. She says she gets a lot of professional jealousy from the police whenever she picks up on something."

"And has she 'picked up' on the children yet?" he asked acidly.

"No—but she's told Donal and me a lot of stuff about our past. And now she's working on a moonstone ring I lost just before Lisa disappeared. She says it's the way she gets into it."

Donner watched as the psychic put her fingers to her temples and shut her eyes. "The image is very clear now. Very clear. I see a ring, a ring belonging to a female. It's under water, under a shallow dark body of water."

He turned away in disgust. The day was getting off to a bad start: first the disturbing interview with Day McAllister and now this. He said to Carla, "You and Donal are both intelligent people. How can you believe in this kind of hocus-pocus?"

She looked at him. "What else do we have left to believe in, Sergeant?"

"You might try Saint Anthony." At her puzzled glance, he explained, "Patron saint of lost objects. A moonstone ring should be a snap for him."

The green wall phone rang. Carla moved away to answer it, leaving Donner to think about his reply. It had not been entirely flippant. There had been a time when he believed implicitly in the saint, the ascetic of old Egypt, who, if asked sincerely, would guide the petitioner to a lost ring, a misplaced key ring—even a missing child. And now? What, if anything, did he believe in now?

He heard Carla say, "Yes, he's here" and gesture to him. He accepted the receiver.

"Kerry? It's Dick Rydell in dispatching. A call just came in—another kid's missing."

The news seared white in his mind. "Good Christ! Where?"

"Disappeared from a haberdashery called Preston's, corner of Grand and West Broadway. It's a boy this time—son of the owner, Preston Hughes. You better get over there."

"I'm on my way."

Two months after his wife died of a rare lymphatic cancer, Preston Hughes came out of the closet.

While Helen was alive, he had done his best to maintain a conventional lifestyle, confining his outlets to an occasional evening in the Tenth Avenue bars and a yearly weekend "business trip" to Fire Island. He had loved Helen in some integral and complex way, and when she died, he mourned her honestly. But being able to shed the heterosexual pretenses that had bound him for years was like removing a pair of tight trousers. For the first time, he tasted the illimitable possibilities of freedom. The world was his. He could do as he pleased.

He made drastic changes in his lifestyle. He resigned his position as a district marketing manager of Sears and invested his savings in a men's imported clothing store in Greenwich Village. He then sold the four-bedroom hi-ranch in Garden City and moved with his infant son, Jason, to a Charles Street "simplex" apartment—a tiny dwelling by suburban standards, but (as the real estate agent readily pointed out) one that was loaded with charm.

164

It was Jason who had given him cause for much soul-searching before actually making these moves. He loved the boy above everything else in the world and worried about raising him in a gay culture. What would it do to him in the long run?

But then he reasoned, gay men, as far as he could see, were kind, loving, and peaceful—and they seemed no less happy than any other segment of the population. In fact, they seemed more so. He thought of his stolidly "normal" neighbors in Garden City. Sports, politics, and the health of their front lawns dominated their conversation—that is, when they could be pried away from the ever-blaring boob tube long enough to have any conversation at all.

But his gay friends made him quite heady with the scope and glamour of their interests. Here was one just returning from a scuba adventure in the Seychelles. Here was another refinishing a Louis XV fire screen rescued from some rural rummage sale. And yet another was setting off to meet graceful and charming friends at some as yet undiscovered Portuguese bistro.

Jason could only profit by exposure to such fascinating people, Preston decided. And if the boy grew up to be gay himself—well, it wouldn't be the worst thing that could happen to him.

And so father and son took up their new life. They were happy. The clothing store did reasonably well, and Jason quickly adjusted to the city.

But after three years it became obvious to Preston that the Village was through as a shopping district. The kids from Jersey and the outer boroughs who invaded the neighborhood on weekends seemed to have money only for drugs, cigarettes, beer, and the vulgar "message" T-shirts that they bought from equally vulgar sidewalk vendors. And the trendy gays and young couples who lived here preferred to shop Bloomies or the elegant boutiques of Madison Avenue.

Preston contemplated his next move. The exorbitant rents of upper Madison ruled that out as a location. But

Soho was newly chic, and a spacious ground-floor loft could be had for a song.

A year later he opened Preston's. It was a shop tailored frankly for snob appeal. The merchandise was selected to appeal to the owners of the Corniches, Porches, and Alfa Romeos that had begun to cruise West Broadway. There were shirts of imported silk and linen, fine leather boots and jackets, sumptuous woolens. The styles were trend-setting, even daring—but never too outrageous. The prices, on the other hand, were.

But the ambience—oh, it was the ambience that set it apart, even in adventurous Soho, from any other shop. The interior was more like an elegant cafe than a haberdashery. Walls dripping with baroque mirrors. Plush gray banquettes on which weary shoppers could fondle buttery leather shoes or contemplate the purchase of a hand-stit 'ed Irish sweater. Casablanca-type fans turning lazily o. the ceiling, a nightingale singing a lush bel canto from a brass cage. And in center stage a magnificent old white Steinway that had once belonged to the great George Gershwin himself.

The shop caught on immediately. But most important to Preston was that Jason seemed to love it as well. The boy delighted in helping out; he could often be found fetching things from the stockroom or carefully balancing a fragile cup of espresso for a thirsty customer. He was six now: a pale, striking boy with enormous eyes and a chin-length fringe of soot-colored hair. The customers found him charming; the regulars asked after him when he wasn't there.

Then this morning—this morning had been frenetic. One of the salesmen had called in sick, and Preston had fired another the evening before, having caught him sneaking a silver-studded concha belt under his shirt. And as usual, whenever they were short-handed, there was an unusually heavy rush of customers. There were lines for the dressing rooms, lines at the cash registers. Both customers and sales clerks became short-tempered. Preston had run himself ragged trying to keep up.

When the first lull came, he had looked around for Jason. It occurred to him he hadn't seen his son in some time. The boy wasn't on the sales floor, nor was he in the storeroom where a cot and a portable TV were kept set up for his use. He had never before gone out of the shop by himself. But no one had seen him in over an hour.

Preston had panicked. One of the clerks had had to hold him by the shoulders to prevent him from running crazy. Another had gone to phone the police—Preston, on the verge of hysteria, couldn't be trusted to talk. Someone had forced a Nembutal on him, and only then had he begun to calm down.

All this Preston Hughes sobbed out to the tall, ungainly-looking detective who stood listening to him. Sergeant Donner was rough cut, but there was something about him that made Preston feel he could deliver all his troubles into his hands.

"I don't deserve to live," Preston confessed. "I should be executed for what I've done."

"You haven't done anything, Mr. Hughes."

"That's what I mean. A lovely summer day—I should have had Jason somewhere with grass and trees and cows and lakes to swim in. Instead I kept him here." He gestured feebly. "A place of commerce."

"I'm sure you've raised your son as you thought best."

Preston shook his head. "A selfish prick—that's what I am, doing only what's best for myself. And this—this is my punishment."

"Mr. Hughes!" Donner said gruffly. "When Jason is found, you can put on sackcloth and ashes, and beat your breast, and do whatever penance you choose. But until then I'm going to need your full cooperation. So I suggest now that you pull yourself together."

The authority in the sergeant's voice cut through

Preston's self-absorbed misery and had a heartening effect. He raised himself. "You're right, Sergeant—if I have to come through, I will. You can count a hundred percent on me."

"That's better. Now I'm going back out to talk to the clerks. When you feel up to it, I'll need you to corroborate their stories."

"Two seconds," Preston promised bravely. But when Donner left him, his resolve began to weaken again. He lay back bleakly on the cot, eyes staring up at the scores of neatly stacked boxes packed into the gridwork of steel shelving. A hundred thousand dollars' worth of inventory, but it might just as well be trash.

He thought of the locked Chippendale secretary in his office; in one of its drawers lay a little Walther semiautomatic. It had been given to him by one of his former lovers, an AWOL Marine and avid gun freak, in the event that—God forbid—Preston should ever have to defend himself. He decided to make sure he really knew how to use it.

Because if anything happened to Jason, there was one thing Preston Hughes was sure of: he was going to put a bullet through his head.

The boy struggled with all his small strength, but the woman's grip was too powerful. She bound his arms behind him with one strong hand while the other raised the scissors. The blades opened and closed, and a lock of soot-colored hair dropped to the ground.

"I don't want my hair cut!" the boy shrieked. "Let me go!"

"You are a boy, and it is fitting that you look like a boy!"

The scissors descended again. The boy wriggled and jerked his head, causing the blade to nick his scalp. He howled with pain and began to cry. The relentless blade kept snipping, and the soft, dark locks rained around his shoulders.

"I'll tell my daddy on you," he sobbed. "I'll tell him, and he'll come beat you up."

"Evil debauching man! *Thou shalt not lie with a male as with a woman; it is an abomination.* Give thanks that I have taken you away from the evil premises to be raised as a man and not as an abomination."

Lisa and Joey watched silently from the sanctuary of the dollhouse. They knew how silly it was for the boy to

169

wiggle and cry. It wouldn't do him any good. You had to do it Her Way. She was the one who made up the rules, and you had to obey.

But even if you did everything she said, she sometimes got mad anyway. She would start screaming that your room was filthy, even though you had no room—just those little beds against the wall—or that you had been playing with her makeup, even though it was kept in a big round box high on a shelf that even with a chair you couldn't possibly reach. And even if you said you were sorry, it did no good. The punishments followed, swiftly, inevitably.

And so they had learned that it was best to keep out of her sight—to play in the darkest corners, to pretend to be taking a nap, to hide in the dollhouse—and only come when she called.

The woman kept cutting and cutting until there was almost no hair on the boy's head—just a dark patchy fuzz that stuck out around his ears. He looked strange and scary, like a little bald old man.

"Lisa," Joey whispered, "do you think she's going to do that to us?"

Lisa shrugged. "I don't know. Maybe."

"Lisa?"

"What?"

"Do you think we're ever going to go home in our whole lives?"

It was the first time either child had ever voiced that question. It made their skin go prickly and cold.

Joey's lip began to tremble. "You know what? I think we're going to stay here forever and ever until we die."

"Until we die," Lisa echoed.

They held each other's hand, squeezing as hard as they could, but even that couldn't hold off the most terrible fear.

For some time after Kerry Donner had left her office, Day sat in a turmoil, going over what he had said. One thing was now perfectly clear—Eben's strange behavior for the last few days. The one thing he'd find most intolerable was the police prying into his personal life—dragging him into what he thought of as their "system." She knew that if they kept pressuring him, he was likely to do anything—including skipping on his parole.

If he did, would that classify him as a fugitive? And if so, would she still stick with him? Day McAllister harboring a fugitive from justice—it was too crazy! She was the type of person who gave back the money when a cashier undercharged her. The type who declared thirty-five-dollar free-lance payments to the IRS and always paid strict attention to the speed limit. The proverbial straight arrow. Even for Eben's sake, could she ever be anything else?

Funny that just a few short weeks ago she had considered herself one of the luckiest women alive, and now everything was in such a bewildering, complex mess.

But she couldn't sit here stewing over it forever. When the detective had intercepted her, she had been on her way to an appointment with Albert Knowlton. If she was interested in keeping it, she'd damned well better hop.

The architects' office was the first shock—an environment of pristine, functional elegance. Every element in it, from the clean wood of the drafting tables to the long-necked metal lamps, was perfectly integrated within a large airy space overlooking the river. It displayed a completely opposite sensibility from the brutish, hulking design of the Sports Center.

Albie Knowlton was the second shock. Day had expected him to be a remote gray-haired businessman, someone with immobile eyes and an unyielding cramp of a mouth. Instead, here was a small, intense, peppy man dressed in jeans and sneakers and an Oxford shirt with the sleeves rolled up. He was warm, open, and forthright. She found herself liking him immediately.

"Soho is a wonderful community," he was saying. "Vibrant. Creative. Probably the most unique neighborhood in all of the United States. My partner and I are thrilled to be able to make a major contribution to it. The vital services our Sports Center will provide . . ."

"That's just it," she cut in. "Have you considered the fact that the center might be more of a *dis*service to Soho? I mean, in terms of traffic congestion, skyrocketing rents, the spread of tacky commercialism . . ."

He smiled in a way that made her feel at once intensely naive. "Believe me, Miss McAllister, these are questions we've spent a lot of time wrestling with ourselves. But we've always come back to one fact. A community is made up first of all of the people who live in it. And it's the people we designed this project for."

"Could you explain that please?"

"Sure. Who do you have living in Soho? First of all,

the Italian families who have been here for decades—long before you or I discovered it. The kids have never had anyplace to go but the streets. But we have designated free use of the center's facilities for them during certain hours. The pastors of the Italian churches are so enthusiastic about it that they're behind us one hundred percent.

"The artists are another good example. Dirt poor, most of them—about the only thing they've got is their lofts. So when real estate goes up, so does their net worth." He grinned. "Even artists these days can't ignore the economic facts of life."

"But does all this justify tearing down a landmark? An irreplaceable part of our city's heritage . . ."

"I'm all for preserving monuments," Knowlton said quickly, "as long as they're not a death trap."

Day sat forward in her seat. "You've claimed the building is structurally unsound. What exactly is wrong with it?"

"It has many, many problems, most of them quite technical in nature. The problem is that over the last fifty years these buildings were not held in the same esteem they are today. In fact, they were considered monstrosities."

"What does that have to do with the condition of the building?"

"My point is that since the buildings were considered worthless, the owners showed little concern for even the basic fundamentals of maintenance. To put it bluntly, they let them go to hell. In this particular case, water seepage from the roof went uncorrected for years. It got into the timbers, which expanded, dangerously cracking the walls, and then rotted out."

"It looks perfectly sound from the outside."

"Are you qualified to judge these things?"

"Well, no, but . . ."

"Take my word for it, Miss McAllister—that building is a disaster waiting to happen."

"What if I were to bring in someone of my own?" she said. "An engineer, to verify all this. Just for my own curiosity."

A scowl flashed briefly across Knowlton's face. Then his smile returned, as generous and open as before. "Ordinarily I'd say fine. In fact, it would be fun to give the press a little demonstration of building structure. It's not often you take any interest in our dry old profession. The problem is, though, I'd need permission from the majority partners. They happen to be extremely hard to nail down, and since we're scheduled for demolition in nine days . . ."

He stood up. "My partner and I are dedicated to architectural excellence, Miss McAllister. "We've built our reputation on it. Though we're destroying a landmark, we will do our best to reinterpret it in terms of contemporary architecture. We're going to provide this community with a *new* landmark, one whose benefits will last long into the future."

Day was convinced—at least, until she had returned to her office and the influences of Albie Knowlton's considerable charm began to wear off. Then certain aspects of the interview began to nag at her. The look that had crossed his face when she suggested bringing in another engineer, the glib, public relations nature of his remarks. In fact, the interview had raised more questions than it had answered. Why had she been so easily swayed? Perhaps the detective's questions had unnerved her more than she'd thought.

But she was over that now. And now she determined that if Albert Knowlton wouldn't supply answers, she'd get them on her own. An idea suggested itself—risky, no doubt highly illegal, but it would get her what she wanted to know right away. She gave a laugh. Day McAllister, inveterate straight arrow, was about to venture into bending the law.

She looked up the number of the engineering firm of Canby, Dole and Sutherton, dialed, and asked for Charles Canby, Jr.

Chip's voice, warm and instantly familiar, came on the line. "Do you believe in ESP?"

"Should I?"

"You tell me. Last night I had my first dream about you in a year."

"Then I guess I have to believe," she said. "How *are* you, Chip?"

"Not bad, though dad's got me working my tender little tail off around here. Seems you can't be the heir apparent in this company without sweating for the honor."

"Do you good. I always thought you had it too soft."

"You're probably right. How about you, Daysie? Still with that glamour boy of yours?"

"If you mean Eben, yes, we're still together."

"Then I guess you're not calling to beg me to come back."

"No, Chip," she said lightly, "I'm not."

"Damn! In my dream, it was you and me on a deserted beach with nothing between us but some seaweed. So much for ESP, huh?"

"Oh, you loon! You know, one of these days you're going to meet someone who realizes what a terrific catch you are."

"I've met hundreds. Damn few have your brains, and none of them has your eyes." When she started to protest, he said hurriedly, "Okay, I promise no more sordid passion. What can I do for you, old friend?"

"I need sort of a professional favor."

She told him briefly what she wanted, and he gave a low whistle. "You don't ask much of your former lovers, do you?"

"Listen, Chip, if you don't want to do it, I'll understand."

"What time do you want this nefarious deed carried out?"

"About seven?"

"Seven it is. And in case you've forgotten what I look like, I'll be the one with the seaweed in my hair."

Gil meticulously blocked out a toilet, sink, bidet, and oversized sunken bathtub on a set of design development drawings; then he realized he had placed them in a walk-in storage closet instead of the bathroom. He threw down his drafting pencil in disgust.

In the next room his daughter Alexis droned the same four notes over and over again, as she had been doing all afternoon. The sound set his teeth on edge. It was no wonder he couldn't get anything done.

His temper lately seemed set on a permanently short fuse. Though each morning he routinely swallowed two Valium pills, by midday he began to feel tight and irritable. Anything in the office could set him off, from the mildest demand of a client to the smug expression on Albie's face as he finalized the details on the Sports Center. Yesterday Gil had found himself snapping at Teddy—serene, gracious Teddy!—and decided he'd better try working at home for a while.

But he was not faring much better here. The day was hot—the first real asphalt-melting scorcher of summer. Though the Fedders in the window of his study hummed busily, the sun poured in through the skylights, sending rivulets of sweat down the back of his neck. A horsefly buzzed through the air. And then there were those infernal noises coming from his daughter's room!

The tuneless song stopped suddenly. With a sigh of relief, Gil picked up his pencil; as he did, the horsefly drew an insolent circle around his head. And then, suddenly, the four notes began again, over and over and over.

He bolted to the door, flung it open, and screamed down the hall, "Cynthia! Can't you get her to shut up?"

His wife appeared at Alexis's door. "What are you yelling about?"

"That goddamned noise is driving me crazy. Do something to keep her quiet!"

Thia shut Alexis's door behind her and came into the study. "Keep your voice down. You're going to upset her."

"Thia," he said slowly, "I am trying to work." There was a tight edge to his voice that he couldn't control; he spoke each word as if there were a period after it. "I am trying to earn the money to keep the roof over our heads and the food in our mouths. I don't see how I can do it with that racket going on."

"Don't you think you're overreacting?"

"No, I do not. I'm sick and tired of having my career continually jeopardized by my daughter."

Her eyes fixed coldly on his face. "What do you mean by that?"

"I mean like that scene she caused in East Hampton. Under other circumstances it could have thrown off the whole deal. Luckily Spetzi happens to be such a damned nice guy . . ."

"Oh, that's good!" she blazed. "Well, let me tell *you* something. I caught him in the room where Alexis was sleeping. He said he was just checking up on her, but I think he was going to touch her."

"What makes you so sure?"

"I don't know, but there was something about the

way he was standing there, *look*ing at her. I mean, I could just tell."

"And what did you do?"

"I told him to get out."

Gil slammed his hand on the desk so violently it made her start. "That's exactly what I'm talking about!" he said. "Here's some poor guy going out of his way to make his guests comfortable, and you—you're so paranoid about that kid, you insult him and order him out of his own goddamned house!" He felt a sudden sweep of dizziness and leaned both arms on the drafting board for support. "I don't want to argue," he said weakly. "I just want some peace and quiet. Can't you take her down to the park for a while?"

"It's not time yet. Dr. Wigget has her on a very strict schedule."

"Go off it for today. What difference would it make?"

"It makes a lot of difference. Wigget says the most important thing for her is consistency. Especially now when she's been getting so much better . . ."

"Thia, she is not getting better," Gil said emphatically. "She is never going to get better. Our daughter is an idiot. She is mentally retarded. And she will be for the rest of her life."

Thia's face grew blank. "That's not true."

"It *is* true. When the hell are you going to face it? And face the fact that there are places that can care for her a hell of a lot better than we can."

"You mean an institution."

"Whatever you want to call it."

"I'll see you in hell before I let you send her to an institution!"

"Sometime's I think I'd damned well rather be in hell than this house of bedlam!"

She raised her face to his. "No one is keeping you here."

"And I sure don't know why I'm staying."

"Then go!" she shouted. "Go, damn you, and leave us alone!"

He stared at her a moment, then rushed past her and down the hall to their bedroom. He yanked the largest valise down from a closet shelf and began stuffing it with clothes—whatever his hands happened to fall on—the trousers to his tuxedo, a baseball cap, a torn windbreaker, odd handfuls of shirts and socks and underwear. When it was full, he strapped it shut and returned to the study to gather up his work. Thia was no longer there. He supposed she had gone back in with Alexis.

He packed his briefcase with trembling hands and stumbled out. The four tuneless notes, repeated again and again like some unearthly signal of distress, followed him all the way downstairs.

The golden-haired child, lost in her private song, rocked back and forth in her little chair. Thia watched her, not turning her eyes away until she heard the steps on the stairs and the door slam shut downstairs. Then she stood up and placed her hands on her abdomen.

Something was happening within her body. A shifting and enrichening—changes so subtle she intuited rather than felt them. Changes that she remembered from the first weeks after Alexis had been conceived— before there were any other signs of pregnancy.

No, she thought, it can't be happening.

She pressed her palms hard against the walls of her stomach. *No!* she cried to herself. She was strong, she had a will of her own.

She wouldn't let it happen.

There was a mummy in the corner. During the day it hid behind the big silver pipes that came down from the ceiling, but at night Jason could see it there very distinctly, milky-white and tremendous, waiting there in the brightest corner of the room until Jason slipped back to sleep. Now Jason struggled to keep his eyelids open. He knew that if they closed, the mummy would come forward, lumbering, stiff-legged, past the other children until it got to him, and it would touch him with its horrible bandages. But he'd be asleep, and he wouldn't be able to do anything about it.

Sometimes a mummy got into his room at home. But all he had to do was call out and his dad would come and make it disappear. One time Gerald, who was his dad's best friend, was the one who came when he called, and he left a magic key on the dresser that kept the mummy out for a long time. Gerald was nice. He made Jason a Chinese dragon kite, and he played the harmonica and made faces with his eyes and nose that made Jason laugh.

He must have done something very bad to have been sent away like this. Maybe it was because of that man who had come into the store. The man had a bald head and said he was going to buy a million dollars' worth of stuff because Jason was such a handsome boy. And then he had put his hand down the back of Jason's pants, right inside his underpants and onto his behind. Jason had been scared and had run away, but maybe someone had seen it and told his dad, and that's why he had been sent away.

If he could get home, he would tell his dad he was sorry and maybe he wouldn't have to come back here.

He had a happy thought. They were supposed to go to a rodeo—his dad had already sent away for the tickets—so he'd *have* to come and get Jason before that!

He peered at the corner. The mummy was still there, waiting, impassive. What if he called out to the woman? Would she come? But he was scared of her, too. She didn't look like anyone else he knew. When she was mad, she hit him or gave him a heavy book to hold until his arms hurt badly. But even when she was happy, she made them do funny things. Yesterday she had made them all sit scrunched up facing a wall for a long, long time. It was an air raid drill, she said. His neck had begun to get sore and a cockroach had ran underneath his knee. But if he moved, she had said, a bomb would drop on him, and he was scared of that too.

He wished he could go home.

Suddenly he froze stiff—the white monster shape in the corner had moved! He was sure it had. Maybe tonight it wasn't going to wait until he was asleep. Maybe it was going to come over right now and touch him!

His hands gripped the metal sides of his bed while his heart thumped loudly, beating out the long, endless minutes in fear.

Chip Canby hadn't changed a bit. Same thinning side-parted hair and horn-rimmed glasses, same burgundy Lacoste shirt, same Brooks Brothers loafers. In all respects he was the same boy Day had known when she was at Briarcliff and he was taking his engineering degree at Columbia. And now, as then, his looks told everything about him. Superstandard WASP: prep school, Ivy League; good tennis player, a little backgammon, fair skier; polite, friendly, cheerful; Republican; destined by birth to make a pile of money.

He had been the perfect match for Day. Their backgrounds meshed like twin cogs; they had acquaintances, interests, summer haunts in common. She had known boys like Chip when she was four and enrolled in Miss Greerson's dancing school, and she had been meeting them ever since. And when she introduced him to her parents, they took to each other as only members of the same and exclusive caste can—with mutual approval and tacit appreciation. Even now her mother sometimes asked after "that delightful engineering boy you used to see."

Day supposed it was out of a sense of the correctness

of it all that she had continued dating him so long. Months passed before she had even allowed herself to admit that she was discontented.

When he began to talk about marriage, she realized it was time to break it off. She had a vivid image of what being Mrs. Charles R. Canby, Jr., would entail: cocktail parties and tennis weekends, a white frame house in Connecticut, children with thinning hair and horn-rimmed glasses—a lifetime of polite, ice-skating laughter.

Chip had never quite understood why she had rejected him. His logical engineer's mind couldn't find the flaw in the formula. At last he simply shrugged it off with the infuriating insinuation that she was going through a "Bohemian" stage—and that at some time she would return, if not to him, at least to the class in which she belonged.

She could tell from the way he smiled at her as he ambled up Greene Street that he still held to that conviction, and she felt a momentary burst of resentment. But it disappeared when his face broke into the broad, unqualified grin that she remembered so well.

Good old Chip, she thought.

He gave her a mock salute. "Second-story man reporting for duty, sir."

He carried a nylon bag on his shoulder filled with clanking, cumbersome objects. "Are you sure you've never done this before?" she asked.

"These, my dear, are the tools of my legitimate trade," he retorted. "This is my maiden attempt at breaking and entering." He glanced up at the building. "This it?"

She nodded. In the mauve and gray shadows of the darkening sky, it had a brooding, desolate quality that seemed to warn her away. She felt a shiver, remembering the ghastly white face she had thought to appear at the window pane. Her nerve was beginning to fail.

But Chip had already jumped onto the loading platform and was experimentally rattling the gate.

"Solidly chained up," he said. "Let's see what's around the back."

Day murmured reluctantly.

"Don't worry—the most they can give us for this is five years." When she didn't laugh, he looked at her. "You're not chickening out, are you? After all this?"

She took a breath. "No. Let's try the back."

They followed a narrow, grimy alleyway that wound around the building to the rear courtyard. "Great, there's a fire escape," Chip said. "That'll at least get me up to the roof. If you give me a boost, I can reach the ladder."

She made a stirrup with her hands and was surprised by the agility with which he caught the ladder and pulled himself up. He continued to climb and disappeared over the edge of the roof. She waited in the deepening shadows for what seemed an inordinate length of time. Just when she was sure something horrible had happened to him, a Brooks Brothers loafer reappeared on the iron grid.

"The roof's a dream!" he called, scrambling back down. "They could hold army maneuvers up there with no problem. Are you sure that's where the damage was supposed to be?"

"Pretty sure."

"Well, somebody's been misinformed. Let's see if we can get inside." He lowered the ladder for her from the second-story platform. When she climbed up, he had already begun to jimmy open the adjoining window.

"Canby's the name and danger's my game. There, that should do it!" He had pried a space large enough to fit his body through. He took a large flashlight from his bag and shined it in. "Just a short jump down. Come on."

They wriggled their way into a cavernous black space. The flashlight beam danced across the walls and a filthy, littered wood floor. "I think I read a Hardy Boys book like this once," Chip whispered. *"The Adventure of the Haunted Basement."*

"Don't say that!" Day hissed sharply.

"Don't say what? Hey, are you scared?"

"Terrified. There's something about this building that gives me the creeps." She gave a thin laugh. "The morbid imagination of a crime reporter."

"I won't take too long. Here, you work the flashlight. And watch out for potholes in the floor. I'd like to avoid breaking an ankle if possible."

She followed him closely as they picked their way around the obstacle course of litter. The pungent odor of mildew and the stench of an old industrial toilet assaulted her nostrils. Now and then a board creaked beneath her feet.

She watched Chip jab a large ice pick into one of the wooden support columns. "Hardly goes in at all," he muttered. "It's solid, aged oak." He climbed up onto an old metal drum and repeated the test on the beams. Again the pick barely sank into the hard wood. "No rot here. These timbers are like steel. Give me that hammer, will you?" She passed it up to him, and he whacked at the metal fastener joining the beam and the column.

"What are you doing?" she asked.

"Sounding for rust. Hear that clang? If these were rusted out, it would make more of a thunk sound. So far, so good." He jumped off the drum, and they continued walking. "Wait a minute," he said suddenly. "Shine the light over there."

She trained the beam to where he pointed, a corner in which the floorboards were warped out of shape and the brick walls stained black.

"Water damage, probably from a burst pipe," he said. "Let's see how bad it is." He took a crowbar from the bag and pried up a few floorboards. Then, kneeling down, he chiseled off a small piece of the wood cross-supports underneath and examined the chip. "Still dry," he said. "These cross-supports were probably soaked for about a month in creosote, which means they'll be water repellent for the next century or two."

"Which means the leak hasn't hurt anything?"

"Just cosmetic damage. It's easy to replace a few floorboards."

"And the rest of the building," she said hurriedly. "You think it's in good shape?"

"Absolutely. The walls look good—a few minor settling cracks but no major structural ones." He took the hammer and pounded on a nearby pipe. The sound rose eerily into the upper reaches of the building. "Hear that? Even the plumbing sounds good. I'd give this place an A minus, maybe a B plus."

"That's great. Really fabulous. Now let's get the hell out of here."

"Not so fast. Let's see if that freight elevator is working and check out one of the top floors."

"Is it necessary?"

"We want to be thorough, don't we? Come on, don't be such a chicken."

"Yeow!"

He grabbed her arm. "What is it?"

"Something just brushed against my ankle."

"You sure you didn't imagine it?"

"Positive. I definitely felt something . . ."

A sound rose from the far corner of the loft—a dismal, relentless scratching, like something caught in the brick walls, something beyond all hope or reason.

"I didn't imagine that!" Day breathed.

"You certainly didn't. Let's make tracks!"

They dashed back to the window, squeezed through, and clambered back down the fire escape. Then they ran, laughing and squealing, back to the safety of the street.

Day caught her breath, wiping tears of laughter from her eyes. "It was a cat," she gasped. "Or a pigeon that got in through the window."

"No way," Chip insisted. "That was a ghost, and I won't hear anyone say different."

They looked at each other and exploded in laughter again. A thought crossed Day's mind. If Chip had ever been like this before, they might still be together. He seemed to sense the thought, for he looked at her with sudden tenderness.

"If it doesn't work out for you with this guy, Eben," he said, "maybe we could give us another try."

"It wouldn't work, Chip," she said firmly.

"Give me one good reason why not."

"Well, because of our names. Chip and Day—it sounds like some kind of singing animal group."

"You're impossible!" he sputtered.

But the thrill of their recent adventure still held them under its spell, and they came together spontaneously for a hug. Then, hand in hand, they walked off down the quiet street.

The door of the old black car parked at the curb opened and a woman emerged. She watched the couple strolling away from her as if her very stare could turn them into stone. Then she turned and went toward the building, her head down and shoulders hunched inward, as faceless as a decapitated doll. She disappeared into the now pitch-black passage of the alleyway.

She had watched the children closely, observed them in their sleep and in their play. She saw that all was not well. Even here, in the hidden place she had prepared, evil forces worked against her, struggled to turn them away from her. She could sense it in their unwillingness to kiss her, to accept her hugs and caresses—she, their natural guardian and protector! She knew that voices were getting to them—through wires, perhaps. Thin, invisible wires, wires so delicate she mistook them for silver strands of cobweb. She heard the rustling in the walls at night and knew that the wires were at work, turning the children away from her, back to the iniquities of the world.

The boy especially. He was steeped in sin. His eyes were blinded by it, his ears deafened. It was almost too late to save him.

She watched him now, sitting quietly, pretending to be playing with a train. But she knew he was concentrating on his hatred—of her and of all that was just and good.

"Kevin!" she called.

He looked up. She knew he was clever enough to look frightened in order to mask his hatred.

"Come over here. I want to talk to you."

He walked with his head lowered, disguising his shame. Oh, he was beautiful. But she had tried to mortify his beauty before it led him into further perdition. She had shorn his head and destroyed the pretty clothes he had worn and clothed him in shapeless little garments of brown and gray. Yet now she saw that it wasn't enough—she must also clip the long lashes that framed the wide, lustrous eyes. She would do that tonight.

Now she said, "Come with me, Kevin." She led him to the back of their home near the stove and the little humming icebox—away from the girls so that they would not hear and be corrupted.

She crouched down close to him. "I want you to listen to me," she said—gently, coaxing him from his hatred. "You have been living with a very bad man. He called himself your father, but he was not a father to you. He was a sinner and a corrupter, an agent of Satan. You must turn your back on this man. You must denounce him for a sinner."

"My dad is not a bad man," the boy replied. Hate blazed from his eyes, far deeper and stronger than she had even suspected.

"A man who lies with other men is wicked," she said. "He is to be despised!"

"My dad is good, and nice, and I love him."

"He has debased the temple of his body—he has made of it an abomination! He is a wicked sinner, Kevin. He will go to hell!"

"No!" the boy cried.

"To hell! Do you know what hell is?"

She pulled him over to the little electric stove, turned a burner on, and placed his hand above it. The coil grew hot; her hand holding his could feel the heat rise, become more and more intense.

"This is what hell is, Kevin," she cried. "It is burning, forever and ever, eternal flame in every part of you."

The boy howled and tried to pull away. She forced his hand down lower, closer now to the crimson hot coil. All she had to do was press it down, just for an instant, and it would be there—an imprint reminding him for the rest of his life what punishment awaited him should he succumb to the abominations of his father. The coil was already so hot it nearly burned without touching. Scarcely another inch . . .

She released his hand. He ran howling away.

Not this time, she told herself. But she would watch him carefully—him and all the others. And if she thought it necessary, she would not shirk her duty. She would apply the greater lesson.

Albie Knowlton arrived at his office fresh from an extremely satisfactory business breakfast at the Plaza with a man of considerable power. Still riding high, he was annoyed to find the girl from the *Soho Sun* waiting for him at his office. He informed her rather brusquely that he was too busy to talk to her now.

"I don't need much time," Day said quickly. "All I want is a comment from you on what I've already written." She held up several typewritten pages.

Albie smiled condescendingly. "I'm sure you've done a very good job. But if you'll excuse me . . ."

"How do you know if you haven't read it?" She thrust the manuscript at him, giving him no choice but to accept it.

With a sigh of great impatience, he glanced at the first page. Then a grim frown settled on his mouth, which deepened as he read through to the end. His face livid, he slapped the manuscript down on a cabinet. "I suppose you realize I can have you prosecuted for trespassing!" he snapped.

"Go ahead," Day said impassively. "I wouldn't mind a little extra publicity."

Albie pulled himself short. He composed his face, flashed his genial public relations grin. "Before we start swiping childishly at each other, let's take a look at this from a sensible point of view," he said. "Now these allegations you've made—you've based them on a cursory examination made by some unidentified engineer under the most adverse of conditions. Now I can tell you that, given a proper amount and adequate light, an experienced professional would come up with an entirely different analysis. As, of course, has already been the case."

"Would you be willing to arrange those conditions for my engineer?" Day shot back.

"I've already explained to you why that's unfeasable . . ."

"Then," she said lightly, "I'm afraid I'll have to stick by my story."

Albie dropped his grin. "I've heard that journalists often bend the truth for the sake of a story," he said sharply, "but, baby, you've gone far beyond that. Your means of getting information was not only highly unethical but downright illegal. And the so-called facts you've come up with—they amount to nothing more than libel. That may be okay for the kind of amateur rag you're with now. But if you've got any ideas of making a real career out of this, let me give you some advice—learn how to be a professional."

He turned and retreated icily into his private office. As he sank onto his stool, his first feeling was one of relief that Cassidy wasn't around. With his partner's bleeding-heart guilt complex, he probably would have spilled everything.

But just how much damage had been done? His mind quickly assessed the various factors. A local paper— couldn't have a circulation of more than twenty thousand—no influence to speak of. And even if it should attract some attention, it couldn't do it in enough time to cause any trouble. The building was coming down in six days; once it was just a patch of rubble, all the allegations in the world wouldn't be worth a damn—no one would be able to prove a thing.

But maybe it would be worthwhile to make sure. He had a name someone had given him. Nothing heavy, it was promised, just a little scare—enough to be effective. There was always a way to do these things right.

He picked up the phone.

Bob DeRitis uttered an oath in the Neapolitan dialect of his grandfathers.

He hated to be disturbed while he was working—particularly when the work was going as well as it was today and his concentration was at its peak. But whoever was rapping on the big metal door of his loft meant business. His growled invective only caused them to knock louder.

He felt a sudden pang of nostalgia for the years when he had been a failure—when he had been able to spend long days and nights undisturbed, the hours his to work or waste as he pleased. But since the success of his last show he had been plagued by a barrage of phone calls, letters, telegrams, people coming to his door, usually at the most inopportune times. A drift of envelopes and hastily scrawled phone messages had completely snowed in his battered Plexiglas coffee table and was slowly making its way across the floor. How the hell was he expected to get anything done if they insisted on turning his life into Grand Central Station?

The rapping continued.

"All right, I'm coming!" he bellowed. He jammed

his brush into a jar of water, stormed across the loft, and threw open the heavy door.

He stared at his visitor in utter stupefaction.

He knew immediately who she was. Christ, who could forget that ponytail swinging down from the middle-aged face, or the eyes, black winged like a Halloween bat? He remembered how she had caught his eye coming out of Susan's gallery; how, when he had absentmindedly followed her, she had turned and challenged him. How her eyes seemed to pin him to the street and hold him immobilized like some sort of cosmic death ray from the twenty-fifth century.

"Aren't you going to invite me in?" she asked brightly.

"Oh, sure," he managed. "But what—I mean, what are you doing here?"

The question seemed to take her by surprise. "You wanted to paint me, isn't that what you said?"

"Yeah, sure, but . . ."

"Well, I've decided to accept the offer."

Bob ran his hand through his hair, more bewildered than ever. "How did you know where to find me?"

"I've watched you. I've seen you go in and out. I've seen the lights go on in this floor whenever you've gone in."

He felt a crawling sensation start up the back of his neck. To think of those strange eyes planted on him— how many times? And for what reason? It came to him suddenly: she was crazy. Completely off her rocking chair. The best thing to do would be to get rid of her as quickly and as tactfully as possible.

"Maybe you don't understand," he said. "What I paint is nudes. If you posed for me, you'd have to take off all your clothes. And I'm sure you don't want to . . ."

"Well, of course," she said, and sailed past him into the loft.

Now what? he wondered. Call Bellevue and have the boys in the white coats come take her away? But another thought pressed on him: he was still tempted to see what he could do with her as a subject. She was here, she was willing. . . . His head swam with ideas. Crazy she might be, but he just couldn't let an opportunity like this go to waste.

"Like a beer?" he asked.

"Oh, yes. That would be fine."

"Righto. Just make yourself comfortable."

He went into the kitchen, pulled out a bottle of Miller from a tiny refrigerator. One of these days, he told himself for the hundredth time, he'd get around to really doing the place up right. One of these days . . .

His visitor had wandered into the half of the loft apportioned to the studio. She stared at the charcoal and gouache studies that were tacked up to the whitewashed brick walls, moving from one to the next as if she were at an exhibition. And then she froze; her face bleached to chalk.

"Whore of Babylon!" she shrieked. "Daughter of Satan's profanity!"

What the hell? Bob set down the glasses he'd been carrying and raced over.

"Satan's harlot!" Her hand, shaking, pointed to an easel set up in a corner. On it was the double portrait of Susan Capasian. No longer unfinished, it now breathed with a sumptuous life of its own, paint and canvas transformed into a shimmering diapason of light, texture, color.

"Remove it from my sight!" she cried. "I shall not bear witness to the defilement of virtue! Remove the devil's handmistress."

Completely bonkers, Bob decided. He picked up a sheet and threw it over the canvas. "There," he said. "Is that better?"

She turned to him. "You must rid yourself of the base profanity."

"Okey-doke. Out with the trash in the morning, I promise. Now, how about that beer."

He went back to the kitchen and finished pouring two

glasses. When he returned with them, she was standing with a pleasant Sunday-come-visiting smile on her face, all traces of her recent outburst gone. She accepted the glass and sipped daintily as if it were a cup of English Breakfast tea.

Bob drained his glass, feeling the need for fortification. "Well," he said, setting it down. "Should we get down to work?"

"Why, yes," she said.

He shuffled his feet uneasily. "Would it be okay if I posed you on that bed over there?"

"Of course." She walked over to the unmade bed and settled graciously on the edge, as if some perfect but unseen servant had announced dinner and she were seating herself at table.

"Should I take my clothes off now?" she asked.

"That would be . . . uh, helpful. You can undress in the bathroom, if you want. There's a big towel in there . . ."

"That won't be necessary."

Since she didn't seem to mind, he watched her undress. She undid first the buttons of her white Peter Pan blouse, then crisply stepped out of her long, swirly plaid skirt. Underneath she wore a strapless bra, the padded, pointy kind that reminded Bob of platinum blond sex symbols of the fifties. And—holy Christ!—a girdle, pink with satin panels and bows and pink garters to hold up her stockings. Last time he'd seen one of those must have been the night after his senior prom.

Bra, girdle, and stockings came off with as prim efficiency as if she were removing a pair of gloves. She reached up to take out the barrette that fastened her long ponytail.

"Leave that in!" he ordered. Her hand dropped; she looked up at him expectantly. With a detached, professional eye, he surveyed her. The body was very good. Heavy breasts beginning to lose their elasticity. A rounded belly scarred with faint stretch marks. Thighs slender and puckered with the fatty crevasses the ladies' magazines had dubbed cellulite. The painting was definitely going to work.

He selected one of several primed and stretched canvases that were stacked against a wall and picked up a charcoal pencil. The artist took over completely. He no longer saw a woman but a subject, a composition— a pattern of line and shape and color. He directed her to lie back on the mattress. "Great. Terrific. Now put one arm over the top of your head—no, the elbow more toward me. No, no . . . look, I'll show you. Like this."

He bent over her to position her. As he did, her hand encircled his neck, and suddenly he found himself pulled onto her, her arms holding him tightly, her mouth pressed importunately against his. He smelled the bordello scent of a flowery perfume as his senses aroused to the warm, naked female flesh beneath him. Why not? he thought wildly. What was there to lose? He began to respond. His hands sought her breasts, her thighs.

But it was crazy—*she* was crazy! It would be like taking advantage of a child. And besides, what if it was a trap? What if she intended to do him some kind of harm while she had him vulnerable?

A cold fear ran through him. He broke out of her embrace and scrambled to his feet.

"Listen," he babbled, "I appreciate the invitation, really I do, but I've got this rule never to fool around with my models."

She lay back very still, hands covering her breasts and pubis. Her eyes stared up at him, flat as phonograph records, hard and dead as vinyl.

"You don't want me," she said.

"Sure I do. I mean, you're very attractive and all—it's just that I've got this rule. I mean, ordinarily I'd say great, let's go . . ."

"Let her put away her harlotry from her face, lest upon her children I shall have no pity!"

"Yeah, sure. Absolutely."

"Turn around!"

His blood turned to ice. "What for?"

"I want to put on my clothes."

He turned slowly, half-expecting to be met with a bullet in the back of his head, a penknife between his shoulder blades. But there was only a rustling, then the sharp, receding click of her stiletto heels across the floor, the door opening and slamming shut.

He was drenched in sweat. Though it didn't make sense, he had the feeling of having had a very close call.

It was a sign.

Caroline Losey hurried out into the glare of the day feverish with purpose, a coal burning hot in her breast. The sign had been quite clear—as clear as a spoken command or a finger pointing the way.

There were urges that came upon her—to be with a man, to be touched by him. Desires that seared through her like the sword of the devil, that drove her to paint her face and fly into the arms of temptation. At first she didn't understand and had tried to fight them. But now she knew they were a test to determine if she were worthy of her task.

Once she had turned to her husband with desire and had been refused—and this had tormented her because she did not yet understand.

They continued to live together as man and wife. Steven continued to make more money, and Caroline began dressing better. They ate their meals together, and they continued to share a double bed. But though Caroline waited, he never again turned to her to take her in his arms. Night after night, she lay awake beside her indifferent husband, her mind turning over and over again like an engine that refused to shut off. What had she done to deserve such a thing? Why was she being punished?

Finally, in those long, still, wide-awake hours, an idea took form. Perhaps she was not being punished but tested. Perhaps her trial was to lead to a higher calling, something that would be revealed to her in time.

And it was. A young man came to her door calling himself a missionary. An unhealthy whiteness of complexion served to amplify the startling blue current of his gaze—a gaze that to Caroline contained a proclamation. She bought without question the blue paperbound book of tracts he offered and poured through it in search of a message. Certain passages leapt out at her—those from Isaiah and the sterner prophets that condemned flagrancy and the gross acts of the body. She read that the mother who turns to harlotry shall be deprived of her child. And slowly she came to a conclusion: she had experienced desire, and that had made her impure. She had craved the pleasures of the flesh, and that had made her unfit to be a mother.

But she had been saved from her own path of iniquity. And a voice, as clear as the clear blue gaze of the messenger, spoke in her mind: she had been chosen as the perfect mother.

The idea warmed her. Perfect motherhood. Yes. She had received the sign and she would obey.

But one thing disturbed her. At times she felt a rage toward her beautiful baby daughter so vast that she could hardly contain it. She searched her text, and once again she was rewarded with an explanation. What she felt was righteous anger. To raise a child in the way of perfection, the rod was as important as the caress. The child who misbehaves must receive just punishment.

And so she no longer checked her anger but vented it in punishment of her naughty daughter. Georgene grew older knowing equally what it was like to be lavished with kisses and whipped for the least transgression.

And Caroline grew ever more certain of her chosen mission.

Once again she was certain. Once again she had offered herself to a man and had been refused. It was a sign that said that she was still pure, still worthy of her task.

"*Collect unto you the children,*" she whispered to herself. "*Take them from profanity and raise them in the way of the righteous.*"

Such was her mission. And such she would obey.

The car waited for her. The 1956 DeSoto with its rounded back, newly painted black like a glossy, lumbering scarab. Inside, she flipped open the glove compartment, removed a black kerchief and a pair of black sunglasses whose lenses swept up at the corners like a cat's eyes.

Deftly, she pinned her long ponytail into a tight chignon, then wrapped the kerchief around her head so that not a hair was visible. With a Kleenex she scrubbed the lipstick from her lips and the rouge from her cheeks and slipped the dark glasses over her black-ringed eyes.

She was ready.

She got out of the car, her mind working clearly, thinking of her tasks, of all she had to do. There could be no mistakes. Everything would go perfectly, as it was meant to.

First, the provisions. The children must be fed; such was her duty.

At the end of the block was the grocery store she always frequented. Lostrito's, run by an ancient couple who spoke no English and took no interest in their customers other than to count out their change. In Lostrito's it was dark and cool; she could shop in peace. Not like these lit-up modern supermarkets with the snooty young girls and nosy boys at the checkout counters.

She hurried there now. Having become familiar with the jumbled shelves, she quickly filled a basket. Good, wholesome foods: two gallons of milk, the largest box

of Quaker oats, and a long loaf of whole wheat bread,
giant jars of peanut butter and grape jelly, six cans of
Campbell's tomato soup, and six of chicken noodle—
plain but healthy nourishment, the kind she had been
fed herself as a child.

Old Mr. Lostrito shuffled up to the counter. As
always, he kept his head bowed as he rang up the order,
as if to raise his eyes to a customer would be to trespass
upon some old-world rule of propriety. But this time
his withered face split suddenly in a grin. He looked up
at Caroline with an old man's puckish delight.

"Beeg family, eh?" he cackled. "Lotsa cheeldren."

She stared at him in horror. The old man quickly
lowered his head. Muttering a little to himself in
Italian, he finished bagging her purchases and retreated
to the back of the shop.

Caroline grabbed the bag and rushed back to the car.
The incident, small as it was, had been a bad omen.
Undoubtedly, there were forces at work—unfriendly
forces sent to test her, to distract her from her purpose.
She would have to be strong and crafty to circumvent
their powers. She would have to keep all her wits about
her.

She nosed the bulky car into traffic and swung it
around the corner. At a corner of West Broadway, she
parked by a fireplug and sat very still while the motor
idled quietly.

She was invisible now. All was under control.

She was waiting.

The boy's name was David Biskin. He was undergrown for his six-and-a-half years, and his kinky, reddish hair bushed out unevenly from his face. A diet of Sabrett hot dogs, Dr. Peppers, and chocolate-covered graham crackers had given his cinnamon-colored complexion a spongy gray quality, as if he had spent many of his years in the dark. He walked beside his mother, almost running to keep up with her savage strides, taking great care not to let any part of his body come in contact with hers. But an irregularity in the sidewalk made him stumble, and, in righting himself, his hand accidentally grazed her hip.

She whirled and smacked him on the shoulder. "Stop pawing me, you little creep!" she screeched.

The boy looked at her with brilliant eyes. Then he seemed to shrink into himself, like a flower closing for the night.

Anita Biskin continued her furious pace. The sidewalk beneath the thin soles of her shoes felt like coarse sandpaper; the noise of the street thundered in her ears. She had been four days without a high, and she was hurting bad. Her nerves were like shattered glass, her head was a bruise. And the damn kid wouldn't leave her alone.

Lousy, stinking kid! It seemed the cruelest twist of fate that, at only twenty-seven, she should be tied to this creature, a kid whose big black eyes were always begging for something: a meal, a new shirt, a touch. It was monstrous that she should have lines on her face and stretch marks on her belly and be tied to a stinking hole of a basement in this sewer of a city so that the only way she could stand it was by pumping a constant thick stream of heroin up her arm.

It wasn't the way she had planned it. She was going to be a stewardess, fly for Pan Am, or the wings of man, or the friendly skies of United. She had dreamed of taking off one morning for Singapore and touching down the next in Hawaii, of being free as the birds and the wasps and the very dust in the air. But then Winston came along, big black nigger with his lousy guitar, promising he'd become a superstar, have her riding in limousines and living at the St. Moritz. Instead he gets himself killed over some crappy gun deal in a hallway over on Avenue C, leaving her nothing behind but his junk habit and his mongrel bastard kid.

It fucking wasn't fair.

The kid was dragging behind her. "Hurry up!" she snapped.

He scurried up on skinny legs as she turned into a doorway. It was a shop called MacIntosh, which specialized in antiques of the Art Nouveau period. The boy knew from previous expeditions what he was expected to do. While his mother "shopped," he was to wander into another area of the store, preferably where there was breakable merchandise, and distract the sales help.

In this case it was easy. There was only one person in the shop—a small, prim man with a head of scraped blond hair like the fuzz of an Easter chick—obviously the proprietor. His eyes fastened on the boy nervously, leaving Anita free to work. She slipped a brass filigree

mirror down the front of her dress into the pocket of a
specially constructed bra. A slender and lustrous Tiffany vase disappeared up one of her loose sleeves. A
Horta ink stand, brass tendrils intertwined like an-
other-worldly plant, vanished up the other. That was
enough. She called to her son.

"Come on, David. I don't want you breaking any of
the nice man's things."

The shopkeeper nearly wept with relief as she swept
the boy out of the premises. Asshole, she thought. The
time he'll really cry is when he discovers what's missing. Well over five hundred dollars' worth of artifacts
lay nestled against her body—the thought gave her a
thrill of anticipation. If Pico was in any kind of mood,
he might give her up to twenty bags for it.

But she had to hustle. Pico had said four-thirty, and
she knew he wouldn't hang around one second later.
She grabbed the boy's elbow and ran with him down
the street.

Here was some luck. On the corner of West Broadway and Canal a juggler dressed in medieval costume
was putting on a performance. Pinwheels of red rubber
balls revolved around his head, while a crowd of a
dozen or so stood oohing and aahing. She deposited the
kid in their midst, ordered him to stay put.

Ten minutes later, Anita came flying back up Canal
Street. The transaction had been a success, and now
she could hardly wait to get home. But though the
juggler was still on his corner with the rubberneckers
gathered around him, David had disappeared. She
glanced furiously up and down the block. What kind of
stinking trick was this? It was just like the rotten kid to
pull a number at a time like this.

Well, screw him, she decided. He knew where to find
her. When he got hungry, he'd come on home fast
enough, that's for sure.

And if he didn't, she thought, heading up the street,
he could damn well starve.

At the end of a frustrating day Kerry Donner found himself on the block of Susan's gallery. It was closed and the gates were drawn, but upstairs in the front windows of her floor a light was burning. He had seen her that morning on his usual rounds, but now something compelled him to stop and press the button of her intercom. It was more than just the desire to look at her face and hear her voice again—lately there didn't seem to be a time when he didn't want to do those things. It was rather a feeling—call it even an intuition—that she needed him, that his being with her now would make a difference.

She met him by the elevator, trying to keep her face turned away from him. But still he noticed the hastily scrubbed cheeks, the red-rimmed eyes.

"You've been crying," he said.

She gave a wan smile. "You weren't supposed to notice."

"Why not? It's nothing shameful."

"But I'm supposed to be so tough. Especially after all these weeks."

"Nobody's that tough," he said. "If it didn't get to you once in a while, it would be unnatural."

"It's the silence!" she burst out. "Everyone's gone now—the police, the reporters, all my friends. I can't stand television, and I can't even listen to music anymore. But when it gets so quiet, I start listening—as if any minute I'll hear her footsteps or her voice calling from her bedroom. And then I start wondering if I'm losing my mind." She looked up, her eyes set and hard. "I wish she was dead!" she declared. "If I knew she was, I could mourn her and maybe get back to some sort of life. It would be better than this constant not knowing."

He regarded her gravely and said nothing.

"Aren't you shocked?" she prompted. "Don't you think it's appalling for a mother to wish her own daughter dead?"

"If I believed you meant it," he said, "maybe I would."

"Oh, hell!" She turned away from him, toward the long black expanse of windows. "Who knows if I mean it or not? I haven't had a single coherent thought since this all happened. My mind's a total wreck."

He noticed a large safety pin gathering in the back waistband of her jeans. "You've lost weight," he said.

She shrugged. "A couple of pounds."

"Haven't you been eating?"

"Oh, you know—I don't go out much anymore. And cooking for just myself seems like so much trouble that sometimes I don't even bother."

"Here's a proposition for you. Let me cook you dinner tonight."

She gave a startled laugh. "You mean it?"

"I mean it. I've got a place down by Wall Street. If you're willing to come down there, I think I could throw together a pretty fair meal."

"But I wouldn't want you to go to any trouble . . ."

"Trouble it's not," he said. "I love to cook. And I

especially love trying out my creations on other people.
How does stir-fried shrimp with almonds and snow peas
sound to you?"

"Like ambrosia."

"Ah, I see you're one of those hard-to-please types."
He grinned. "There's just one catch, though."

She tilted her head expectantly.

"You've got to change your clothes. Take off those
old jeans and put on something you like. Anything that
makes you feel good."

"Oh, I can't," Susan said quickly. "Not while she's
gone. I'd feel . . . I don't know, like I was betraying
her."

He came to her, put his hands on her shoulders. His
grave, dark, mismatched eyes held hers. "I won't let
you give up on yourself," he told her. "I've told you
before that unless you keep fighting every step of the
way we don't stand a chance."

She wanted him to keep holding her forever. She
wanted to throw herself in his arms, nestle close to the
broad expanse of his chest and be protected. Instead
she nodded and made her way to the bedroom. As she
slipped on a pretty lilac-colored shift, she wondered at
her readiness to do as he asked. These days everyone
offered her advice. Don't try to do anything, it'll only
make it worse, one would say. Keep busy, it's the best
way, another would insist. Go on a good drunk, one
friend suggested. Whatever you do, don't turn to
alcohol, someone else warned. Their words slipped
through her, leaving nothing behind but a vague sense
of distaste. Why, then, was she so willing to take Kerry
Donner's advice to heart? And why, when she appeared in her dress, did she feel so glad when he smiled
one of his rare, all-encompassing smiles?

They drove downtown in the dirty white Chevy
issued to Donner by the department. The financial
district was deserted at this hour.

Kerry Donner lived in a small wooden building, an

anachronism dwarfed by the superstructures around it. A Blarney Stone bar occupied the first floor. It's rude neon sign was the only evidence of life on the empty street.

They climbed three flights of stairs. He unlocked a door and ushered Susan in.

"You live in a loft!" she exclaimed.

He gave a quick laugh. "I guess it is a little incongruous for a cop."

"That's not what I mean. It's what you said the first time I met you—that day at the Wyles'. About how unnatural it was for people to be living in old factories."

"I still think that," he said. "It's just that I don't always practice what I preach."

She regarded him intently. "I don't think I'll ever figure you out."

"That's funny. I have a very strong feeling that you already have." He turned abruptly and gestured around him. "So," he said, "what do you think?"

Watching her take it all in, it occurred to him for the first time to be proud of what he had accomplished. He had worked both lovingly and hard on the place, and it showed. There was the pressed tin ceiling, salvaged from a Bowery demolition, that he had painstakingly washed with vinegar before putting up, so that the beautiful fleur-de-lis pattern was visible even in the dimmest light. And the kitchen, ingeniously constructed in an otherwise wasted corner—its row of copper pans dangled in descending order of size like a family of gleaming opossums. And the smooth-grained pine shelves housing his jazz collection—Charlie Parker to Cecil Taylor. The two solid walls of books . . .

"It's wonderful," Susan breathed. "It's so much like you!" Then they both broke into a laugh as her eye fell on his rumpled sports jacket, his hopeless tie—such a contrast to the orderly loft. "You know what I mean," she insisted.

"If so, I'm deeply flattered," he said. He went to a small cabinet bar, took out a bottle of Lillet, and poured it over ice in long-stemmed glasses. "I want you to go put your feet up," he said, handing her the sparkling drink, "while I see about rustling us up some dinner."

"Can't I help?"

"Nope. Tonight you're to be totally and unconditionally pampered. Doctor's orders."

She browsed through the books, watching him at work through the corner of her eye. He was obviously well at home in the kitchen. There was a sureness in the way he handled foodstuffs and utensils—the sureness of those for whom the preparation of food is both an art and a pleasure. Delicate and delicious odors began to arise from the big steel wok on the range. The plates he brought in a remarkably short time to the table were a feast for both the eye and the nose.

There was a practiced grace, too, in the way he lit tall, tapered candles, folded linen napkins, decanted a chilled Napa Valley Chablis. Susan wondered with a brief thrill of jealousy how many other women he had entertained here in just this way.

But for the first time since she could remember, she had a genuine appetite, and she joined him readily at the table. The food was as delicious as it appeared, and she hungrily consumed several forkfuls. Then she glanced at the title of a book that she had pulled from one of the shelves. "Teilhard de Chardin, *The Divine Milieu*. What's this all about?"

"Theology," he said, biting into a crisp snow pea. "Basically, it postulates the cosmic oneness of God and the universe."

She pursed her lips. "All these books on the wall—Paul Tillich, and Nietzsche, and somebody Bergson. Have you actually read them all?"

"Pretty much. A lot of it, actually, was required reading."

"In college, you mean?"

"Sort of." He hesitated, then added: "I studied for several years in a seminary."

Susan set down her wineglass and stared at him. "You mean, to become a priest?"

"That was the general idea."

She was silent a moment, digesting this information. Certainly some things about him that had puzzled her before now made sense—his startling erudition, for instance. But in other respects Kerry Donner was more of a puzzle than ever.

"Why did you leave?" she asked.

"The specific reason? I fell in love."

"Oh," she said—somewhat more glumly than intended.

"She was the sister of an old high school friend," he went on. "Someone I'd known nearly all my life. One day I was home on a visit and dropped by to see old Freddy. Margot answered the door. She hadn't changed much from the last time I'd seen her—no bobby socks to stockings transformation or anything. It's just that suddenly she seemed to be the most exquisitely unique creature on God's earth. I felt I could no longer exist without her.

"I spent the entire week's visit hanging out at the O'Keefes', keeping as close to Margot as I decently could. Then I went back to the seminary, spent a month swinging back and forth from high elation to guilt-ridden despair. Finally I screwed up my little bit of courage and told the master of novitiates I wanted to leave." He paused; his eyes held the reflection of the candles' lambent flame. "I remember the feeling of shame I had while I packed my bags. As if I were doing something cowardly, despicable. A thief in the night. And when I went to say good-bye, the other novitiates avoided my eyes. These were men who had been my friends—we had worked and eaten and prayed together. But now they wouldn't look at me while they shook my hand. It was the worst moment of my life."

There was silence.

"And the girl?" Susan prompted.

He made a wry mouth. "When I declared myself, she was shocked. Which shouldn't have surprised me. She was a sheltered Irish girl trained to think of the clergy as beyond all worldly matters. And in her eyes I was as good as in the priesthood already. From the way she reacted, it was as if the Pope himself had suddenly exposed himself from the balcony of St. Peter's."

Susan laughed lightly. "What did you do?"

"Oh, I holed up in the Bronx for a while, licking my wounds. Eventually, certain things managed to penetrate my thick skull. Like the fact that my passion for Margot O'Keefe wasn't so all-consuming after all. In fact, it was just a cover-up. I had really made the decision to leave All Saints a long time before, but couldn't admit it to myself. My subconscious had to drum up an *affaire de coeur* to justify it."

He picked up the wine bottle and divided the remaining contents between them.

Susan sipped meditatively. "How did you come to join the police force?" she asked. "It seems like such a strange choice for someone just out of a seminary."

"Not for an Irish kid from Inwood," he said, grinning. "And anyway, cops and the clergy have a lot in common."

She glanced at him skeptically. "You'll have to explain that."

"Okay, look at it this way. Both wear funny clothes, both are considered somewhat other than human by the general population, and both are applied to in times of trouble and expected to come up with solutions.

"Another thing—they both have a constant ringside ticket to the human soul. I'm continually a witness to people's most secret vices. All their private little perversions and degradations. They tell me things they wouldn't tell their wives, their husbands, their best friends . . ." He paused, put his glass to his lips as if afraid of what else he might say.

Susan waited a moment. "Do you ever regret it?" she asked. "Not staying in the seminary, I mean."

Regrets? A dozen images flashed through his mind at once. The dawn light seeping thinly into a bare cell. The feel of the rough habit against his skin; pulling the cincture of his habit tight while muttering the morning orison, "My yoke is sweet, oh, Lord, my burden light. . . ." The brotherhood of the midday colloquy, the meditative peace of the minor silence . . .

"No," he said decisively, "I don't regret it. I made the right decision."

The rare smile fled across his face—Like a shooting star, Susan thought, that disappears so quickly you can't be sure you've even seen it at all. Then, at once, it seemed urgently important that he know everything about her. When she began to talk, it poured from her: the raggedy first months in Manhattan, the highs and lows of her year with Bob, and how she had fled from the abortionist's table. The building of the gallery from scratch, every step a struggle, each tiny gain a triumph —all of it she told him.

They took *café filtre* and brandy and settled on huge, white, floppy floor pillows and continued talking. They spoke of feelings now—the private, deep-seated impulses that govern a life. He told her about being on foot patrol—how, instead of being happy when he made a collar, he'd feel an overwhelming sadness. "So many of them were hardly more than kids. You could see in their faces that their entire lives had led up to nothing more than this one moment—dumped in the back of a patrol car, hands cuffed behind their backs, waiting to be shipped off to some stinking, overcrowded cell." And in turn Susan described the horrible chasm of loss that had swallowed her when Joey disappeared.

The first touch was spontaneous. Hand upon hand, fingers intertwined. The touch led to a kiss that lingered, grew passionate, drew them toward and into each other. He gathered her as if she were made of a precious, fragile substance lighter than air, carried her to the big, handmade pine bed. And then there was no time: just the enduring comfort of flesh against flesh, the tenderness of giving pleasure, the gratitude of receiving. Fingers explored, eyes discovered. It was as if their bodies had known each other in some other form long ago and had existed in flesh only to be reunited. It was right.

Afterward they lay cradled together, her head in the hollow of his shoulder, his hand curved upon her breast. Breathing together, not wanting to give up the moment. And after a while, they slept.

The phone jangled them awake. Donner roused himself to answer it and Susan listened anxiously to his terse conversation. "When?" he said. Then: "Damn! Yeah, yeah, I know. Give me fifteen minutes."

He turned to her, his face drawn. "Another boy's missing. I've got to go."

"Yes," she said.

It was barely light outside. She watched him—big, dear man—make his way through the dim room, shower and dress rapidly. He returned and kissed her forehead.

"I'll call as soon as I can," he whispered.

She nodded. When he left, she snuggled into the other side of the bed, still warm from the indentation of his body. But she knew she wouldn't get any more sleep.

Now there were two she had to wait for.

David was starving. He always was—he couldn't remember a time in his life when he had had enough to eat—really enough. But the lady had promised him a chocolate ice-cream cone—a double scoop and all his! He could hardly wait to get to the place they were going.

His mother ate ice cream all the time. When she wasn't sick, all she wanted was chocolate. But she ate it fast, in big greedy gobbles, and seemed to forget he was even alive when she did.

The car was stopping now. He was disappointed to see it was a big, dirty building that looked a lot like the one he lived in. And the alley they were walking into was just like the one behind his own basement.

"Is this where you live?" he asked.

"This is where we *all* live, Bobby," she said.

He was about to blurt out that his name wasn't Bobby and that he didn't live here, but he caught himself in time. What if she had made a mistake, and the double-scoop cone wasn't for him but for some other boy? His years on the street had made him cagey. He knew what it took to survive. And so he kept his mouth firmly shut as they got into a funny-looking elevator and began to go up.

The lady pushed open a heavy door. David saw some bright-red chairs and a table and some other furniture, also painted pretty colors, and the room was bigger than all the rooms at home put together. But it was as dim here as it was at home, and the light came from the same naked light bulbs. And there were other children. He was sorry to see that. He really hoped he wouldn't have to share his cone with anybody.

"Look who's here, children," the lady yelled. "It's Bobby! Come and give him a kiss hello."

David shrank back. He wasn't used to people touching him.

"Can't I have my ice cream now?" he asked.

The lady took off her glasses. Her eyes were funny and ugly underneath, with black rings like the bruises on his mother's arms. "Children must never make demands upon their elders," she said. Her voice had changed. It sounded now like Anita's just before she got her worst sickness and started to scream and throw things and forget he existed.

"You promised," he said boldly.

Something dark came across her face. In an instant he knew that there would be no ice cream. And he knew, too, what this place was. It was the orphanage. Anita had warned him many times that one day he would be taken there, and she had filled his head with stories of the horrible things that happened to children there.

He turned and broke for the door. But the lady was fast. She grabbed him by the shoulders and held him, though he turned and twisted and kicked her in the shins. She shook him hard and shouted to him in words that made no sense. He braced himself for a beating. But instead he was being dragged across the room, forced into a tall wooden chest, the door locked upon him.

"I shall cast out the rebellious seed," he heard the

lady shout. "The wild child shall be sent to the outer
darkness to learn the ways of the just!"

It was black as pitch and hard for him to move.
But he drew himself into a ball and lay still—very,
very still. Here, too, he knew, he would learn to survive.

Part III

SOHO: A HISTORY (continued)
By Day McAllister

8—8—8—8

For 60 years this neighborhood lies
moldering in an obscure limbo. Forgotten by
the city, its streets clogged with trucks, the
columns and fanciful pediments of its
once—proud buildings now blackened and
corroded by smog and soot, it is a desolate
industrial slum. The bleakness of its
landscape is relieved only when the colored
lights of the festivals spill over from Little
Italy, its neighbor to the east.
And so it may have stayed. But in the late
1950s a new group of people discover the
neighborhood. They are neither manufacturers
nor retailers nor prominent bourgeoisie. They
are artists. Perpetually out of pocket, and
perpetually in need of space to turn out
canvases and sculptures that are becoming

[MORE]

221

9-9-9-9

increasingly monumental in size, they seize
upon the huge, sunny lofts of the Iron Valley.
Their trained eyes see through the layers of
grime to the lovely, idiosyncratic
architecture beneath. They are content to
share the streets with trucks.

Word gets around. The early pioneers are
joined by their friends, then by friends of
their friends. And then glamour sweeps into
the neighborhood in the form of The Famous:
Robert Rauschenberg. Lowell Nesbitt. Louise
Nevelson, who converts a Spring Street
sanitorium into a house of mysterious caves.

And then, suddenly, everything happens at
once. The first galleries open—not the small,
cramped showrooms of uptown, but huge, spare,
airy loft spaces designed for the display of
grand-scale art works. Trend-setters add the
downtown galleries to their Saturday route,
then stay to live; they are followed by the
affluent and the curious. And then there are
sleek bars and fancy cafes, expensive
first-class restaurants, shops offering witty
and original clothing, refinished barber's
chairs, rare pâtés, Head Comix and Wet
magazine, giant Plexiglas pencils, furniture
from the furthest reaches of the
imagination—and wave upon wave of tourists.

By the late 1970s, Soho has come of age.

—30—

It was a false alarm.

The little boy had awakened early and, feeling rest-less, had gotten out of bed. Somehow he managed to unlock the front door and went out to prowl. When the detectives found him, he was curled up fast asleep on the sticky tar roof of the building. They brought him down to his frantic parents.

With nothing more to do, the four detectives who had answered the call filed back out to the humid street.

"Gonna be another scorcher," Casiopo observed. "I'll tell ya, on a day like this it doesn't pay to get up early. I coulda used another couple hours in the sack."

"Yeah, but at least we're gaining," Franklin said. "Yesterday we were 0 for three—now we're one for four."

"You kidding? This don't count. The kid wasn't really missing."

"Sure he was. We had to *find* him, didn't we? Christ knows what coulda happened to him if we didn't."

"Christ, there goes Franklin with his butchered kids

223

routine again. You know you got a morbid mind, Frankie?"

"Yeah? Well, how's this: What's red and sits in a corner and gurgles? Give up? A baby eating razor blades."

"Jesus, you're really sick, Franklin."

But they all laughed.

Kerry Donner, coming up behind, understood their retreat into black humor. It was a way of channeling off some of the intense anxieties that rode with this case. Everyone was on their ass, from the newspapers to the local pols to the neighborhood ad hoc committees. The FBI was nosing in, claiming jurisdiction on the grounds that it had to be organized crime. The commissioner's office, the mayor, even the governor were screaming bloody murder.

And still kids kept disappearing into thin air.

He found a pay phone and dialed his own number. When Susan answered, he felt a thrill; the memory of last night returned to him in a rush.

"Did you get some more sleep?" he asked.

"Not much," she said. "I was too worried. The little boy . . .?"

"He's okay. We found him up on the roof asleep."

"Oh, that's good."

"Yeah." He sighed. "Do you know what I'd give to have every single one of them turn up like that?"

"I think I do," she replied.

He told her of the new developments he'd been briefed on by the precinct detectives. A parking ticket had been issued to the same car in the neighborhood on the days both Lisa and Jason disappeared. A good description of a man seen talking to Jason in the shop that morning had been obtained; a sketch would soon be circulated to the media. These were his gifts to her, these small morsels of hope, and she accepted them with gratitude.

"Will you be coming back here?" she asked. "I've kept the coffee hot."

"I wish I could, but it's shaping up to be a hell of a day. I'd better get to my desk. But I'll be up to the gallery as soon as I can."

"I'll be waiting for you."

He paused, a heartbeat. "Susan?"

"Yes?"

"I love you."

"Yes," she said. "Oh, yes."

Eben Link could hardly move, so many children were climbing about his legs.

"Hey, you little terrors, give me a break," he laughed.

But more of them clustered around him, shouting, "Give me a swing, Mr. Link! Can I have a swing?"

As they knew he would, he finally relented. One by one, he scooped them up and whirled them, squealing and giggling, high in the air. Then, one by one, he delivered them to the mothers, fathers, baby-sitters, and older siblings who waited at the playground gate to bring them home.

Last of all was little Alexis Cassidy. She came so docilely—her tiny hand wrapped snugly in his and a smile on her angel's face—that his heart went out to her. Funny, he thought, how nature sometimes seems to try to compensate for its own thoughtlessness. As if by making this child so exquisite it had wanted to insure that at least she would always be loved.

Alexis broke from him suddenly and ran on tiny legs to her mother. Thia Cassidy thanked him as she always did in her grave, politely distant manner. It was not until she had turned away that Eben realized how unwell she had seemed: thin and pale, her mouth compressed in a tight arc. He wondered if she had been sick recently.

"The husband's left her," someone said.

He glanced down. Caroline Losey stood beside him, arms folded across her chest.

"What did you say?" he asked.

"The Cassidy woman. Her husband's walked out on her. Left her high and dry with the child."

There was a tone of smug satisfaction in her voice that Eben found disturbing. He grunted neutrally.

"Can't say *I'm* surprised," Caroline went on. "Not with her airs and those high-and-mighty ways of hers. No self-respecting man would put up with *that* for very long, I can tell you. Though I must say that *he's* not above reproach himself. Not by a long stroke. Been running around with the type of girl who's got no more morals than a common alley cat. The two of them out every night till all hours, carrying on to the devil!"

Eben shifted uneasily. "If the Cassidys have problems, it's really none of our business," he said.

Caroline seemed not to hear him. She gazed fixedly out past the Cyclone fence toward the street where Thia and Alexis had disappeared. "They're not fit parents for that child," she said. "Neither one of them. But they'll find out. Yes, one day they will understand, and then they will hearken to the truth. But it will profit them nothing, for by then it shall be too late!"

She spoke these words with an avenging fervor that amazed Eben. He wanted only to get away from her. Mumbling a few words, he turned and walked quickly inside the center.

Day was right, he thought, she *was* a weird old bird. But the encounter had left him with the chills; there was something appallingly familiar about Caroline's sudden spurt of fanaticism. Of course—it reminded him of his mother during the last few years of her life when, after too many kids, and too little money, and day after uncountable day of fruitless drudgery, her mind had begun to wander. The similarity was hardly surprising. Caroline, poor thing, could hardly be a stranger to tight money—not with those clothes that looked as if they'd been pulled from a rummage sale or at best some old trunk she'd been hoarding over the years. And he supposed she was lonely. She occupied a single room in the Gramercy Plaza, a shabbily genteel women's residence hotel, and he had never heard her mention family or friends. Solitude, endless scrimping for dimes—no wonder she had gone a little crazy. And if the bitter circumstances of such a life surfaced now and then in the form of a few unholy remarks, what of it? It couldn't do anyone any harm.

Still, he had to wonder how she knew about the Cassidys' breakup. And the other details about their private lives, assuming they were true—where did she get those? But then he shrugged to himself, remembering the old gossips in his New Hampshire hometown, how they always seemed to be plugged in to everything that happened—especially the sordid and the scandalous—as if their fading eyes had been granted the compensatory power to see behind closed doors.

He folded an activity schedule that he planned to work on at home, locked his office, and emerged onto Houston Street. Caroline Losey soon vanished from his mind as other, more personal thoughts crowded in. His life was becoming too complex; there were too many ties forming, too much involvement already beginning to restrict him. He felt himself being drawn into that entangling web that most people called normal life. His gut instinct told him it was time to shake loose. Get out before it gets you—that was the guiding principle.

But there was Day. He had no doubts about his feelings for her. He loved her. All the burning, yearning, churning stuff of the rock 'n' roll lyrics, the lofty endorsements of poetry—it was all there. And yet the undeniable fact remained that she was plugged in to everything that he was desperate to avoid: career, family, friends, neighborhood—all the tightly knit systems and structures, the ones that roped you by the ankles and tugged till they had you sprawled on the ground, bound, helpless, and final.

Shit!

Maybe it had been a mistake to let her move in with him. But, damn it, he did love her. Love, cherish, revere, adore—everything that was supposed to make you feel good. It's just that he didn't know whether it was enough.

And then he saw the two men.

Both were of about medium height, built upon broad, solid lines. They leaned limply against a new, white Toronado, two idlers relaxing in the sun. But in contrast to such seeming indolence, their eyes were alert, sharply focused.

Instinctively, Eben knew they were cops. And that they were waiting for him.

He veered across the street. As he suspected they would, the men straightened and followed him. For the length of several blocks, they trailed him closely, rounding a corner when he did, stopping ten paces away when he stopped. Finally, passage on the sidewalk was blocked by the van of a refrigerated truck parked at a loading ramp. Eben could get around it by shimmying between two cars at the curb, then dodging traffic. But he was sick of the cat-and-mouse charade. He turned and faced his silent shadows.

"What do you want?" he demanded.

They regarded him impassively. For a moment he imagined that he had just foolishly challenged two innocent strangers. But no, the eyes were a dead giveaway. His instincts had to be right.

He tried again. "Look, I already told Donner I had nothing to do with it. If he thinks something else, let him take me downtown. Otherwise, tell him to get off my fucking back!"

One of the men—the shorter and deceptively more innocuous-looking of the two—hunched his left shoulder slightly, as if shrugging off a kink in his neck. "If we knew this Donner, maybe we could do that," he said. "Trouble is, we don't know him."

"But we know you, Mr. Link," the other said softly. "And we know your girl friend, the writer."

Eben glanced at them, confused. "Day? What's she got to do with this?"

"She's writing a story about a building, right?" the first one said.

"Yeah, but . . ."

"We hear she's got her facts wrong. We hear that if she goes with this wrong story, it could do some damage to a good friend of ours. We'd be really sorry to see that happen."

Eben suddenly realized his mistake. "You're not cops, are you?" he said.

The second man gave a humorless grin. "You could say we're kind of a private force."

"What do you want with me?"

"We were thinking you might use your influence to get your friend to change her story. Go with something a little more accurate, if you see what we mean."

"Hey, I don't tell her what to write. She does what she wants."

The first man gazed at him thoughtfully. The lids of his eyes drooped, as if he had scarcely roused himself from a deep sleep, but the pupils shone with a hard, unwavering light. His left shoulder hunched again briefly. "Why not try a little persuasion and see what happens?" he said. "You could be really surprised."

"Why the fuck should I?"

"A stupid question, Mr. Link. You're an ex-con on parole, and odds say you want to stay on parole."

Eben felt his muscles contract, ready equally to attack or take flight. "That's a shit scare," he said harshly. "I've done nothing to get sent back up."

"Are you sure about that?" The first man took a step closer. "You don't think maybe your parole board might hear about you associating with known criminals? Or they could find out about that dime you been carrying in your back pocket."

Eben thrust a hand into the back pocket of his jeans, drew out a thin cellophane packet. He threw it to the ground. "I'll kill you!" he hissed, and sprang at the shorter man. The other slipped behind him, pinning his elbows, while the first man slammed a punch into his solar plexus. Eben doubled over with pain, dry-retching.

The first man picked up the cellophane packet from the sidewalk. He shook it fastidiously, then placed it inside his jacket. "Just don't forget to deliver our message," he said.

Day burst into the loft fairly dancing on air. "Eben!" she cried. "Gabe's giving me the entire front page with a seventy-two-point headline and eight columns inside. He says it's the biggest scoop we've had in a year! God, you should have seen Knowlton's face when I showed him the story. He turned green. I mean positively chartreuse! I got him, Eben, I really did!"

She drew closer to the old oak table where he was sitting bent over something. He turned toward her, and she froze. "Oh, my god!" she gasped. "What are you doing?"

"What does it look like?" he said coldly.

The pistol with its brutish snub nose and dull handle seemed to insult his fine, long-fingered hands. But there was no denying the familiarity with which he held it. He looked at her a moment, then picked up a scrap of old shirt and resumed cleaning the barrel.

Day felt the blood stop cold in her veins. "Your parole," she whispered. "If they catch you with a gun, you'll be sent back to jail."

He shrugged. "Better to go like this than be sent up for a frame."

"What are you talking about?" He didn't reply. She pleaded, "Eben, you've got to tell me what happened."

"It's none of your concern."

"Don't say that. Anything that happens to you is of course my concern." Her thoughts raced wildly. "Is it that detective Donner? Did he threaten you with something?"

He glanced up. "You know about him?"

She nodded. "He came to ask me some questions about you. I told him he was crazy if he thought you had anything to do with those kidnappings."

He looked at her a moment, then stiffened. "Yeah, Donner's on my ass. But he's not the only one. I'm getting fucked from all sides."

"Eben, what's *happened?*" She grabbed his arm and he wrenched it away. His face wore the wild expression of a creature calculating its survival. "You want to know?" he said with a short laugh. "I got cornered by two goons today. They threatened to set me up to the parole board, and then they punched me out."

"Oh, God, are you hurt?"

"Nah. But it's not going to happen again."

"Who were they? What did they want?"

"They were sent by your pal Knowlton. He wants me to try to make you change your story."

Day's hands flew to her temples. "I'll call Gabriel. I'll tell him to stop the story. I'll tell him I made it all up, it was a joke."

"Fuck that. I don't want you fighting my battles for me."

"But they're my battles, too. Whatever happens, we're in it together."

He turned his face to her. His eyes were narrowed, his teeth bared. "Get this straight. I don't work as a team, and I don't go for that you-and-me-together bullshit. I'm staying loose. If you don't like it, you can check out any time you want."

She stared at him, wooden and speechless with terror. Then she jumped as Eben hurled the pistol at the opposite wall, and it hit with a crash. He dropped his head into his hands.

"I thought they couldn't get me if I didn't play by

their rules anymore," he said. "I thought if I stayed outside their system I'd be safe. But, Christ, I was wrong. No matter what you do, they'll always find a way to get you."

Very gently, she touched the fine, high arch of his cheekbone. He turned and clutched her fiercely around the waist while she stroked his hair and face.

"Don't ever leave me," he whispered.

"I won't," she said.

She awoke in the middle of the night, smelling the acrid smoke. When she opened her eyes, she saw the first faint wisps curl toward her bed. Her throat froze in terror. But the children must be saved! Quickly, she must get them out of the burning house, out beyond the lawn to the clear ground and safety.

She rose and went to their beds, shaking each small body. "Get up, children. Hurry, it's a fire. Wake up, we must get out. No, don't get dressed, we have to hurry!"

The children, still half asleep, sensed her terror. One of them began to whimper. But there was no time to comfort them. She herded them before her, stumbling in the thin beam of the flashlight, till at last they were out the door and into the night.

But something was wrong. There was no grass beneath her feet and when she looked up there were no stars. They were still inside a building, and the crackle of the flame had disappeared. Perhaps, she thought, there never had been a fire. Or perhaps it was the misfortune of some other woman that she had heard about, and it had lingered in her mind.

And yet she could remember every detail so clearly. Just as if it were happening all over again.

It is seven o'clock of an early summer evening. Steven is not home yet. It has been clear for some time that he has been meeting his needs with other women, and Caroline has just found out the name of the latest one—a trashy, freckled girl just out of high school who works at Sculley's department store.

Caroline, all efficiency, has fed Georgene and put a pork chop casserole to warm in the oven. Now, as has lately become her habit, she mixes herself a Seven & Seven while she waits. It makes the furniture around her look softer, as if she could mold it with her fingers. She has another, sips it slowly, and no longer cares that the casserole is getting dry. But Steve has never been this late before. Perhaps if she has one more drink and sips it very, very slowly, it will bring him back. But she has run out of 7UP, so she pours straight rye and gulps it back to lessen the taste. And suddenly her soft contentment turns into sodden despair. She is sad, so very sad. She wants only to see her little girl, to hold her close. And so she runs, swaying a bit, into Georgene's room.

The child looks up guiltily. She has stolen her mother's lipstick and has painted her face—lascivious, wanton color smeared upon her innocence. She tries to rub it off with her fingertips. But Caroline erupts in fury. She beats the child's buttocks until her hand is red and raw, and yet it seems that for such harlotry greater punishment is called for. The child must be taught. For a lesson she must stand locked in her closet until bedtime.

Caroline returns to the kitchen, feeling spent now, and still so sad. She pours herself another tumbler of rye. But this one makes her ill. The room is whirling, and the floor has lost its foundations. Perhaps if she eats something—not the thick, dry casserole, ugh. She opens a can of Campbells's tomato soup, turns the gas burner on high. In a minute—it seems like only a minute—the soup is bubbling over the top of the pan, so she grabs the handle with a dishrag. But somehow the fringed end of the dishrag touches the flame, and it is on fire, so she drops it, pan and all, into the garbage; but that catches on fire too, and somehow the curtains over the stove have also started to burn. And now there is smoke making her choke and cough, and so she staggers out the back door, but just for a minute, just to clear her head, for she knows she must go back and get the child . . .

And then it all stopped.

No, there was more. *She is lying on a field of damp grass, and a siren is wailing close by, and Steven's face is looming above hers. "Where's Georgie?" he is screaming. "Did she get out, too?"*

But there is no grass here. She is lying on a floor—a dusty, wooden floor—and Steven is dead. It was dark, the light had gone out, but she can hear the children crying and whimpering, and she knows they are all safe.

"Don't cry, my precious darlings," she whispered. "I'll take you all back to bed."

Perhaps if he threw himself into work, he could take his mind off the god-awful mess that was his life. Gil brought the table light down closer to his head, but the delicate tracings on his drafting table swam in the glare. It was no use. He snapped the light off and sat, his head in his hands.

If he couldn't work, what *could* he do? He had succeeded in narrowing his entire life down to this office. Albie had been his best friend. All his other "friends" were actually acquaintances garnered in the course of doing business. Almost everything he had thought, done, dreamed about in the past few years had been somehow connected to making this partnership a success.

And there had been precious little left over for his family. He had justified his neglect of them by putting the blame on them, by telling himself that it was their problems that had driven him away. But really it was his own greed—a hunger for success so consuming that he had been willing to sacrifice his wife and daughter in order to feed it.

How smugly he had believed that buying his wife

some new clothes was the best he could do to help her. He could have tried tenderness, patience, support. But he hadn't had the time. He was far too busy.

He stood up and was suddenly overcome with dizziness, an attack stronger and longer-lasting than any that had come before. He shook out two yellow pills from the plastic vial and tossed them back with a swig of the Cuervo he kept in a file drawer. In a moment he felt the welcome relaxation of his nerves, like sharp-edged icicles melting in a soft sun. His face no longer felt like a stiff, ill-fitting mask; his fingers regained their pliancy. He felt much better—or at least he did except for what seemed to be an ominous message floating in his mind. It was all balled up like a crumpled telegram so that he couldn't quite make it out. He concentrated on smoothing it out, reading what was written on it.

Addict, it said. *You're hooked on this pathetic housewife's medication. No way you can get by without it, you poor bastard.*

Beads of sweat broke out on his forehead. Not true, he told himself. The stuff had gotten him through a rough time, that's all. Once things picked up again, he could go it alone. Tomorrow, in fact—tomorrow he'd start cutting them out completely.

The words in his head jeered: *Just like you cut out cigarettes, right?*

He glanced at the burning Marlboro in his hand and dashed it to the floor. He felt suddenly dirty; his face reflected in the dark expanse of window glass was shadowed and drawn. But it was still a face that spoke of the West—of high winds and clear open spaces. He thought now of the prairie and the skies of home with a longing and a love that he hadn't felt in years.

The two-lane road stretched straight as an arrow through field after field of wild flowers: bonnets, five-finger, bluebells, black-eyed daisies. But he was making for the huge red fireball of a sun that was settling like a lady onto the wide, flat prairie. He was driving the Chevy pickup—the old one with the BB hole in the windshield; and his brother Rich sat beside him, fiddling with the radio—nothing on but preachers and jug bands, so he gave up and stared out the window at the thunderheads rolling in from the north. "Holy Jeez!" he cried out suddenly. "Look at that!" And Gil, braking hard, got out of the truck to investigate. It was two white diamondback rattlers coiled up within each other— mating, he guessed. He saw in their slow, oozing dance an interlock of life and death that was beautiful beyond all words. But then there was a report, and those fat white coils were blasted to the heavens. He turned and saw Rich leaning on the smoking Winchester, a big grin plastered on his face like he'd done the world some kind of favor.

Why did the image seem so vivid to him now? It had happened so long ago. He remembered telling Thia about it and how she had understood in the uncanny, intuitive way she had that that was the night he decided to leave home. When was it he had told her? That's right, it was on their honeymoon. The cabin at Jackson Hole that was freezing cold. But they had snuggled like children beneath the comforter. She had worn the Red River longjohns he had given her as a joke, and when they were off, her body felt electric, impossible. He had held her for hours, simply held her, and thought, Mine. My wife!

There had been other women in the past years, but they were passionless affairs that never lasted long and left him feeling emotionally flat. Just sex, after all. And what did that mean? A natural function of life, no mystery about it. People do it everywhere, all the time, in palaces and motels, in fields and alleyways . . .

Except that sometimes when you do it you make a baby—a perfect, golden-haired child with sound limbs and a sturdy heart, and it becomes the center of your life, the joy and force of your being. Until you learn the truth: that the perfect creature you've created is missing a mind, will have the intelligence of perhaps a reasonably clever monkey. And the rage and horror you feel shows

*in your eyes; and though you want to fall down on your
knees to your wife and cry, I'm sorry, it's my fault, all
you can do is back further and further away.*

He picked up the bottle of Cuervo and took a deep
swallow. It was going to be a long night, and he was
going to need a lot of fortification.

The phone rang for what seemed like hours. It finally
stopped, only to start again a few seconds later.

Gil blinked awake. His limbs were stiff, and there
was a vile taste in his mouth. He couldn't quite place
where he was.

The metallic glint of a file drawer jolted his memory.
He was sleeping on a couch in his office. Somehow he
had managed to crawl back here last night—the only
home, he thought wryly, he had left.

He groped for the phone and a cigarette at the same
time, reached the Marlboro first and lit it. Then,
holding the receiver some distance from his ear, he
tried to focus on the abrasive voice that issued from it.
It was someone wanting his comments on certain
allegations that had been made about his firm—
something about the latest issue of the *Soho Sun.*

The words made absolutely no sense. "I don't know
a thing about it," he replied.

Spetzi gazed disconsolately at a canvas done in bright swirling colors that was displayed on an easel. Bah! It was such trash. Blatant. Unpardonable. A connect-the-dots drawing had more integrity.

He threw a drop cloth over the canvas, depressed by the simple sight of it. What, he wondered, would those wizards of light and color—Turner, Monet, Winslow Homer—have made of such a meretricious display as this? And those master draftsmen of art history—Vermeer, Pollaiuolo, Daumier, the idols of his youth—wouldn't they have sneered at such flabby drawing, lips curling in contempt at the sight of such cheap shortcuts in perspective?

And yet the artist who had perpetrated this monstrosity could not be blamed. He was simply a twenty-four-year-old exceptionally talented and ravenously hungry graduate of the Pratt Institute who had faithfully accomplished that for which he had been commissioned: to imitate with precision the elements of an original Spetzi work of art. That he had been more than successful was evident to his employer at a glance. The print that was to be made from this painting would have an enormous appeal, would sell in the tens of thousands.

In short, it would sell like hotcakes. Spetzi chuckled grimly as he composed an aphorism: "I am the fast-food of the art world. The Burger King, the Kentucky Fried Chicken of culture."

Gloom curled around him like an importunate cat. It was a lamentable fact that he had sold out whatever talent he had possessed, traded in every scrap of integrity for an easy win. And it was irreversible. His name would be forever debased, a synonym for *schlock*.

But just then a spear of sunlight slanted in from the skylight; as it widened, bathing the well-appointed studio in a liquid gold, it served to remind him that the rewards of prostitution had not been small. On the contrary, they had surpassed his wildest expectations, lavishing a material extravagance upon him that even his dreams had not encompassed. And if the truth be told, he had never possessed enough talent to become another Vermeer—or even an Honoré Daumier. He would always have been a second-rater. And, therefore, when confronted with the choice, hadn't he been merely sensible to go for the money? It had been a calculated, perhaps even a cold-blooded, decision, but in the face of reality, not an unsound one.

Thus reassured, he let his mood pass with the late afternoon clouds.

As he walked toward the stairwell, the intercom crackled briefly, then gave up his butler's inflectionless voice. "Excuse me, sir—there's a Mr. Knowlton here to see you. I told him you were not to be disturbed, but he insists it's a matter of some urgency."

Spetzi sighed. Knowlton had the potential of becoming a first-class pest. Such people had to be trained; they must realize he could not be expected to jump at their convenience.

He flipped the intercom switch. "Tell him to wait in the red study. I'll be right there."

He found his visitor pacing tensely, a strained look on his face. He stopped abruptly and held out a folded newspaper. "Have you seen this?"

Spetzi glanced at the headline, then quickly scanned the first four paragraphs. "So," he said. "What does this mean for us?"

"A lot of problems. The goddamned phone hasn't stopped ringing all morning. We're getting flack from every committee and agency in the city. The worst is that the Zoning Board is claiming that it passed our case on a forced referendum and has revoked our demolition permit until it can be reviewed."

"What about your man in City Hall?"

"He's withdrawn his patronage. At least until this matter has been smoothed out." Albie lit a cigarette with visibly unsteady hands. "I can't believe a shitty little local paper could raise such a stink. I mean, who the hell even reads it?"

"You're behind the times, Knowlton," Spetzi muttered. His mind was already hard at work, reviewing possibilities, weighing and eliminating options. For a moment he was silent. Then he declared, "As I see it, we have no choice. The building must be destroyed before there is any further investigation."

"I told you, we've lost our demolition rights. No wrecker in the city will touch it."

"There are other ways than a wrecking ball to get rid of an encumbering structure. A fire is the most obvious alternative, and also, I believe, the easiest to arrange."

Albie recoiled. "We can't do that! It would look too suspicious. Even if they couldn't prove anything, people would speculate. My reputation would be ruined."

"Would your reputation fare any better if these charges were allowed to be investigated?"

"Christ, no!" Albie began to pace again in a distraught manner, his eyes staring at the floor. Suddenly he looked up. "You say you could arrange it?"

"I'm fairly certain."

"When?"

"The sooner the better, obviously. Tomorrow evening, just after dark."

"Where should I be?"

"Right here. This is how we'll arrange it: I'll have a largish gathering here, which both you and your partner will attend. That way you'll be very visible at the time the fire breaks out. I can't protect you from falling under suspicion, but at least you won't be personally implicated."

Albie nodded whitely.

"Now the man I have in mind . . ."

"I don't want to know the details!" he protested.

Spetzi drew a contemptuous smile. "Then I won't trouble you with them. Be here tomorrow evening at seven. And do try to look as though you're having a good time. I can't bear my guests to be gloomy."

But when left alone, the artist's intrepid smile crumbled and deep lines of tension appeared in his forehead. He sank weakly into a velvet wingback chair. It had been necessary to maintain a calm facade to Knowlton, whom he judged to be on the brink of doing something rash, but in truth the news had left him extremely agitated. He had committed his own agents to this deal—those silent, unsmiling, colorless men who hovered in his life like forbidding guardians. Should he go to them with the intelligence that this deal had been so ineptly mishandled and that their participation in it was in danger of being exposed? He shuddered to think of the consequences.

Agents, guardians. Why didn't he stop kidding himself and admit it—they were his owners. They had been since the day thirteen years ago they had first presented themselves to him. He had still been Coy Seiglitz then, of course—a moderately successful commercial illustrator whose talents seemed ideal for Madison Avenue. Though he could never quite manage to draw a beautiful duck, he could nevertheless always be counted upon to produce an attractive duck—even a clever or engaging one, a duck that would catch the eye and sell a product.

He would never get rich, but he possessed a realist's sense of his own limitations and knew he had no cause to complain. And yet he couldn't help periodic spurts of envy and resentment over the growing success of certain of his former classmates. Bob DeRitis in particular. It seemed suddenly that he could no longer pick up a paper or magazine without a mention of this hot new painter popping out at him. What burned him was the reverence with which the critics had begun to speak of his work. And there was the slightly patronizing way Bob treated him when they happened to meet, just as if they were still back at school, and Bob was the darling of the fine arts department. All this smoldered in Coy's soul like a corrupting ember.

And then one day, as he was struggling over a dog food ad, two men in dark suits walked into his tiny Upper West Side studio. Deus ex machina—speaking of something "to your advantage." If he would consider leaving commercial art and going back to painting, they proposed to act as his agents. Their function would roughly approximate that of a good gallery. In other words, they would obtain commissions, promote his name, manage the sale of his uncommissioned work so that it commanded the highest prices. In addition, they offered to set him up in the studio of his choice with an initial retainer. The sum they mentioned was precisely twice his gross earnings of the previous year.

How or why they had gotten his name, they didn't say. Nor did he ask. From the start he knew intuitively that questions were not to be a part of his role.

Still, he imagined that there had to be a catch. These strangers with their somber suits and down-to-business attitudes were unlikely patrons of the arts. Their intention must be to use him for something—as a front, perhaps, for some illegal enterprise. But the money was tempting, and the dog food spread he had been laboring over bored and disgusted him. Moreover, the *Times* that morning had carried an article by the éminence grise of the art world on the most exciting of the new young painters, and Bob DeRitis had been prominently mentioned.

He shook hands on the deal. That was all it took: no contracts, no written agreements, no lawyers. But it was enough.

Taking a pseudonym was his own idea, and his "agents" accepted it without blinking. The message in their attitude was clear: Call yourself anything you like. Just turn out the work when we tell you to.

And there was work—a lot of it—right from the start. The breadth and variety of his agents' contacts and influence astonished him. Commissions rolled in from the top interior decorators of a dozen countries. He did paintings for the covers of *TV Guide, Time* magazine, and the Los Angeles phone book, and one for an African island republic that was made into a stamp. He was commissioned for three murals for a new Playboy Club, monumental paintings for the lobbies of civic centers, smaller works for the reception rooms of blue-chip industrial corporations.

There was only one rule: all his work had to be done in the gimmicky semi-impressionistic style he had developed for his commercial illustration. When once he tried his hand at something different—an abstract canvas for the reception room of a Wall Street law firm—the man sent to pick it up glanced at it briefly, slashed it with a pocket knife, then calmly ordered another to be ready by the end of the day.

At the same time, he was being agilely molded into a celebrity. Invitations to the right openings, receptions, gala dinners, and charity balls appeared in his mailbox. His name popped up in society and gossip columns. He was an item in *Vogue*'s "People Are Talking About" column, a regular in *Women's Wear Daily*'s "Eye" section.

The established art world—the snobbish, internecine

circle of critics, curators, and top gallery owners—viewed his rising star with derision. His work was scoffed at, dismissed as a joke, wallpaper. But though these exalted ranks were closed to him, Spetzi was quickly becoming one of a handful of living painters whose name was known to the general public. People who had never heard of Helen Frankenthaler or David Hockney could nod their heads instantly at the mention of Spetzi.

And he was becoming rich.

Still he was nagged by a persistent worry: he had not yet been able to figure out what his agents stood to gain by his success. True, they commanded a straight twenty-percent commission off the top of his earnings, but he knew that the tens of thousands this amounted to was an insignificant sum compared to what he imagined were their usual enterprises.

And then, after four years, the Spetzi studio turned to graphics: lithographs, posters, limited-edition prints. And abruptly he understood. This was where the big money in art lay. A poster that becomes popular can sell as many copies—at fifteen to thirty dollars a throw—as a best-selling paperback book. A print in a limited edition of five hundred or one thousand, signed and numbered by a well-known artist, can command up to a thousand apiece. It is mass-market art, affordable to the man on the street: the student with ten dollars to decorate a wall of his dorm room, the lawyer with a thousand to cover the naked spot above his couch. The profits in it were staggering.

By this time the Spetzi signature had become as familiar worldwide as a name brand, and the market for his graphics proved enormous. His income leaped almost overnight to over a million a year. But by his own calculations, for every dollar he was receiving, his agents were taking in ten. They had sole control over the distribution of his work, and it was implicit that he was not to question the flat financial statements he received on the thirtieth of each month.

He did some further figuring. Over the course of an average working lifetime, at his present rate of production, he would become a quarter-of-a-billion-dollar industry.

And with this calculation, he experienced a sudden realization. They would never let him go! He was as good as a printing press to them—like coining money. For as long as he lived, they would never allow him to break those slender, but indestructible threads that kept him bound to them.

He tried a small test. He contracted with a dealer in Zurich to deliver two canvases—a negligible deal with an obscure gallery, but the first he had negotiated without the intercession of his "agents." The morning the paintings were to be shipped, his assistant frantically summoned him to the studio. The canvases still on easels had been eaten to a horror by some sort of corrosive acid. As he stared at them, the phone rang. It was Zurich. The dealer was canceling the contract. He refused to specify his reasons, but he sounded scared to death.

The warning was clear. He would never be free of these men unless they chose to let him go. The more he realized the truth of this, the more desperate he became to be free. He searched his brain for a solution —and at long last came up with something. What if he could buy them out? Not with cash, of course. But with kind—other ventures that would insure them equal, if not greater, profits. Certainly they were reasonable men, they played by a sense of honor. If he were successful in this deal and others like it, they would have to acknowledge the debt. His release from their unspoken contract would only be a fair repayment.

This sports complex deal was the down payment— the first step to his freedom. It must go through—there was no alternative. He was prepared to do anything, use any means in his power to insure its success.

So determined, he retired to dress for dinner.

For the third time that morning Thia Cassidy put her hand on the phone, and for the third time withdrew it. There was really nothing more to say. Gil had made himself ruthlessly clear. He hated Alexis, wanted to send her away; and every time Thia thought of his words, her heart turned to ice.

• But another memory kept insinuating itself, weakening her resolve to shut him entirely out of her life. It was the memory of how he had stood up for her that day by the side of Spetzi's pool—how his hand had slipped into hers, and how, for that instant, at least, they had been a family, bonded against the world. But that was a freak, she reminded herself—a single moment when he'd been feeling chivalrous or sentimental or something, and it didn't mean a thing. Nothing at all.

There was another reason she had been tempted to call him—she was three weeks late with her period. But ever since her first intuitions that she might be pregnant, she had concentrated her entire will against it. If she believed hard enough that it wasn't true, then it wouldn't be. And at last this morning she had felt a cramping in her lower abdomen, an undeniable signal

249

that her period was coming on. No doubt the tension of the past month had thrown her cycle out of whack; she knew that that was not uncommon. But, oh, the relief!

She would not call him. She had no news for him, nothing to ask of him, it was over.

Her thoughts were interrupted by the sound of a dull thud upstairs. Alexis had knocked something over or thrown something from her bed. The part-time housekeeper, Mrs. Mooning, was busy in the laundry room and couldn't hear a thing over the simultaneous hum of the washer and dryer, and so Thia would have to go investigate herself. But the thought of hauling herself up the steep spiral stairs was suddenly oppressive. She felt startlingly bad. The cramping had become stronger now—more like a sharp needling pain—and the Tylenol she had swallowed an hour ago had done nothing to dull it. She guessed it was going to be an unusually heavy period—another miserable legacy of the last few weeks.

With a groan, she lumbered to her feet, but as she started for the stairs the doorbell rang. Never rains but it pours. She sighed and dragged herself across the room to open it.

But the pain in her belly grew suddenly intolerable— a razor slicing quickly and decisively through her organs. She dropped to her knees, clutching the doorknob. Pain splashed in hot colors, its intensity not possible, beyond all other sensations. I'm going to die, she thought blindly, but it was no longer important. She was alone with her agony, sealed within its silent world, not hearing even her own scream as she slid gratefully into darkness.

Passersby on West Broadway did a double take at the huge canvas that seemed to be bobbing along of its own accord. But then they grinned as they saw Bob DeRitis behind it, puffing and perspiring under the weight of the frame. The day was hot and insufferably close; he paused to wipe his red face, then continued on, turning at the end of the block into Susan Capasian's gallery.

Susan's assistant jumped up in alarm, and the few browsers in the gallery turned to ogle. Bob swept his cargo past them all, took a sharp right, and guided it into Susan's office.

She leaped up from behind her desk.

"Happy Birthday, Merry Christmas, and a most felicitous Chinese New Year!" he called. "This, sweet Susan, is for you."

He settled the canvas against the wall and, with a flourish, removed its drop cloth. Susan drew in a quick breath. It was the double portrait of herself that had once hung there. But he had finished it—and if, in its unfinished state, it had been remarkable, now it was indisputably a masterpiece. The flesh glowed with a thousand subtleties, the eyes were living, each toe and finger was an exquisite whole in itself.

Susan touched it, delicately, half expecting to find the figure warm and pliant. "Oh, Bob!" she breathed.

"Like it?"

"What can I say? You don't like something like this. You drown in it."

"Well, it's yours. Always has been, of course. I just borrowed it back for a while."

"But I can't take it. It's museum quality—it should be shared. And think what this would mean to your career to have it accepted by the Modern, or even the Met . . ."

"The hell with that," he said gruffly. "I did this for you, not for my goddamned career."

"But why?"

"I guess to prove something to you. Don't know what exactly. Maybe that I've changed. Or grown up. Anyway, that I don't leave things half finished any-more."

"But you don't have to prove anything to me, Bob," she said softly.

"Yeah, I do. I mean, I want to." He felt suddenly awkward and jammed his fists into his pockets. "Oh, shit, Susie—isn't it obvious? The first second I saw you again I knew I was still crazy about you. It was like all those years in between never even happened. Running away from you was the stupidest thing I ever did in my life. But I'd like a chance to start again, to make it all up to you."

A look of startled dismay crossed her face.

"I know," he said quickly, "that it's tough for you to deal with any of this while Joey's still missing. I thought a lot about that and figured I'd wait . . . until there was something. But, hell, Susie, she's my daughter, too. I've been rocked by it pretty bad. And I thought maybe if we shared it—went through it together—maybe it wouldn't be so hard."

Susan shook her head. "It's impossible, Bob."

"It is too soon, isn't it?" he said glumly.

"It's not just that. There's someone else."

He seemed for a moment not to understand her. "Another guy, you mean?"

"Yes. Someone else I've become involved with."

He flushed deeply and ran a hand through his wiry hair. "So . . . is it serious?"

"I think so."

"Yeah. Well, Christ, what did I expect, huh? I come waltzing back after all these goddamned years, and you're supposed to jump into my arms? I've got a hell of a nerve."

"Bob . . ."

"You don't have to say anything, babe. I'm a thick-headed son of a bitch." He grinned tenderly at her. "Just tell me one thing—is this new guy of yours good enough for you?"

"Yes," she said with a smile. "He really is."

Bob wandered dismally back into the afternoon torpor, hardly knowing in which direction he was heading. What do you do, he wondered, when you've poured your soul out to a woman and she gives you the well-deserved raspberry? Go get stinking—that seemed logical. Where then? Someplace dark, seedy, and anonymous. There were a couple of bars in Little Italy that fit the bill. He headed toward Mulberry Street.

On an impulse, he stopped first into Lostrito's grocery, ostensibly to buy a pack of cigarettes, but in truth to slip into the Old World for a moment, to speak Italian with Mr. Lostrito, and be comforted by reminders of his own childhood and long-dead grandparents.

"Buona sera, signore!" he called out.

The old man hobbled to the counter, his face beaming. *"Eh, Roberto, come sta?"*

"Not well, today, signore," Bob continued in the old tongue. "My heart is broken. I have been turned down by the only woman I love."

"Ah, and so you are sad. But maybe you will try again with better success, eh? Maybe the lady is playing hard to get?"

"No, signore. The lady is far too kind for such a thing and far too honest. I've lost her."

"In my opinion, Roberto," the old man said, "it is the lady who is the loser."

Both men glanced up as the bell over the door jangled. Bob stared curiously at the customer who had just entered—a woman whose costume could only kindly be called eccentric. Despite the heat, her head was wrapped skull-like in a thick silk scarf, and despite the dim light, she peered through enormous dark glasses. To his surprise, she seemed startled—actually alarmed—to see him. Her hands flew to her face; she turned and darted back out the door.

"What the hell?" he exclaimed in English.

Mr. Lostrito stared after the vanished woman with a look of extreme agitation. *"Strega!"* he muttered. "Better that she doesn't come back at all."

Bob gave an uneasy laugh. "A witch, signore? Surely you don't mean that?"

"She is a strange one, I swear to you," the old man said vehemently. "When she first came into my shop, she bought only a few things—a carton of milk, a tin of tuna fish. But each time she returns, the basket grows larger, until she is buying many gallons of milk, many loaves of bread and tins of fish. But that is not all. The food she buys is for children, yet she never brings the *bambini.* And when one speaks to her, to wish a good day, she sends the evil eye from behind her black glasses."

Bob remembered all too well the unlodgeable force of old-country superstitions. He tried to make his voice light. "I have no doubt of what you say, signore. But this neighborhood . . ." He gestured toward the streets outside. "It has changed greatly. Now it is full of many people with strange ways."

The old man spat on the floor. "That is true, Roberto, and I don't give a damn for any one of them. It is fortunate that I am old and will soon die, for I would not like to live long among such filth."

Bob's face fell. This was not exactly the cheering up he'd been hoping to receive. He mumbled the required politenesses, purchased his cigarettes, and wished the old man a good day.

On Mulberry Street he found a suitably dark tavern, empty except for a dolorous-looking bartender and one man slumped asleep beside a glass of beer. Several hours and six double Scotches later, Bob was swimming in a pleasant, purgative haze of self-pity. It was his own fault, all his fault. Susan was the most wonderful, sensational, beautiful woman in the world—never find another one like her, half as good even. What good was success if he couldn't have her? But, oh, he had treated her so badly, he deserved everything he got.

And his daughter. He thought of Joey with a choking sob. The little girl with his own anthracite eyes now gone, and he might never see her again. If only he could turn back the clock to have just one hour with her, twenty minutes . . .

But a strange thing was happening. As he thought of his daughter, the image of the odd woman who had come into Lostrito's shop kept flashing in his mind. He couldn't shake it. Maybe he was just drunk, but it seemed to him she had some association with Joey.

He borrowed a pencil from the barman and sketched the face as he remembered it on a cocktail napkin. Yes, there was something familiar about it—the jawline and the lift of the chin. He drew in some hair over the wrapped head, first a short, curly coiffure, then long and straight. And then suddenly his fingers seemed to move of their own volition. He sketched the entire face again, this time adding a long ponytail and round, flat, black-winged eyes instead of the dark glasses.

He shuddered. It was her, all right—the crazy

woman who had come to his loft, the one who told him she'd been watching him. No wonder old Lostrito thought she was a witch!

But what made him associate her with Joey?

Then he remembered: the first time he had seen her was at Susan's gallery when she had been bending over his daughter, talking to her in a familiar way.

What was it Lostrito had said about her? Damn it, he was too drunk to remember. Wait a minute. He said she bought food for kids, a little at first, then more and more each time. And she didn't like to be spoken to. And that crazy outfit—what if it were really some kind of disguise?

Jesus! It was almost too crazy to possibly be true. But he sure as hell better find out. He grabbed the cocktail napkin and ran out of the bar, not stopping till he reached West Broadway and flung himself, gasping, against the door to Susan's building.

He breathed a prayer of thanks when she answered the buzzer. Ignoring the elevator, he raced the five flights up to her loft.

From her expression as she met him at the door, he realized he must look like a wild man.

"You're drunk," she said.

"Yeah, but forget that. I've got something to tell you."

"Bob, I'm not alone."

"I don't care." He stepped resolutely inside, hesitating only when he saw Kerry Donner coming toward him. He turned back to Susan and handed her the cocktail napkin. "Ever see this person before?"

She glanced at it. "It's the woman from the day-care center. The strange one . . ."

"Caroline Losey," Donner supplied, looking over her shoulder.

"That's right." She looked back at Bob with bewilderment. "But why . . ."

"I think she might be the one who took the kids."

Susan caught her breath.

"Any information you have I'll want to hear," Donner said.

Bob ran through his story as concisely as he could. He was becoming more sober by the minute, he realized—probably from the effort of having to think clearly. No sooner had he finished than Donner nodded to Susan. "I think we'd better get to her right away."

"I'm coming too," Bob said.

"You're too drunk," Susan told him. "You'd just be in the way. Please, Bob . . ."

"She's his daughter, too, Susan," Donner said gently.

She looked at him, then nodded, relenting.

But Bob shook his head. "No, you're right, I'm in no condition. Just let me know the minute you find out anything, okay?"

"Of course we will." Susan hurried to the door, then stopped and turned briefly. "Bob," she said. "Thank you."

Gil had a moment of shock as he entered his wife's hospital room. Thia's face looked so thin and white against the pillow—ravaged, actually. He had a sudden fear that somewhere within the green, impersonal labyrinth of this hospital she had been hooked up to a machine that had gone awry—that instead of pumping life-giving nourishment into her opened veins it had instead drained her of something vital.

But she was going to be all right. The tiny female resident who had performed the surgery had assured him of that. And she had taken great pains to explain to him just what had gone wrong. An ectopic pregnancy, it was called. The fertilized egg becomes somehow implanted in the lining of a Fallopian tube instead of dropping down into the uterus as it normally should. The fetus and placenta continue to develop, causing the tube to expand until, inevitably, it bursts. This, in turn, causes heavy internal bleeding that, if not checked in time, could be fatal.

But Thia had been lucky. The housekeeper, hearing her scream, had found her unconscious on the floor and had had the presence of mind to dial 911 for an ambulance. Thia had been rushed to St. Vincent's, where an immediate operation to remove the entire tube and corresponding ovary was performed. She would recover fully. However, there was one complication—and here Dr. Svetyana's crisp professionalism had softened just perceptibly—she might have difficulty conceiving again. And if she should, her chances of another ectopic were greatly increased.

But Gil emptied all of this from his face as he saw Thia's eyelids flutter open. He grinned down at her. "How do you feel?"

"Woozy from the waist up. Below that, nothing." She gave a weak smile and touched at her damp forehead. "I must look a disaster."

"You look great. Hey, I would've been here sooner, but I just got the call. It's been kind of a madhouse at the office. The hospital had a hard time getting through."

"That's okay. I've hardly been conscious anyway."

He hesitated. "The doctor told me you were seven weeks gone. Why didn't you tell me you were pregnant?"

"Because I didn't want to be. And I thought, if I just didn't believe it was true, it wouldn't be." She gave an unhappy laugh. "Look how successful I was. I'm as good as my own abortionist."

"Don't talk like that," he said quickly. "Nothing you did could've caused this. Or stopped it either. These things just happen."

"Yes," she murmured, "they happen to me. Oh, I'm a wonderful mother. Look how I've destroyed all my children."

"Come on, baby, you're talking crazy. The anesthetic's got you all muddled . . ."

"No, Gil, I know what I'm saying." Her voice was so direct that he stared at her. There was such an utter anguish in her eyes that he turned pale.

"You were right, you know," she said slowly.

"Right? About what?"

"About Alexis. When you said it was my fault she's the way she is."

He gazed at her perplexed. Then he recalled the last bitter, slashing fight of several years before—the words he had spat out in anger. "I was mad and wanted to hurt you," he said. "You didn't think all this time that I really meant it?"

"But it doesn't matter, it was true. I just never told you."

"Told me what?" He leaned closer to her.

"How it happened." She shut her eyes a moment, as if summoning strength against the memory. When she reopened them, they were brilliant with tears. "It was a couple of months after she was born," she went on. "I was in the living room giving her a bottle when the phone rang—that wall phone we used to have in the old kitchen, remember? Anyway, without even thinking, I laid her down on the couch while I went in to answer it. And when I got back, she was on the floor. She had fallen. She was crying a little. And . . . oh, God, you know what the doctors said!"

He felt a shuddering rush of emotion. "They said the damage could've happened anytime, before she was born even, or during delivery. You don't know for sure that was the time."

She shook her head. "I can't explain it, but I *do* know. And that's why I've been so bad to you. I felt that since I took Allie's life away from her, I owed her mine in place. And until now I never thought how unfair it was to you. You were right to want to get away from me."

"Oh, baby!" Gil said. "All this time I thought you were blaming me." Her eyes widened. "There're so many bad genes in my family," he explained. "You know about my Uncle Lon who went crazy and all the alcoholics on my mother's side. And . . ." He stopped. He had been about to confess his own dependency on tranquilizers, but decided to wait. Enough had been said for one day. "We've been doing a lot to each other," he said heavily. "Isn't it possible that we can stop trying to fix the blame somewhere and start right again? I'd like to try. We can go someplace new—someplace where all the crap we've been through will seem like a bad movie."

She looked at him tenderly. "I'd like that, too."

He reached for her hand and it rested dry and snug within his. Funny, he thought, how some of their best moments seemed to involve simply holding hands.

"You look tired," she said. "Have you been working hard?"

"Yeah. There's a problem that's come up with the Sports Center that's got us running ragged. But it can all wait," he added defiantly. "I'm staying here with you till they kick me out."

"Oh, no, I'm about ready to fall asleep again. There's no use your sitting here staring at me unconscious."

"Are you sure?"

"Yes, you should go. But, Gil . . . ?"

"What is it?"

"Would you go home and check on Alexis? I had to leave her with Mrs. Mooning, and you know she's kind of strange . . ."

"Sure, I will." He kissed her forehead. "Sleep well, baby. I'll be back first thing in the morning."

But as he emerged from the hospital onto the angled streets of Greenwich Village, his cheerful face crumpled. It was a close, sticky night, and the stagnant air smelled foul and unhealthy to breathe. It seemed a tangible reflection of the state of his life. The harder he tried to swim out of the thick soup of problems that surrounded him, the more deeply he became mired within it. If only he could burrow down in some warm, dark place and sleep for several days, or weeks, or months without waking. He was simply too worn out to continue.

But there was still this wretched party of Spetzi's to go to. First words Albie had spoken to him in weeks, and it was to insist he show up at some trendy affair. It nagged at him that Albie had some scheme to rectify this Sports Center debacle that he might unleash at this party. So he supposed he'd better go.

He turned off Seventh Avenue onto King Street. From the corner of his block he could see his apartment. Strange, he thought, that there were no lights in the windows. He let himself in and called out "Hello?" but there was no answer. He switched on lights. The hall and living room were deserted. On the kitchen table he found a note scrawled on a paper towel:

> *Dear Mrs Casidy,*
> *My husbind called and he wants me home now to make his dinner so I got to go. Alecksis had her dinner all ready and she is sleeping in bed so she will be fine. I'm sory I can't stay no longer but my husbind is very mad.*
> *Yours truely Mrs. Janet Mooning PS I hope you get better soon.*

Damn the woman!

Gil hurried upstairs. He heard Alexis babbling in nonsense syllables, but from Thia's bedroom, not hers. He switched on the light and groaned. She had pulled a box of dusting powder off Thia's dressing table and overturned it on herself. She and everything around her were covered with a fine white powder. She flapped her arms, crowing happily at the clouds that billowed up from her.

His hands began to tremble, but he caught himself with a deep breath. No pills, he repeated to himself. Whatever happens, don't go for the pills. Cope with it. Take it one step at a time.

He cleaned up as best he could, then undressed Alexis and plunked her into a warm bath. What the hell was he going to do with her? He knew nothing about baby-sitters, and at this hour of the night it was probably too late to hire one anyway. He'd have to bring her with him. Albie would have a cow, but there was no other solution.

He dried her off and dug up a clean pinafore for her to wear. In lieu of a fresh shirt for himself he used Thia's deodorant, then brushed his teeth with her toothbrush. He half-carried, half-dragged his daughter out the door.

"Go home!" she wailed, pulling back toward the house.

"We can't go home now," he said. "We're going to a nice party. You can take a nap there if you want."

"Go home!" Alexis screamed. "Tia! I want to home!" She plopped herself obstinately down on the pavement.

"Get up, damn it!" he snapped.

She shook her head vigorously.

"I said get up!" He yanked her harshly by the arms, and she began to howl. "Stop that!" he cried. "You stop that crying, or I'll smack you good." He bent threateningly toward her, his hand raised. And then he jumped back with a shock.

In the malignant haze of the streetlamp above her he saw a death's head materialize.

He stood frozen for a moment, his heart pounding; then, with a nervous laugh of relief, he realized it was only his jangled nerves playing tricks on him. What he had taken for a skull was actually a woman in a scarf and round dark glasses leaning from a car window.

"Is there anything wrong, Mr. Cassidy?" she called out.

Gil took a step closer. "Do I know you?"

"I don't think we've ever met. But I know your daughter." She took off her dark glasses and stared up at him with flat, depthless eyes. "I'm Caroline Losey. I work at the Synergy Center."

"Oh, yeah, the day-care place." He felt suddenly foolish, certain that she had noticed him jump back in fright. His eyes wandered to her car—an ancient DeSoto, late fifties model, newly painted black. As outmoded as a dinosaur, yet somehow familiar. "I think I've seen your car before," he said.

"That's possible. I frequently drive through this neighborhood on my way to the market." She glanced behind him to where Alexis still sat crying on the sidewalk. "That child ought to be in bed."

"I know." He began to babble. "Everything kind of happened at once tonight. Her mother's in the hospital for an ectopic pregnancy, and it was too late to find a baby-sitter, you know, so I've got to bring her with me . . ."

Caroline got out of the car and, sweeping by him, leaned over Alexis. "There, darling, it's all right. Look who's here. It's Caroline."

Alexis broke off in mid-sob and peered at the familiar face.

"That's better, darling—no more tears. Let's have a happy smile." Caroline looked back up at Gil. "Mr. Cassidy, would you like me to mind Alexis for you tonight."

His face brightened. "Oh, God, would you? I mean, if it's no trouble, of course, I'd be happy to pay whatever you think . . ."

"That's not necessary. I'm very fond of your daughter. It would be a pleasure to stay with her." She shook off a gold charm bracelet from her wrist and gave it to the child. Alexis clutched it with a happy cry. "You see, we're going to have a splendid time together. Don't you worry about a thing, Mr. Cassidy."

"Hey, I don't know how to thank you."

"Don't even think about it. Now here comes a taxi. You scoot, and I'll see to putting this child straight to bed."

He handed her the keys to the apartment with another outpouring of thanks, then sank with luxurious relief into the backseat of the cab. Well, he thought, maybe things are finally starting to look up.

He turned to wave good-bye to the woman whose long, voracious arms were already wrapped tightly about his daughter.

There had been bad years—a lot of bad years—but Caroline had only intermittent memories of them now.

First, there was the hospital—a terrible place where people kept saying, "I'm sorry, I'm sorry," though she really didn't understand what they meant. And then a lawyer's office—a fat man lowering himself cautiously into a creaky chair and telling her there was no money left. Her only inheritance was a factory building in New York City that had accrued to her husband in lieu of payment on a tax case, but which was worthless—in such a seedy neighborhood that no one would buy it. And then the mean little jobs behind counters and typewriters, the ugly boardinghouse rooms and short-tempered landladies, and every so often the hospital again, where people's smiles were always riddled with disgust and no one listened to her at all.

But then a year ago the fat lawyer had come to see her again. It was about the worthless old factory building in New York City. All this time it had scarcely earned enough in rentals to pay the taxes, but now it seemed the neighborhood had suddenly upgraded—become, in fact, quite valuable. To get to the point, there was an offer to buy the building for $475,000.

She rode a Greyhound bus to Manhattan to sign the necessary papers; while there, she went to visit the building that had made her suddenly rich. There had been an old-fashioned key among the papers in Steven's safety deposit box that was labeled with the building's address. After some exploration, she found a small door in back that it opened. Feeling adventurous, she went in.

The industrial tenants had not long vacated it. The electricity was still on, the plumbing and elevator worked. It was warm inside—in fact, almost cozy. The thought crossed her mind that a body could live in here if necessary.

But it was walking away from the building, down the street called West Broadway, that she had seen the child—the one that had made her heart stop. At first, it was just a glimpse of flame-colored hair. Then, as she drew closer, she saw the nose, the elfin eyes, the startlingly precocious mouth—almost the spitting image of her own lost Georgene.

She canceled her return bus ticket, took a room nearby, and watched for the child. Before long she knew where she lived, when she left for school and when she returned, where she went to play. And the more Caroline watched her, the more she became convinced that it *was* Georgene. They had lied when they said she was dead. They had stolen her from Caroline and brought her to this wicked place.

The more Caroline pondered this, the more past and present mixed up in her mind. She began to replace her modern wardrobe with items of twenty-five years' vintage picked from the racks of Third Avenue thrift shops. An ad in *By-Lines* led her to a battered 1957 DeSoto sedan. She had the metal body smoothed and repainted a shiny black and the seats reupholstered in palomino-colored vinyl. And one day she faced a mirror, drew on a full bright mouth, lined her eyes with black, and drew her heavy, graying hair up into a ponytail.

Past and present were now fused. She straddled the decades, taking from each only what she chose.

And now she began to plan. She took a volunteer job at a children's day-care center to give her an excuse to be in the neighborhood and continued to watch for Georgene. At night she let herself into the cozy closed-up building to which she had the key, carrying cots and blankets, a tiny refrigerator and a toaster oven, towels and dishes and toys, one boxful at a time.

And then, one radiant, blessed afternoon, her

chance came, and she gathered her daughter back into her arms.

But there were difficulties. The evil ones had spoiled her, turning her against her true mother with their lies and making her proud and willful. She must be turned back to the path of righteousness. And to do this Caroline knew she must be firm, she must not withhold discipline.

There were more plans to be made. Caroline had purchased a farmhouse in a remote area of Nova Scotia. But the evil ones were everywhere. They had controlled the police and even the newspapers with the force of their lies. And so it was not yet safe to travel. They would wait for a time in the secure protection of the old building.

But as she waited the voices continued to speak to her. They sent her signs that puzzled her. Hadn't she fulfilled her task? Was more required of her? At last it came to her in an ecstatic revelation: she had been chosen to be the perfect guardian, not only of her own child, but of others as well. Children in the hands of adulterers, sodomists, and whores cried out for her protection. *Gather them unto ye: lead them from the paths of destruction and the places of iniquity.*

This she heard, the voices and the signs. And she would obey.

Alexis curled happily on the car seat still enthralled with the golden bracelet she clutched in her fist. Caroline, shifting up, stepped on the gas. It had been a sign that she had happened by when she did, just as the man was about to strike this innocent creature. For some time she had known that Alexis was meant to be hers, and once again divine assistance directed her hand.

But now she must hurry. She had revealed herself this time, and the evil ones would soon be in pursuit. There was no more time to wait. The children must be taken away immediately—north, to the place of few neighbors and long, private winters, the place where they would never be found.

She pulled the car into the deserted parking lot beside the building and parked it in the darkest shadow. Then she hurried Alexis out of the car and disappeared with her down the narrow, coal-black alley.

The block was still; the murky light and oppressive polluted air had conspired to clear it of all human forms. A taxi turned the corner cruising for fares and, realizing its mistake, swung back uptown toward more convivial neighborhoods. And then the street was empty once more.

Bland as a shadow, a figure slipped out from a narrow passageway and onto a rusting loading dock. He fit a key into a padlock and lifted a heavy gate.

Now he was inside the building.

His flashlight showed him the basement door. The stairs down were thick with the odors of rot and mold—unused for many years. The air at the bottom was moist, like skin of a living creature.

And now his beam passed over rotting boxes, broken crates, accumulations of ancient building materials left here by carpenters who would never return.

He went to work quickly, efficiently. Crates and rotting boxes doused with paint thinner dragged to a stack near the floor of the elevator shaft. A hot bulb nestled into the center. Simple but effective—no evidence but that of an ordinary electrical fire.

He watched a thin bluish smoke appear, then the first flames lick the ancient cardboard. Satisfied, he made his way out the way he had come in.

But as he prepared to jump off the loading dock, he froze. Two figures had just rounded the corner into the alleyway—a woman and a child. He had narrowly missed being seen.

He wondered briefly what they were doing there—whether they intended to go into the building. But that wasn't his business. He had already finished the job he had been paid for, and anything that happened now was beyond his care.

The manager of the Gramercy Park Residence for Women was a silver-haired matron of shabby gentility. The liberal patting of beige powder on her face only faintly concealed the pink mottled skin of a gin drinker underneath.

She led Donner and Susan down a stuffy hallway and unlocked a door at its end. With a prissy flourish, she gestured into the room inside.

"What did I tell you? Not a single sign of life. She pays off regular the first of each month, and then we don't see a hair of her till the next." The woman aired large dull teeth in a smile. "My maids have a little joke. They say they wish every guest would be so considerate as to not use their rooms like Mrs. Losey."

Kerry Donner stepped into the room. He glanced quickly through the empty dresser drawers and under the bed. He pulled open the closet. It contained a single dress smelling faintly of mothballs.

"When was the last time you saw her, Mrs. Pearson?" he asked.

"Like I said, she stops in on the first of each month to settle her bill."

271

"Do you remember what bank she draws her checks on?"

Mrs. Pearson pulled herself up. "I only accept cash," she declared. "You'd be astonished at how many perfectly respectable-looking people will cheat you if you give them half a chance."

Susan interjected, "Did Mrs. Losey ever tell you anything about herself, Mrs. Pearson?"

"No, dear, we never discussed anything personal. She didn't volunteer, and I, for one, don't like to intrude."

"Anything you remember might help us," Donner continued. "For instance, did she post any letters or charge any phone calls while she was here?"

Mrs. Pearson shook her head.

"Then can you remember the direction she took when she left here last?"

"It's not my nature to keep tabs on my guests," she sniffed. "We have certain rules and regulations that we ask them to respect, as I'm sure any establishment does. But as long as they are quiet and behave decent, that's all my concern. Though just last month I had an awful run-in with a new woman who was making such a racket in her room . . ."

"Thank you very much, Mrs. Pearson," Donner cut in, "but I think we've taken up enough of your time."

He and Susan returned to the car. Susan slumped in her seat, tears of frustration in her eyes. "It's another dead end," she said.

He grasped her arm. "You give up too fast. We still have other people we can talk to."

She raised her head. "Who?"

"One of her co-workers, Eben Link, lives in Soho. We can start with him."

They drove back downtown.

Day McAllister, opening her door to them, looked clearly startled to see Donner. "I was expecting friends," she said coldly.

He noticed that she was festively dressed in an embroidered Chinese blouse and silk pants. "I'm sorry if this is an inconvenient time," he said, "but it's important that I speak to Eben."

Hostility hardened in her beautiful eyes. "Haven't you persecuted him enough?" she snapped. "Or are you going to dog him for the rest of his life, whether he's guilty of anything or not?"

"I know you feel that way, but believe me, I'm not here to persecute him. I need his help."

"Yes, help in getting yourself a promotion. Why don't you just leave him alone!"

"I'm afraid I have to insist . . ."

But then Eben appeared in the doorway behind Day. His arm encircled her waist. "It's okay," he said. "Come in, Sergeant Donner. I'll be glad to cooperate with you in any way I can."

Donner and Susan followed him into the loft. "I do need your cooperation, Eben," Donner said, "but this time it's not about yourself. There's a woman you work with named Caroline Losey."

"Caroline? Sure, but she stopped showing up at the center about two weeks ago."

Susan turned white. "Oh, God, Kerry, do you think she's left town with the children?"

Eben looked at them, stunned by a sudden realization. "Christ, you don't think Caroline's the one who's been taking all the kids, do you?"

"There's some evidence," Donner said, "but nothing conclusive. Still, it's very important that we find her right away."

"Yeah. Well, all I know is she lives in a hotel up by Gramercy Park."

"We've already been there," Susan cried. "The manager told us she never even comes to her room."

"What else do you know about her, Eben?" Donner asked.

"Not much. I never heard her talk about family or friends or anything. I always figured she was pretty much alone in the world."

"What about her background? Where is she from?"

"Somewhere in the Midwest. Begins with an I: Illinois, Iowa, Indiana . . ." He shrugged. "One of those."

"But you must know *something* more about her," Susan insisted. "All the time you were working with her . . ."

Day suddenly cut in. "What did you say Caroline's last name was?"

"Losey," Eben said, turning to her. "Didn't you know?"

"I guess I never heard it mentioned before. And it's funny . . ."

"Does that name mean anything to you, Miss McAllister?" Donner prompted.

"Oh, it's probably just a coincidence. But I've been working on a story about a building here in Soho. Some developers were about to tear it down, and I found out some things that stopped them. But the point is that the developers had bought the building from the estate of a man named Steven Losey. And he was from Indiana." She stopped, suddenly embarrassed. "You see, it's nothing—just a dumb coincidence."

"Maybe not," Donner said. "You said the building is in this neighborhood?"

"Yes, just three blocks away, number Eight-sixty-four Greene Street."

"When was it purchased?"

"March one of this year."

Donner turned to Eben. "When did Caroline begin at the Center?"

"Sometime early spring," he said. "Yeah, we were just back from the Easter break, so it must have been the end of March or beginning of April."

"And the building, since its purchase, has been vacant?" Donner asked Day.

She nodded.

"But someone who had access to it—say a key or the combination of a padlock—could stay there virtually undetected."

Susan gave a cry. "That's it, Kerry! She's got the children in the building!"

"No, they're not there," Day said quickly. "I went inside the building while I was doing my story, and it was quite empty."

"Are you sure?" Donner asked. "Did you go on every floor?"

"No, just the first. But . . . I mean, it *felt* so deserted. If anyone had been in there, we'd have heard some kind of noise . . ." She stopped, remembering the eerie sound that had scared them out. The ghost. Could it actually have come from some mortal being, a sound carried down through the plumbing that their imaginations had romanticized? "Anyway," she continued, "they couldn't live there without lights, could they? And you'd see a light from the outside . . ." Suddenly she clapped her hand to her forehead. "Except for the top floor! The top-floor windows are completely boarded up. You couldn't see a thing inside!"

Susan looked anxiously at Donner. He nodded. "We'd better get right over there. Thanks for your help."

When they had gone, Day tore through the loft collecting pencils and notebooks in a carryall. "This could be the story of the year," she breathed excitedly, "and if I get a scoop on it, I'll be able to write my own ticket. Damn it, where's the flash attachment to the Minolta?"

"Top drawer of the white cabinet," Eben said calmly.

"Oh, God, thanks!" She turned and noticed him tying on his sneakers. "Are you coming, too?"

"Yeah. In case there's something I can do to help

out." He caught her expression and grinned. "Hell, I figure it's about time I got involved."

"Yes," she said, grinning happily back. "Oh, hey, what about Timmy and Louise? They'll be here any minute."

"I think they'll forgive us for standing them up this one time. Come on, let's run."

Caroline hurried the children out of their pajamas. In their sleepy state they assumed that they were being taken home, and they were jubilant. They ran back and forth collecting favorite toys to take with them. A quarrel broke out between Jason and David over a model of the Hulk: Jason snatched it out of David's hands, and David retaliated with a swift whack across Jason's shoulders.

"You two stop that this instant," Caroline commanded, pulling them apart. "Children, listen to me. We are not going to take any of our toys. You can have all new things later, so put all these old things down. Georgene, your shoelaces are still untied. David, button your sweater. Hurry, children, hurry!"

At last, they were properly dressed and ready. Caroline counted noses and, taking Alexis by the hand, marched them in a double row to the elevator. For the last time, she glanced behind her. It had served her well, this cavernous space. It had provided good shelter from the wickedness of the city. She glanced at the thick columns marching down its length like

staunch guardians and allowed herself a moment
of tender regret to be leaving them forever. Then she
turned and swung open the heavy freight elevator
door.

A cloud of hot, brown smoke billowed into her face.
With a scream, she covered her stinging eyes and drew
back. Plumes of smoke and orange cinders were shooting through the cracks in the freight elevator floor, and
she could hear the sharp crackle of flames licking up the
elevator shaft. She sank to her knees. The children
were shouting and tugging at her, and one of them
had begun to cry. But she was oblivious to them.
She saw only the smoke, heard only the approaching
fire.

*She was lying on the grass. The smell of smoke was in
her nostrils, and the wail of a siren grew steadily louder.
When she opened her eyes, Steven's face loomed over
her, his mouth contorted, his eyes wild with fright.
"Where is Georgie?" he was screaming. "Did she get
out?"*

The picture should stop there. But this time it went
on, like a horror movie with the scariest part about to
come on the screen. But unlike at the movies, when she
covered her eyes it didn't stop her from seeing what
came next.

*Steven gripped her shoulders and shook her like a rag
doll. "Answer me, damn you!" he shrieked at her.
"Where is she?" And then her lips were moving. "In the
house," she told him. "Where in the house? Tell me
where?" But she couldn't tell him about the closet. He
didn't understand such things—how the voices commanded her to be firm with the child, how punishment
was for her own salvation. No, Steven would be furious
—he might leave for good, leave her alone to be mocked
at and pointed to as a wife who couldn't keep her
husband, a woman who had failed.*

"I don't know," she said.

And then Steven was running across the lawn. As the

first fire engine came screaming onto the block, he disappeared into a wall of black smoke, never to come out again. And she continued to lie on the grass, staring at the burning house with her husband and daughter trapped inside.

She was unable to move an inch.

Kerry Donner's white Chevy skidded into the parking lot beside the building. Susan glanced up to the top floor. Its boarded windows, like blindfolded eyes, stared unseeingly back. Suddenly, as if she heard a call, she threw open the door and ran out.

"Susan, wait!" Donner reached for a flashlight under the seat and followed her. He caught her by the shoulders.

"Let me go!" she cried, struggling. "Joey might be in there."

"I know. But listen to me first." He turned her toward him, forcing her to look up at him. "Listen to me, Susan. There's something you must be prepared for first. We don't know for sure if the kids are in that building. But if they are, they might be dead. Do you understand that? We might find Joey's body in there."

She stared up at him, ashen. "I have to know," she whispered.

His fingers tightened on her shoulders. "I love you," he said. He released her and helped her up onto the low loading platform in front of the entrance.

Susan ran her hands against the corrugated metal gates. "How do we get in?"

"I don't see a padlock. Could be it's already open." He bent down and gave the handle a tug. The gate cracked open, then slowly began to rise. As it did, a plume of smoke curled lazily out into the night.

"My God, it's on fire!" Susan gasped. She ducked into the lobby, coughing as the smoke filled her nostrils.

"Stay low," Donner shouted.

She bent from the waist as he directed, shielding her face with the sleeve of her blouse. "Can we get upstairs?"

"It looks like the fire's in the elevator. The stairs are pretty clear, but we'd better hurry. This could spread fast."

Susan ran toward the stairs. A cinder whirled through the smoke and fell on her hair; Donner, coming up behind her, slapped it off. Then, following the lead of his flashlight beam, they began the climb, fighting for breath in the harsh, smoky air.

Their eyes and throats stinging, they reached the heavy metal door at the sixth-floor landing. Susan rattled the knob and found it locked. She pounded frantically with her fists. "Joey! Can you hear me? Are you in there?"

There was no reply, and her heart sank. And then there was the sound of several pairs of small feet running toward the door and the collective cry of small voices. With a burst of joy, she picked out one voice above the rest: "Mommy! Mommy, I'm in here!"

"Thank God!" she breathed with a sob.

"Mommy," Joey called, "there's a fire in here, and we can't get out. And Mrs. Losey's sitting on the floor and won't move."

Susan pulled at the doorknob again. "I can't open it, darling. It's locked from in there."

Donner called, "Joey, I'm a friend of your mother's.

We're going to get you out, so don't worry. Do you see where the lock is on the door?"

"It's way up high. I can't reach it."

"Can any of the boys get it?"

There was the sound of jumping feet, then a chorus of voices. "No, it's too high."

"Okay, then. How many boys are there?"

"Two!" they called out.

"Good. I want both you boys to get down on your hands and knees and make a platform with your backs. Get very close together. Okay? Are you ready?"

"Yes," the two replied.

"Good. Joey, are you the tallest girl there?"

"No, Lisa is," she called.

"Okay, then, Lisa, you climb up onto the boys' backs. Boys, you keep very steady. And, Joey, hold her hand so she doesn't fall. Are you doing that, Lisa?"

"Yes," she said.

"Can you reach the lock?"

There was a pause. Susan threw a frightened glance at Donner. And then there was a clicking as the tumbler turned inside the cylinder. Donner tried the knob. It opened.

"Okay, now jump down very carefully, Lisa. And everybody stand back from the door." As he heard them scramble away, he flung the door open. Susan darted inside. The children clung to her fiercely as she tried to hug them all at once.

Donner crossed the loft to where Caroline Losey was kneeling, still staring at the source of the swirling smoke. Her body was as rigid as if changed to stone. He touched her shoulder. "It's time to go now, Caroline."

The strange, flat eyes swung toward him. "Georgene is in the house," she said. "But I don't know where."

"That's okay. You're coming with us now." He gently drew her up to her feet.

At that moment the lights blinked out, plunging the loft into total darkness. The children began to scream.

"Don't be afraid," Donner called out, shining the

flashlight beam toward them. "We're going to make a train. Everybody hold hands with each other. Now don't let go until we reach the bottom of the stairs."

The flashlight cut a small swath through the gloom, leading the little parade toward the stairs. As the last of them filed out, the heavy door slammed shut and locked itself again behind them.

A small crowd, attracted by the smoke that now billowed freely from the opened gate, milled curiously in front of the building. A shout went up as, one by one, the children and three adults popped out from inside.

The crowd parted and gaped as Donner led Caroline, moving like a sleepwalker, through their midst. He placed her gently in the backseat of the car, then jumped in the front and radioed for help. Susan shepherded the children safely across the street, away from the wisping smoke. Only then did she allow herself to gather her own daughter into her arms and, sobbing with joy and relief, cover her with kisses. The other children huddled close to her as strangers began to surround them. Reluctantly, she parted herself from Joey and hugged each of them in turn, murmuring assurances and comfort.

After a moment, Joey tugged on her sleeve. "Mommy?"

"What is it, darling?" she said, reaching for her.

"There's another girl still up there."

"No, sweetheart, we all got out."

Joey shook her head. "She's still up there, and somebody's got to get her."

Susan kissed her forehead. "Oh, Joey, it's not a *real* girl up there."

"Yes, it is!" Joey broke from her mother and ran toward Eben Link, who was making his way through the crowd. "Mr. Link, go get the other girl down. She got left behind."

Eben glanced at Susan, who shook her head. "It's

not a real girl. Joey makes up imaginary playmates, and
she thinks one's still caught in the fire."

"She *is* real!" Joey insisted. "Mrs. Losey brought her
just now."

Eben knelt down to her. "Who did Mrs. Losey bring,
Joey?"

"The retard," she said. Then her hands flew to her
mouth; she was not supposed to say that word. She
began again. "The girl who was at the Synergy Center.
She sat in the dirt and made funny noises all the time."

"Do you mean Alexis Cassidy?"

Joey nodded. "'Lexis. She was there, and when the
lights went off, no one got her, and she's going to get all
burned up."

Eben looked back at Susan. Her expression had
changed to alarm. "Lisa! Boys!" she called. "Did Mrs.
Losey bring another child with her today?"

They all chorused yes and began to take up the cry:
there was another little girl still up in the building.

"I'll go get her," Eben said.

"No, you can't," Susan said quickly. "It's too dangerous. The fire was spreading rapidly—the stairs could
be completely blocked by now."

"Let me take a look at least."

Day, who had been standing behind him during most
of this exchange, grabbed his arm. "Don't go in there,
Eben," she pleaded. "Wait for the fire trucks."

"It could be too late. Don't worry," he assured her,
"I won't take any crazy risks. Give me the sash to your
pants. I need something to cover my nose."

She undid the wide silk belt at her waist. He wrapped
it like a bandana over his nose and mouth and tied it
securely behind his head. Then, shoving his way
brusquely through the crowd, he leaped onto the
loading platform and ducked under the half-opened
gate.

The heavy smoke made his eyes tear. Blinking, he
paused a moment to take his bearings. The blaze,

forking up through the floor, had enveloped the entire southeast corner of the building and was working swiftly north. In its eerie, flickering light he could see the stairwell. A trail of flames was eating at its base, but otherwise it appeared clear. Without further hesitation, he leaped the flames and raced up it into the total darkness of the upper floors. The fierce breath of the fire chased his heels as he continued upward, crashing from wall to wall in the dark, coughing as he climbed and gasping for breath. Fourth floor, he counted—fifth —one more to go. Exhausted, he hauled himself up the final flight by the banister and slammed headlong into a metal plate door.

"Alexis!" he called. He banged on the door, trying to find some way to open it. It was no use, he quickly realized—and futile to expect Alexis to help him.

He retreated to the fifth floor, which, once he left the stairwell behind, was relatively free of smoke. And the huge unobstructed windows let in ample light from the surrounding buildings. He lowered his bandana, took a breath, and began to think.

The answer was so obvious it made him start. The fire escape! He could smash through a window to it and be up it in five seconds. Then his spirits sank again. No good, damn it—the top-floor windows were solidly boarded up. There'd be no way to get through them.

What else? Elevators: There were two shafts on each floor. Through the breaks in one of the doors he could see the red glow of the fire being sucked up the shaft. But the other was in the opposite end of the loft where the flames had not yet found ground.

He ran to it and, with little difficulty, pried open its old plywood door. The shaft contained a small, broken-paned window. It let in enough light to illuminate the three cable strands: one the main, one the safety, one the electric power cord. If he could leap out and grab hold of one of them, he could then shimmy up it to the next floor. As a kid, he had often climbed ropes tied to the limbs of trees or looped around chimneys and swing from them as free as a chimpanzee. He remembered the sensation vividly and knew he could do it now.

But what if he missed the cable? His eyes traveled down the pitch-black shaft. What would it be like to free-fall sixty feet into a black pit? Might as well be sixty miles by the time you hit the bottom. His heart began to pound. He had promised Day he would take no unnecessary risks. And God, how he wanted to live! To go on having idyllic Sunday breakfasts in their sun-speckled loft, and watching her beautiful eyes when they made love, and savoring everything else that made life sweet.

And for what would he be risking his life? A pathetic, brain-damaged creature who could never contribute to society, who would never be more than a burden to those who had to care for her . . .

No, she was a soul. A child who could love and be loved.

And if you talk about contributions, his own to date hadn't been so staggering. Hard to make any when you dedicate your whole life to not getting involved. And wasn't that what this was really all about? He could back off now and spend the rest of his life with a pillow over his head—or he could take the plunge back into some sort of useful society.

Now or never.

He ran his tongue over his cracked lips, then backed off several paces, clearing away the rubble on the floor with his feet. His eyes fixed on the cables glittering on the far side of the shaft. They looked suddenly distant, and the pit that yawned in between seemed vast as an ocean. His body told him he couldn't do it; fear, like fever chills, ran through him.

And then, with a sudden determination, he ran forward and leaped out into the blackness.

His hands slammed onto the taut cable faster than he had gauged. He scrambled to grab hold, fighting the searing shock of pain. But the momentum was too great. The metal bit through his hands. His fingers, stretched beyond endurance, peeled back as if made of rubber. A blinding wave of fear and anger swept over him as he realized he could no longer hold on. With a sharp cry, he let himself drop.

But instead of nothingness, his feet found support.

For a moment, he could hardly believe it. Was he already dead? No, he realized sheepishly—he was standing on top of the old freight elevator, stopped some three feet below the open door.

He began to laugh, insanely, unable to control himself. He was alive, goddamnit, and the climb up that cable was going to be a fucking piece of cake!

Finally he forced himself to calm down. Time was wasting. He wiped his soaked hands on his jeans and grasped the cable, this time working himself hand over hand up to the next level.

As he expected, the shaft here was also closed off by a door. He reached out with one hand and took hold of the power cord that ran, with a greater degree of slack, in tandem with the main. His legs carefully wrapped around it. Then, transferring his support, he grasped it with both hands and began to swing, Tarzan style, kicking out at the door with each arc. On the fourth swing, the wood splintered through. Pushing off with both feet from the back wall, he heaved himself through and crashed his body onto the floor.

Damn, that hurt! He pulled himself stiffly up. Nothing broken or sprained, thank God.

And then he realized he heard a child crying.

"Alexis!" he cried. With the windows boarded, he could hardly see a thing. He stumbled toward her crying till at last he could make out the dim radiance of her golden hair. Crooning her name, he reached down and picked her up. Her arms clutched tightly around his neck. Then, guided by instinct, he groped his way toward the stairwell door, felt for the inside lock, and came out onto the landing.

Now what? That fire was hungry—chances are it had

eaten its way up the lower stairs by now. So if you can't go down, the only way is up.

He carried Alexis up the last flight to the roof, emerging into the night air as gratefully as a ship-wrecked man staggering onto shore. As he approached the cornice, a sound swelled up from the street below, a sort of roar that he couldn't quite identify. He gazed cautiously over the edge. A bewildering spectacle met his eyes. The street was packed with people, all of whom were waving and cheering as if he were an actor at a curtain call.

And then the red fire trucks nosed their way in with ear-splitting screams. People scurried out of the way, ladders were hoisted, and earnest, responsible-looking men in heavy black slickers were scrambling their way up toward him.

It seemed to Eben that they were coming to rescue him, not from the fire, but from himself. To draw him back to the center from the dangerous, self-absorbed perimeters into which he'd wandered. All that he had rejected, everything he'd been running from—here it was, take it or leave it. The choice was up to him.

Suddenly, with a great laugh of freedom, he made his decision. He reached out his arms to his rescuers.

Part IV

While Joey squirmed, Susan dabbed at her face with a cloth, tucked her T-shirt into the waistband of her jeans, and—though it was already perfectly straight—recombed the part in her hair. The truth was that she could not keep her hands off her daughter. Only by touching her was she convinced that Joey was actually here, alive and safe, and not a mirage, a ghost, or a dream that would vanish with the first light of dawn.

Bob DeRitis, waiting on the couch, displayed as much fidgety impatience as his daughter. "Now remember," Susan said to him, "don't let go of her hand until you're actually in the theater. And don't leave her alone in the seat to go for popcorn or anything else. If she has to go to the bathroom, go with her and wait outside until she comes out. Oh, and I'd better give you a sweater for her in case the air conditioning is too much. You know how these theaters are."

Bob gave a snort. "You sure you don't want to come along? Just to make *sure* there are no slipups, I mean."

"Don't tease me, Bob," she begged. "You know it's still hard for me to let her out of my sight."

"Yeah, I know," he said seriously. "And I really

appreciate your letting me have some time alone with her."

"If it wasn't for you, neither one of us would have her."

"Yeah, well—it was lucky, I guess."

They looked at each other with fond embarrassment. Susan still couldn't get over how much he had changed. He was working harder now than ever before, and the work he was producing was of a breathtaking quality. And he was in the process of overhauling his loft so that it would be a place of comfort and function and light—a good place, she knew, for a child to visit.

"Mommy," Joey piped up. "Can I bring my new compass with me to the movies?"

"What for, sweetie?"

"I need it."

"But why, sweetie?" Joey shrugged. "Is it for Tweenie to play with?"

Joey's wide black eyes turned solemn. "Oh, no. Tweenie died. She fell down into a big crack in the floor and was dead."

Susan shivered. Every now and then Joey did or said something that brought home just how terrible an ordeal she had been through. What the final legacy of the past month would be, it was too soon to tell. But it tortured Susan to think that in five years' time, or ten, or twenty, Joey might suddenly suffer the delayed aftereffects of the trauma.

"Of course you can bring your compass," she said gently.

For herself the whole thing was far from over. There were still endless demands from the press—and because they had been so cooperative during the search, she felt obliged now to return the favor. And the police would soon be requiring a lengthy deposition from her—even though it was unlikely that Caroline Losey would ever stand trial. She had been confined to the psychiatric ward of Bellevue. Kerry Donner, who checked in on her daily, reported that she was under heavy medication and as yet unable to understand where she was or what had happened to her. But the press had managed to unearth most of the pieces of her life, and it was such a tragic story that Susan had been almost moved to forgive her.

Yet she knew that the queer, mad figure would, for a long time to come, continue to haunt her dreams.

Joey ran back out of her bedroom clutching the shiny instrument in her hand. Bob swooped down on her.

"We'd better make tracks, gorgeous, or Mr. Walt Disney's gonna start his movie without us. And what a couple of sorry kids we'd be then, wouldn't we?"

Joey smiled up at him, still somewhat shy of this funny, friendly, but still strange man who called himself her father.

From the tall arched windows of her loft, Susan watched them emerge onto West Broadway and scolded back her lingering worries. She had to let her go sometime, and who better to trust her to than Bob? Then she saw another man approach them—a big, tousled-haired man who hugged Joey, shook hands with Bob, then waved them on their way.

She sighed. Kerry, she could see, had dressed in his usual haphazard fashion with the usual disastrous results: uncreased brown trousers, an old shirt with a ghastly stripe pattern, shoes that even the Salvation Army would hesitate to accept. The first thing she'd do, she decided, would be to take his wardrobe in line. Throw everything away and start all over again. A casual but distinguished look would be nice. She would choose clothes that were comfortable but had a sense of style and polish to them.

But now he had spied her in the window and was waving vigorously with both hands, a grin lighting up his mismatched features, and he looked, she had to admit, completely wonderful.

On second thought, she told herself, she might just keep him exactly the way he was.

Day and Eben smiled wearily as their friends lifted glasses to them in a rousing toast. It was yet another in a succession of dinners and parties that were being given in their honor—this one a buffet in the charmingly appointed loft of Yves and Martine, featuring a huge tub of couscous and a case of Tattinger that everyone had chipped in for. New York needs heroes, whether it be a penant-winning ball team, a lone man scaling the face of the World Trade Center, or a young couple rescuing long-lost children from a burning building. The tremendous publicity had focused a klieg light on Day and Eben, and they were still blinking from the glare.

Day picked a fluted radish from the tray of Martine's artistically prepared crudités and ducked for a moment from the swirl. She watched Eben. His eyelashes and eyebrows had been singed off by close contact with the flames, giving his splendid features a futuristic look.

"I still can't get used to people coming to *me*," he was saying. "I mean, after years of being practically invisible, suddenly I've been getting offers from everywhere. People wanting me to give an interview or do an ad. Hell, even the fire department's been hinting they've got a job for me."

"Which one will you take?" Yves asked him.

"I don't know. Frankly, it's all pretty intimidating. I've avoided getting involved for so long, it's become a habit." They all laughed. Eben went on: "To tell the truth, I'm kind of leaning toward the fire department. Not to spend the rest of my life as a fireman, but I wouldn't mind going into something like arson investigation. I've been talking to a couple of the investigators in this thing, and the way they work is really fascinating."

He drifted out of Day's earshot. She nibbled a carrot stick, still hardly able to believe that it had all happened. The Sports Center was dead; the children were alive—happy endings that she had played a pivotal role in bringing about.

And yet she couldn't help dwelling on a number of ironies. There was the fact that, with even an hour's difference in timing, her interference might have resulted in not only the destruction of the building she was trying to save, but the horrible death by fire of innocent children. And the fact that, since the fire had destroyed any evidence that could have proved the allegations in her story, the developers were likely to get off scot-free. Of course, they were being investigated for the more serious charge of arson, but it seemed that no conclusive proof could be turned up for that either. The charred body of a derelict had been discovered in the basement; the official theory now was that a cigarette dropped by this unfortunate man had touched off the blaze.

It was frustrating to know better and not be able to prove a thing. But that much she'd have to live with.

A friend came by and clapped her on the back. "Just heard you've landed a job on the *Times*'s city desk. Good going!"

"Thanks, Tony," she said, smiling, "but it's not really a job yet. They're giving me a three-month trial.

At the end of that I'll be reviewed for a permanent position."

"Yeah, but knowing you, you'll do such a bang-up job, they'll be begging you to stay on."

She murmured modestly. But in her heart she had enough confidence in herself to believe he was right.

And so it was another happy ending—this one for herself. The dream job offered to her by the world's greatest newspaper.

With another irony attached.

All this time she had convinced herself that it was the fear of losing Eben that was motivating her to pursue this story, that an advancement in her career would be a consolation prize for being left behind. But when Eben had appeared above the cornice of the blazing roof, she had not waited to make sure of his final safety. On the contrary, she had found herself running for a pay phone, intent on calling in her scoop to the city editor of the *Times*.

And so, at last, she knew herself. She had discovered that it was possible to live for herself rather than through the man she was with. And that instead of being left behind, *she* might be the one moving on.

The funny thing was that it still seemed kind of frightening. Either way, it seemed, the prospects for loneliness were great.

Then, all of a sudden, Eben was beside her, his arm around her waist. As if he knew what she had been thinking, he gave a brilliant smile. "We're together now, and it's good," he told her. "So what difference does it make what happens later on?"

She turned her eyes to him. "Eben, you are so damned smart!" She laughed and squeezed him as hard as she could.

For the last time, Gil Cassidy left his offices on the river and walked the uptown traverse through the heart of Soho.

It was hard for him to believe that he would never again sit at a drafting table in that virginal white space, working, thinking, dreaming, while the great silver snake of the river spangled gorgeously below. But it was true. He had just signed over the lease to two young graphic designers and accepted his half of the payment for the fixtures and furnishings. And already the new tenants had imposed their more lavish tastes upon it. They had moved in potted orange trees and hanging ferns and an ornate bird cage stocked with nervous, jewel-green finches.

The firm of Cassidy and Knowlton was thus officially expunged from the physical world.

Five days ago Gil and Albie had signed the legal documents severing their partnership. Albie had shaken Gil's hand and wished him luck with such relief written in his eyes that Gil had almost laughed. Without the dead weight of his partner's scruples holding him down, Albie would now be free to lie and bluff his way totally clear of the disastrous Sports Center venture.

Though it looked now as if—thanks to Spetzi's two unsmiling partners—they were all going to escape with their skins. Without being told, Gil knew that it was somehow their doing that the arson investigation had suddenly and irreversibly lost momentum and that a new buyer for the property had appeared, as if by conjuration—one who had not only offered an incredibly good price, but whose plans to preserve what was left of the building by converting it to living lofts were a masterpiece of public relations.

But these reflections gave Gil little satisfaction. If Albie *had* arranged for the building to be torched, he deserved to rot in jail. And as for himself—he who had cheerfully delivered his daughter into the hands of a madwoman, abandoning her without so much as a second thought—he deserved the full retribution of heaven and hell.

But no more self-recriminations. For the sake of his family, he must start believing in himself again. Look forward, never back—that much he owed them.

And in his pocket lay his future: a letter from his brother Rich, an engineer in Houston. Gil had reread it so often he knew most of its contents by heart:

> . . . *goddamned glad you're coming on home. I know you had to get those bright lights out of your system, but I always figured when the chips were in you'd haul your ass back West where you belong. We both belong here, buddy. This dry old country is our blood and bone, and it's only the pure Texas air keeping us honest. But end of sermon. What I really want to say is, I'm excited as all get-out over our new partnership. The day of solar construction is now, buddy, and you and me, we're hitting it at the dawn. The Cassidy boys are gonna set the conventional housing industry on its ever-lovin' ass. Cassidy Bros. Inc., that is.*

And so it was final.

At the end of the month they would move to Houston—he and Thia and Alexis. There they would try to start over, to live again as a family. There was a good school for exceptional children in the city that would take Alexis by day and where Thia could work part-time as a volunteer. Perhaps they might even try to have another child.

Not that it would be easy. They were bringing many problems with them—all the years of withdrawal and guilt and misunderstanding could not be expected to disappear overnight. And there was his Valium habit. A doctor had advised him that weaning himself from it would be a gradual process and a difficult one. It would require a lot of his strength in the next few months.

But he and Thia had joined hands again, co-conspirators against the world. Together they could take one step at a time. Look forward, never back.

He turned off the bustling thoroughfare of West Broadway onto a quieter street. As it always did, the charm of the neighborhood quickly seduced him. He loved these buildings—their graceful idiosyncracies had no equal. Houston was a young city, built of smooth steel and mirrored glass. Nowhere could you look up and discover a pink iron lily blooming from a brick wall; a gargoyle glowering down from a cornice; a fluted white column supporting nothing but its own fanciful capitol. These were the things he would miss.

And now he knew where he was heading. He turned up Greene Street and found himself in front of the remains of the Byer Thread Building. But *remains* was too unjust a word, for enough of the structure had survived to make it fair to say that the building itself still existed. The brick shell had come through virtually intact; and, miraculously, much of the cast-iron facade had also withstood the flames. And the broad oak support beams, though charred, were still staunchly upright.

The sight of it made Gil suddenly happy. These

buildings were built to last, he thought. Despite the most destructive efforts of human weakness and stupidity, they survive.

And then, all at once, all the hope for the future that had so far eluded him suddenly flooded his soul with a thrilling weightlessness. The building had survived, and, in so doing, triumphed.

And with luck, he thought eagerly, so could he.